SADE

Anne Giwa-Amu was born in 1960 in Deri, South Wales, the daughter of a Nigerian barrister and Welsh mother. Her formative years were spent in Nigeria where she experienced some of the horrors of the Civil War. Soon after the war, her parents returned to Wales. She has worked in Hotel Management and Further Education and is currently a Law student at the London School of Economics and Political Science in London. *Sade* is her first published novel.

SADE

Anne Giwa-Amu

ACE

SADE
ACE BOOKS: 0 9529174 0 8

Published in Great Britain by Ace Books 1996

Ace Books
133 Condell Road, London SW8 4HS

A CIP catalogue record for this book is available
from the British Library

Set in 11-on-13½ pt Garamond Book by
Morning Star Media, London

Printed and bound in Great Britain by
Cox & Wyman Ltd, Reading, Berkshire

THIS BOOK IS DEDICATED TO
MY PARENTS AND MY DAUGHTER

MANY THANKS ARE DUE TO THE FOLLOWING:

My mother Anne Giwa-Amu, my daughter Virginia Jibowu,
Kase Lawal, Mohammed Idris, Paddy Davies, Everest Ekong,
Abdulmumini Yunus, Toyin Akomolafe, John and Rose Uddoh,
Stella Oni, Shailesh Chavda, Peter Pek, Eddie Iroh,
Kayode Soyinka, Chuks Iloegbunam,
Geraldine Ofori, Charles Aniagolu, Ola Opesan,
Yoliswa Siyolwe and the Africa Centre.

ONE

OBLIVIOUS TO THE world, Sade strolled around her father's garden. It was intensely green and the enchanting smell of flowers filled the cool evening air. Like the garden of Eden, the trees were heavily overburdened with ripe tropical fruit. Surrounding the garden was a red hibiscus hedge which effectively concealed a barbed wire fence.

Sade approached the front of the house and the dogs began to bark. Her uncle's blue Mercedes-Benz pulled up in the gravel driveway and her twin cousins Taiwo and Kehinde jumped out. They slammed shut the doors and Innocent, the five foot Ibo houseboy, rushed to meet them. In his khaki uniform he cowered in acceptance of his inferior status.

'Welcome Sah!' he shouted, looking up at their tall imposing figures.

He had never seen them before, but he knew that they had to be very important people to have arrived in a Mercedes.

'Thank you!' they responded walking past him towards the front door.

At eighteen, the twins looked magnificent. They were both over six foot with strong athletic builds. Their afro hair cut appeared like a halo around their heads and they hid their mischievous eyes behind sun glasses.

On seeing the twins, Sade rushed to meet them.

'Taiwo!' she cried out. 'And Kehinde! I can't believe it.'

'Look at you!' laughed Taiwo sweeping her off the ground in a big hug. 'You've grown into a real stunner.'

He released his grip and she turned to Kehinde.

'What about you two? You must have been driving all the girls wild back in London. Come in. Mum and Dad are in for a big shock when they get back. They're at the club playing tennis.'

She led the way on to the terrazzo porch. Their presence sent the red-headed lizards skedaddling from beneath the pot plants. In the lounge she switched on the electric fan and pressed the bell to call the houseboy.

'What will you have to drink?' she asked as they sat down. Before they had the chance to reply Innocent had appeared from the kitchen.

'I haven't had Star beer for so long I think I've forgotten what it tastes like.' laughed Taiwo. 'Get me a Star!' he ordered Innocent.

'Yes Sah!'

'And one for me!' requested Kehinde.

'Bring me a Fanta! And bring groundnut. You hear!'

'Yes Madam!'

Innocent returned to the kitchen.

'Boy did I miss you two,' Sade laughed. 'I remember when your father first sent you to England, I cried so much because I wanted to go with you. My father got so fed up that he started making arrangements to pack me off to an English boarding school. Only my mother prevented him from doing so.'

'You would have suffered,' Taiwo laughed. 'The cold alone would have driven you home.'

'It was hell!' Kehinde recalled. 'You can count yourself lucky.'

'You have just completed your O Levels haven't you?' Taiwo asked Sade.

'Yes! The results are out next week. I just pray that I've managed to scrape through or my father will kill me.'

'Scrape through? I'm sure you will fly through. No sweat!' Taiwo's voice was filled with excitement.

'I wish I was that confident,' Sade responded. 'Have you had your A Level results yet?'

'Yes!' Taiwo sounded very disappointed. 'Well! You know we needed three A Levels?' He paused. Sade watched him intently. 'I scraped a C in Biology.' He turned to his brother.

'Kehinde! What did you get?'

'In biology? I made a B.'

Sade realised that they were keeping her in suspense to tease.

'You boys are terrible!' she scolded, her dark brown eyes sparkling in delight. 'You haven't changed one bit.'

'Why? Didn't you think we'd make it?' asked Taiwo.

'Of course I knew you would. So is it Oxford or Cambridge?'

'We got into the University of Ibadan,' replied Taiwo who now appeared genuinely disappointed.

Their father had been boasting that they were bound to obtain places at either Oxford or Cambridge. They had performed brilliantly at the O Level exams, passing nine subjects each.

'Congratulations!' smiled Sade attempting to brush over their disappointment. 'So when's the party?'

'Saturday night. It's going to be really something else!' laughed Taiwo.

'I'm so excited. You know my father has not let me out of the house for the past four months.' She knew that her father would never forbid her from attending the twins celebrations.

Innocent returned and distributed the drinks. Sade turned on the record player.

'*Say it loud!*' blasted out the voice of James Brown to the female chorus of: '*I'm Black and proud!*'

'I hope you will invite a few of your friends to our party.' said Taiwo. 'Especially those half-caste sisters that go to your school.'

'You mean Sophia and Marilyn?' It was Sade's turn to tease. 'I thought you would have forgotten them by now.'

'You must be joking. Please invite them,' Taiwo pleaded.

'We met their brother with his Ibo wife on the flight from Lagos. Unfortunately we had not set a date otherwise we would have told him.'

'Their brother isn't married,' Sade puzzled.

'Isn't his name Clive?' asked Taiwo.

Sade went hot with embarrassment and became tongue-tied. Clive was her childhood sweetheart and she had assumed that one day they would become man and wife. She tried hard to maintain her composure.

'They are not married yet,' added Kehinde. 'He said they were on their way to the East to perform the native wedding.'

'That his wife is so handsome!' laughed Taiwo.

'What do you mean?' Sade forced a smile

'She's handsome now!' repeated Taiwo. 'In fact, I have never seen a girl so handsome.'

The twins collapsed in fits of laughter.

'You boys will never change!'

Suddenly a car approached the house and the twins stretched to see who it was. A white Mercedes pulled up by the front porch and her parents got out. The twins appeared nervous, all their arrogance gone.

'Ah!' said Justice Uwaifo as he entered the lounge. The twins jumped off their seats. 'Ah! Taiwo? Kehinde?' Justice Uwaifo appeared astonished by their height. They towered over him.

'Good evening Uncle! Good evening Auntie!' They shook his hand and gave their auntie a kiss.

It occurred to Sade how ridiculous her parents looked in their white tennis outfits. Her Nigerian father was now fifty and his large beer belly pushed the waistline of his shorts to his groin. Shamelessly he exposed his scarred bow legs. She had never found her father handsome, though her mother had assured her that he had been so in his youth. Now the front of his head was bald and he had long given up pulling out the white hairs. But then her English mother was no beauty either.

She looked somewhat like a starvation victim, her legs nothing but skin and bone. Sade noticed that her mother was sun burnt and the skin on her face and arms was peeling. Her father approached and she jumped out of his permanently reserved seat.

'Turn off that player!' he shouted at her as they sat down.

The twins were now tense and upright in their seats.

'Your father has informed me that you were unable to obtain places at any British University.' said Justice Uwaifo. He always spoke slowly, emphasising the words he regarded as important. 'We are all very disappointed. Especially as your father invested a great deal in your education. Anyhow! Praise be to God that your father was able to pull a few strings to get you into Ibadan. However, I must say, I am not happy about you going to Ibadan. With these elections coming up in November, that place is not safe. Anyway, since your father has assured me that there is no alternative, I will give you the address of my friend in the UPGA (United Progressive Grand Alliance). He will keep an eye on you there.'

'Thank-you, Uncle!' they chorused.

'But make sure when you get there that you do not involve yourself in any student demonstrations,' warned Justice Uwaifo. 'You are no longer in England. The police will shoot you here.'

'Yes, Uncle!' they chorused yet again.

'Is the UPGA Chief Awolowo's party?' asked Kehinde trying to change the subject.

'Well, you know Chief Awolowo has been imprisoned for treason but his followers formed the United Progressive Grand Alliance of which I am a member.' Justice Uwaifo smiled proudly. 'They are much preferred to that corrupt Akintola with his Nigerian National Grand Alliance and I am sure we will win the next election with a massive majority.'

The twins knew that Nigeria had gained its Independence from Great Britain in 1960 and that tribalism was creating regional violence, but they were unable to keep up with the political situation from their English boarding school.

'Uncle, we brought you and Auntie a small gift,' said Taiwo, handing over a box of White horse whisky.

'That's very kind of you,' said Justice Uwaifo, accepting it. 'And you remembered my favourite drink. Well! Let us drink to your future and thank God for your safe return. Innocent!' he yelled. 'In-nocent!'

Mrs Uwaifo pressed the electric bell and Innocent ran in.

'Yes Sah!' He had a frightened look on his face.

'Get five glasses,' demanded Justice Uwaifo.

Innocent hurried back to the kitchen, returning moments later with five wet tumblers on a tray.

'Go and dry them,' ordered Mrs Uwaifo. 'And where's the tray cloth?'

'Madam?' Innocent puzzled.

He didn't know what a tray cloth was.

'Take them and go and dry them!' shouted Justice Uwaifo.

Trembling and close to tears, Innocent picked up the tray and returned to the kitchen. Within seconds he reappeared with the tray of tumblers. The tray was now covered in a white lace cloth.

'Let us pray.' Justice Uwaifo stood up and the others followed his lead. 'In the name of the Father and of the Son and of the Holy Ghost.'

They made the sign of the cross and chorused 'Amen!'. Suddenly lightning struck, thunder roared and the rain poured down outside. Through her almost closed eyes, Sade could see the pleading look on her father's face as he stared at the ceiling.

'…Lord we thank you for the safe return of our children Taiwo and Kehinde. We pray that you will continue to protect and guide them, in the name of our Lord Jesus Christ.'

'Amen!' everyone muttered.

'Enable them to succeed in their studies, so that we may be

14

proud to call them our children. In the name of the Father and of the Son and of the Holy Ghost.'

'Amen!'

Justice Uwaifo picked up the bottle of whisky and headed for the porch. He stretched out his arm to pour libation and the house was thrown into darkness. This was obviously a very bad omen indeed.

'Innocent!' Justice Uwaifo yelled. 'Oh God! Where is this boy? In-nocent!'

Anticipating his demands, Innocent hurried in with a bush lamp. Justice Uwaifo poured the whisky into the tumblers, the shadows chasing one another on the walls. A sombre gloom took over the gathering.

'Well! Distribute the glasses,' Justice Uwaifo ordered Innocent, who quickly obeyed before returning to the kitchen.

'Cheers! To your future success!' said Justice Uwaifo forcing a smile. Everyone responded by clinking their glasses together.

Taiwo proceeded to give Sade a dress they had brought back from London.

'Uncle, we have to go,' said Taiwo.

'Ah Ah! So soon!' he protested.

'We would have stayed longer, but Dad needs the car. He has to attend a political meeting.'

'But that's not till eight o clock. In fact, I will be chairing that meeting.'

'I think he wants to visit somebody first,' said Kehinde.

'Well! If you insist.' Justice Uwaifo slowly led the way towards the front door.

The twins shook hands before running through the rain to the car. Slowly Kehinde drove down the dark driveway, the torrential rain badly affecting his visibility.

'Did you notice how miserable Sade became when her father arrived?' Taiwo asked.

'Of course, I noticed.'

'He has always resented Sade for surviving whilst her

15

brothers died. Idowu was telling me that one of the village elders accused Sade of being a witch. The man said she laid traps for the souls of her brothers and ate them. Can you believe an educated man would believe such rubbish?'

When the twins had gone, Justice and Mrs Uwaifo went to the dining table. Sade bade them good-night and made her way up the dark staircase. The hurricane lamp she carried made her feel like an insignificant little firefly.

In her bedroom she changed into a long white night-dress. After taming her hair in plaits, she blew out the flame of her lamp and climbed into bed. Lightning struck illuminating her bedroom and at the roar of thunder she pulled the sheet up over her head. As a child she had been petrified by these tropical storms and recalled her father's laughter at her screams. She tried to escape into the other world but her mind was in too much turmoil to allow sleep. The heavy rains thundered down on the grey asbestos roof sending shivers up and down her spine. Yet again thunder roared and lightning cracked. The short breaks were filled with the jubilation of the crickets and toads singing their wondrous song.

Clive to marry an Ibo girl! There had to be some mistake. After all, her parents would have been the first to know. The Udochis were her parents best friends and Clive's sisters would definitely have mentioned it. Suddenly it occurred to her what the problem might be. Clive obviously knew that Justice Uwaifo would never consent to her getting married at sixteen. Clive was already twenty-three and a qualified Barrister. He couldn't be expected to wait another five years until she finished university.

Sade worked out the answer to her problem. She would give herself to Clive. Once she became pregnant her father would be forced to approve of their marriage. Lying in bed she pictured the whole scene in her mind. A white wedding in the Roman Catholic Church with four bridesmaids. There would be her cousins Idowu, Beauty, Queen and Cecilia. But then, she had to have Clive's sisters, Sophia and Marilyn. That would mean six bridesmaids. But if she did not ask her school friends Osas and Lola they would never speak to her again. Eight bridesmaids. The Chief Bridesmaid would be? If she asked Sophia then Marilyn would be jealous, and if she did not ask one of her cousins the whole family would be offended. It would have to be Idowu. Or maybe Idowu could be Matron of honour and Sophia, Chief bridesmaid. But then, the Matron of honour was supposed to be married...

TWO

SADE WAS WOKEN the next morning by the chirping of the weaver-birds, wrangling in the tall mango tree outside. The bright sunlight beamed brilliantly through the pink curtains that covered her bedroom window. She placed her arms over her eyes to escape its penetrating beam. Lying there, she tried to rethink her plans from the night before. Clive! Excitedly she jumped out of bed and rushed on to the front balcony adjoining her bedroom. Her father's police orderly waited by the Mercedes. Looking down the long palm-tree and poinsettia lined driveway she noticed a group of eight prisoners with their warden. Their shirts lay scattered over the bushy plants as they sliced through the long grass with cutlasses. One of the prisoners sat on a cement block tapping rhythmically at a bottle while singing in Edo.

'*This man that enslaves us is a wicked man.*
He eats our food
He carries our food to his wife
His wife cooks our food for his children
God Almighty punish this man.'
'*Yeh! Yeh! God Almighty punish this man.*' the others chorused.
'*God Almighty punish this man's wife.*'
'*Yeh! Yeh! God Almighty punish this man's wife.*'
'*God Almighty punish this man's children…*'
The Yoruba prison warden was unable to understand their

song but when Justice Uwaifo appeared in the driveway the singing stopped. Justice Uwaifo walked towards his Mercedes and the police orderly rushed to open the door. He got into the back seat while the police orderly sat next to the driver. The car went past the gate and the prisoners began a new song.

Sade made her way into the green mosaic bathroom. After cleaning her teeth, she examined them in the shaving mirror. They were perfectly formed and her thick pink lips made them appear whiter than they actually were. She undid her plait and began to brush her hair. It was long and thick, forcing her to brush through one section at a time.

Having stripped off her night-dress, she stared at her reflection in the mirror. It was like a pool reflecting beauty; her beauty. She stepped into the shower and turned on the water. Reaching for the bottle of shampoo, she poured some onto her hand and worked it into her hair. The water cascaded off her body leaving a sea of lather in the shower basin.

Wrapped in her pink towel, she returned to her bedroom. The dress that the twins had bought for her lay discarded on the floor. She tried it on. It would have been a perfect fit except that it was too short. She knew that her father would never allow her to wear it. Swirling around in front of the wardrobe mirror, she admired her perfect figure. The black dress looked stunning on her. She recalled her mother's necklace and bracelet and decided that she would wear the dress to the twins' party.

Downstairs Sade found one place setting left on the breakfast table. She looked at the teapot hidden beneath a knitted tea cosy. The tea would be stone cold.

'Innocent!' she yelled sitting down at the table. She emptied some cornflakes into the bowl and Innocent appeared from the kitchen.

'Good morning Madam!'

'Morning!' She hardly looked at him as she spoke. 'Go and

make fresh tea.'

'Yes Madam!' He removed the teapot and returned to the kitchen.

Sade covered her cereal with diluted condensed milk before reaching for the sugar bowl. Two soldier ants marched defiantly around the rim and she crushed their rebellion with her spoon. She looked at the vase of freshly picked Blushing Hibiscus. Anyone seeing them in the morning would swear they were pure virginal white. Yet by evening they had turned into the most flirtatious pink. Sade abandoned her breakfast and made her way into her father's study. She picked up the heavy black telephone receiver and tried to call Sophia. The line was dead. The night storm had obviously brought down the telephone lines. Her mother would have to drop her in the club. Clive would probably be there with his sisters by mid-day.

Sade found her mother in the lounge reading a novel. As usual, she was surrounded by a cloud of smoke from her cigarette. Mrs Uwaifo's daily routine had remained unchanged for years. Her life revolved around the needs of her husband and daughter.

'Morning Mum!'

'Morning luv!'

There was a tenderness in Susan's eyes whenever she looked at her daughter. Sade sat down.

'Did Mrs Udochi tell you that Clive is getting married?' Sade tried not to appear too concerned.

'Clive? Who said he's getting married?'

'Taiwo!'

'Funny! His mother was at the club last night and she never said nothing.'

'Can you drop me in the club later?'

'We'll see!' She returned to her book.

Although in her late thirties Susan now looked closer to fifty. Her face was drawn and haggard, her breasts had dropped and

20

her lean body had lost its shape. Her straight nose and thin lips were from her English father, but her blond hair and blue eyes were from the German mother that had deserted her. Susan was a plain looking woman and made no attempt to improve her appearance with make-up. Most of the time she wore a caftan. After fifteen years in Africa she possessed a mottled tan but still she burnt red under the African sun.

Sade watched her mother. She could not help wondering whether she had ever been in love. Whether she had ever shared intimate secrets with her girlfriends or been part of any silly girlish pranks and giggles. It didn't seem possible! She must have always been just as she was now–mature, sensible and boring.

But Sade was wrong. In her youth, Susan Smith was full of fun. Every Saturday night she was at the dance halls, rocking and rolling the night away with her stepsisters, Angela and Christine. They shared secrets! All secrets but one that is, for Susan could never bring herself to confess her love of a black man. She had heard her father's opinion about blacks all too often.

'Bloody Niggers!' he would shout. 'Nothing but a bunch of monkeys. Ought to go back to the jungle where they come from.'

Bob Smith had never been further than Blackpool with his family on holiday, but as far as he was concerned he knew all there was to know about blacks. He had seen it all in the pictures. How the native cannibals jumped about in the jungle stark naked amongst the screeching monkeys and roaring lions. As far as Bob was concerned the best things that happened to blacks were slavery and colonisation. He saw it as the only way to drag them into the civilised world.

It was a cruel irony for Bob that Susan met Felix at his corner shop. Times were hard and he had recently removed the sign which said 'No Blacks' from his shop window. When Felix came through the doorway, Christine was sitting in the shop knitting. She did not see a man come through the door, she saw a gorilla dressed up in a black suit. Dropping all her stitches she fled to the kitchen. Astounded by her reaction Felix also felt the urge to flee. He looked behind him expecting to find a monster with a great axe.

'A golliwog!' he heard Christine shout.

Susan and Angela peeped through the long curtain hanging across the doorway.

'Where's Dad? There's a nig-nog in the shop.' Christine persisted in the background.

'What the hell's the matter with you? Your Father's down the betting shop,' came the voice of a mature woman.

'There's a nig-nog in the shop. Go on Mam! Go and get rid of him!'

With her daughters watching from a safe distance, Mrs Smith nervously approached the front counter. She was too scared to throw the 'nigger' out in case he turned nasty.

'What do you want?' she demanded, staring anxiously into his dark eyes.

'A pint of milk please.'

Mrs Smith hesitated. Suddenly she reached for the bottle of milk and placed it on the counter between them.

'And a loaf of bread, and a tin of sardines,' said Felix.

Susan watched as her stepmother placed the items before him wondering whether he intended to pay. She kept an eye on the bunch of bananas hanging down above his head, expecting him to leap up and grab them before jumping out of the shop screeching in delight. Yet he kept asking for such 'civilised' items. He didn't ask for the monkey nuts or even an orange.

Felix handed Mrs Smith a pound note and she stared at his dark hand. Nervously she fidgeted with her hair before suddenly snatching the note. She banged his change down on the counter.

Felix left the shop feeling dejected and humiliated. After

22

years of colonial rule he had accepted white superiority and in turn he had accepted his own inferiority. He continued to patronise Mr Smith's shop because there was no alternative. The months went by and the family grew accustomed to his daily visits. They realised that he was different to the natives shown on television. He was not suddenly going to jump over the counter and cannibalise them.

Susan's fear of Felix gradually subsided and the very mystery of him excited her curiosity and captivated her mind. She wanted to know where he had come from and what he was doing in her country. When she discovered that he was a university law student, her curiosity turned to admiration. She found herself yearning for his daily visits and gladly accepted his invitation to dinner.

On the appointed evening, Susan Smith walked quickly down Hayter Road, head lowered to avoid detection. She wore a chiffon scarf to protect her beehive, held in place with sugar and water. Susan was nearly five foot seven, with large breasts and wide hips. Her eyes were startling blue and heavily made up with false eyelashes and blue eye shadow. At twenty-three she was dressed in the height of fashion.

Arriving at the terraced house where Felix lived she banged on the door and Felix rushed to open it.

'Good Evening!' He was obviously delighted to see her.

'Evening! Bloody freezing, ain't it?' She made her way into the hall-way.

'Yes! And the smog is terrible, I could hardly find my way back home.' His voice was deep, filling her with shivers of delight. Their eyes met and Susan smiled affectionately. He pushed open the door to his bed-sit and she strolled in. The room was warm but stank of paraffin from the heater. She handed him her thick winter coat and scarf before sitting down on the edge of his bed. He hung the coat up in his wardrobe and sat down next to her.

'When are your exams then?' asked Susan looking at the pile

of law books on his desk.

'My finals are next year but after that I have to be called to the Bar.'

'There's posh!' She slipped her arm through his. 'So do they have many lawyers in Africa?'

'Not really! In the past our Oba used to settle disputes but colonisation forced us to adopt the English legal system.'

'What's an Oba?'

'It means king.'

'Like King Kong–aye?' She teased, pushing her splendid bosom against him.

'Not like King Kong! Our Obas used to be very powerful.'

'Yeah?'

Felix was enraged. They sat in silence for a while. Susan felt sorry that she had offended him and tried to change the subject.

'So do men and women kiss in Africa?'

'No! We bite ourselves.'

'Bloody hell! I suppose you learnt kissing in the pictures?'

Before she could say another word, he covered her mouth with his. Slowly he pulled her backward, her arms coming up around his neck. With his ebony shade resting against her ivory form, they kissed and caressed under the beautiful glow of the paraffin heater. Susan felt like the sacrificial lamb submitting to the powerful lion that devoured her.

THREE

SUSAN HURRIED OUT of the chemist's in a state of confusion, her worst nightmare realised. She was pregnant for a black man! Her mind drifted in torment as she tried to imagine what the child would look like. She passed a wall of graffiti saying: Keep Britain White! Arriving at the terraced house where Felix lived, she banged desperately on the front door and Felix opened it.

'Susan!' he grinned.

'I'm bloody pregnant,' she cried falling into his arms.

Felix shut the front door and helped her into his room.

'Are you sure?' He sat down next to her on the bed.

'Course I'm bloody sure. I've just come from the chemist, haven't I?'

'What do you want to do?' Felix rested his chin on the palm of his hand as he spoke.

'Dunno! If me Dad finds out, he'll bloody kill me! I've got to get rid of it.'

Felix jumped to his feet and began to pace the room.

'I will have nothing to do with this!'

'What do you mean?'

'Don't you know that an abortion is a criminal offense? And I've heard of many women ending up dead having back street abortions.'

'What am I gonna do?' Susan cried standing up to face him.

'First, have it! If you cannot look after it then find someone to adopt it.'

Susan stared at Felix. Didn't he know that no white family would want to adopt his black baby? She sobbed bitterly at the thought of her child growing up in a Dr Barnardo's children's home.

Felix tried to comfort her, leading her back to the bed.

'Let's get married,' she pleaded.

Felix didn't respond. He thought about his wife and three children in Africa. When he first arrived in Great Britain, he had missed them tremendously but now his perception of them had changed. The way that black people were portrayed in Britain made him ashamed to be an 'associate'. He wanted to be honourable and respected, like the white man. Felix looked into Susan's blue eyes. They were tense with anxiety. Her alabaster skin and blond hair never ceased to fascinate him. She appeared alien and above the primitive. An English wife! She would certainly be a prestigious thing to possess enabling him to enter the elite white world. As his previous marriage had not been legally registered, he could not be found guilty of bigamy and the native law and custom allowed him to take as many wives as he could afford.

'Well?' Susan frowned.

'Nothing would make me happier.'

Susan was ecstatic. She grabbed his chin, giving him a big kiss. Never in her wildest dreams did she expect to marry a lawyer. Her first boyfriend had been a chimney sweep and he was quickly followed by a rag and bone man.

'Shall I come and see your father?'

'No!' Susan panicked. 'I'll tell him.'

She gave him a kiss and set off.

Susan arrived at home to find the shop shut. Using her key she let herself in. The family were in the middle room, huddled around a coal fire. Bob Smith was reading the local newspaper whilst his wife and daughters were knitting.

'Hello!' Susan could hardly wait to break the news. 'Had a proposal today!' she announced sitting beside Christine.

'He must be bloody desperate,' her father responded, hardly lifting his head from the newspaper.

'Don't take any notice of him,' retorted her stepmother.

'You're joking ain't you?' asked Christine.

'No!' Susan lit a cigarette.

'Well, go on then. Who's the lucky man?' Her stepmother sounded eager.

'He's a lawyer.'

For the first time, Bob Smith looked directly at Susan who fidgeted nervously.

'Lawyer aye?'

'Well, he's going to be a lawyer. He's at the university.'

'Where've you been hiding him then?' demanded her father.

'Haven't been hiding him! He's been in the shop millions of times.'

Susan tried to avoid all eye contact.

'And you never said nothing? You're a dark horse!' her father stared at her and Susan averted her eyes. 'You're bloody pregnant ain't yah? Your mother said she'd noticed something.'

'He'd marry me even if I wasn't pregnant. He luvs me.'

'Leave her alone Bob,' her stepmother scolded. 'If she wants to get married, good for her.'

'You'd better bring him home then,' demanded her father.

'Yeah! Tell him to come for dinner on Saturday night.'

Overspending on the weekly budget, Mrs Smith even splashed out on a bottle of wine to accompany the three course meal. She was determined to show this law student that she had some class.

Eight p.m. on Saturday, Felix knocked at the door and Bob rushed to open it. He did not realise that the 'nigger' on his doorstep was his prospective son-in-law.

'Shop's shut!' he told him aggressively.

He did not want his future son-in-law arriving to find out that he accepted black customers.

'Good evening Sir,' Felix smiled.

'I said shop's shut.'

Susan peeped out from behind her father.

'Dad! It's Felix,' she said, pushing past him.

'Jesus Christ! You bloody slag!' Her father pushed her off the doorstep and locked her out.

'Oh my Gawd!' gasped Mrs Smith, peeping out of the shop window. 'The filthy rotten dirty slag. Bringing a bloody golliwog here! What the hell will the neighbours say? I told you that girl was no good.'

Susan cried as she watched her step mother pulling Angela and Christine away from the window. Felix took her in his arms and they walked the short distance back to his bed-sit. The following morning they got married at the local registry office with two strangers acting as witnesses to the sombre occasion.

A few days after the wedding, Felix was walking home from the bus stop when he realised he was being followed. A gang of teddy boys were just a few yards away from him.

'Come here Nigger!' shouted the ring leader. The others jeered. They ran towards him swinging bicycle chains above their heads. Overcome with fear, Felix grabbed onto his precious leather brief case and took to his heels. Luckily he was close to home.

Susan heard the door slam and rushed out of the bed-sit. Felix was leaning against the front door panting desperately. He looked terrified.

'We're gonna get you Nigger!' the teddy boys shouted outside. 'What the hell's going on?' asked Susan, her face pale with fright.

'Teddy Boys! We have to get out of here!' he responded running into the room.

'Oh my Gawd! Me Dad must have sent them!'

The couple packed up their few belongings and went to stay with a Nigerian friend living in Notting Hill in London. During the day Felix attended lectures whilst Susan walked the streets looking for a place to live. She found a few rooms but when her black husband turned up the rooms were always 'gone!'.

In desperation the couple accepted a bed-sit in a rat and cockroach infested house in Latimer Road. The cold, damp room was in the attic heated only by a single bar electric fire. The mattress on the old wooden bed stank of urine and apart from an old oak wardrobe the room was bare. The bathroom on the second floor was furnished with an old stone sink and a cast-iron bath that sent hot water cold within minutes. The brightest aspect of the bathroom was the wooden floorboards, covered in blue linoleum paint. On the ground floor was the kitchen, sparsely furnished with an old grey enamel stove and a huge stone sink. Leading off the kitchen were the doors to the larder and the dirty, cold lavatory outside.

Life was a bitter struggle. With no radio, telephone or television there was no escape from their dreary existence. Without a washing machine or vacuum cleaner Susan laboured each day performing the same mundane chores. Her only entertainment was a lonely walk through the park dreaming of the wonderful life ahead when Felix would qualify as a barrister.

At about 4 a.m one morning, as Felix lay sleeping, Susan made her way downstairs to use the lavatory. She was hugely pregnant and in pain but her midwife had informed her that the baby was not due for another three weeks. She had already called the midwife out on three false alarms, so now she felt that she had to be certain. She did not wish to disturb Felix, because he had been studying into the early hours of the morning. With his final exams approaching, he had become tense and irritable. Gripping her belly, she sat on the lavatory. The tiny room was freezing cold. The bare concrete floor was stinking with urine and the plaster was dropping off the walls. Susan attributed her pain to Felix's fish head soup. They practically survived on fish heads which were given away by the fishmongers for cat food. With no idea of the time, she did not realise that she had been sitting on the lavatory for over two hours. The pain intensified and she screamed in vain for help.

She knew that the child was coming and there was nothing she could do to stop it. Leaning against the wall with her legs apart, she squatted. She gave an almighty push and the child slipped into the world. The baby gave a little cry. Then, taking a deep breath, it began to bawl.

Susan screamed again and this time Felix did hear. With his dressing gown wrapped around him, he rushed outside to the toilet. Pushing open the door he found Susan holding on to a slimy mass.

'Jesus!' he said. He stared into Susan's face for some guidance on what he should do. He had never witnessed a delivery but he knew that the umbilical cord had to be tied close to the baby and cut. By now Susan had delivered the placenta which hung down from the baby and rested on the floor. Felix raced into the kitchen where he found a sharp knife. He cut a thin strip of cloth from his pyjama trousers and hurried back to Susan. He tied a knot close to the child's body and cut the cord.

'It's a girl!' Susan cried as she handed Felix the screaming child.

His moment of silence betrayed his innermost feelings. He had wanted a son.

When the midwife arrived two hours later, there was little for her to do. Felix had cleaned up the mess and got mother and child upstairs. They couldn't afford a cot, so the baby was placed in a wooden draw.

A few weeks after the birth, Felix's brother Samuel came to visit with his wife Miriam and their twin sons, Taiwo and Kehinde. Samuel was now a qualified doctor and about to make the return journey to Nigeria.

'Don't worry!' he teased Felix who made no attempt to hide his disappointment at having a daughter. 'The next one will be a boy, as will the next one after that.'

'Have you named her yet?' Miriam asked Susan.

'Nah!' Susan replied. 'Felix's Dad sent a name from Nigeria.' She turned to Felix. 'What was it again?'

'*Adesuwa!* It means born to wealth.'

'What I want to know is where's the fucking wealth?'   Susan giggled, rolling her eyes as she spoke.

Felix looked embarrassed.

'You know our people back at home think once we come to the motherland we are in God's pocket.' laughed Miriam. 'They think the streets of London are paved with gold. Only God knows how we suffer in this country. I can hardly wait to get home. At least there I can find a girl to run after these children.'

'Your mother sent a name as well, didn't she?' Susan nudged Felix.

'Yes! *Olasade*. It means honour is like a crown.'

Felix put his arm around Susan and looked into his daughter's deep royal blue eyes.

'Olasade is a nice name,' said Miriam. 'You can abbreviate it to Sade.'

'Sade!' repeated Susan softly. 'It sounds nice like that.'

Susan felt sad that her baby had not been welcomed by one white person, yet Felix's friends and relatives kept arriving one after another with their small gifts. She was very aware that they were now outcasts to white society.

FOUR

SUSAN GIGGLED AS she read something in her novel. Sade fidgeted impatiently and stared stonily at her mother.

'Mum! Can we go now?'

Susan stubbed out her cigarette and folded over the top corner of her page.

'All right! Go and get my bag.'

Sade ran upstairs, grabbing her mother's handbag from her parents bedroom. In her own room she stuffed her bikini and towel into a raffia bag. She returned downstairs to find that her mother had returned to her novel. Sade shoved the hand bag onto her mother's lap.

'Come on then!' Sade's voice was demanding as usual.

'For Christ's sake! What the hell's the matter with you? If you don't bloody behave I won't take you,' Susan scolded before slowly standing up. 'And what about your lunch?' she fretted walking towards the front door.

'I'll eat at the club.'

'So you'll need money?'

Sade nodded and her mother handed her five shillings.

They set off, winding down their windows due to the heat. The prisoners waved and shouted greetings as they past.

All that Sade could think about was Clive! Like hers, his handsome face incorporated the broad African features of his Nigerian father with those sharp delicate features of his English mother. His six foot frame was firm with muscle and no-one else possessed his seductive, deep brown eyes or those tempting lips. Sade had taken it for granted that one day they would be man and wife. Ever since she could remember Clive had been a part of her life. With his sisters they had spent hours at the club, swimming or playing tennis and although they had never made love, they were in love with one another.

Sade felt apprehensive as they approached the club.

'I'll collect you at five,' said her mother pulling up in the car park.

Sade got out and banged shut the door. She made her way into the bar. There was no sign of Clive. Neither was he upstairs in the billiards room. At the pool-side Sade found Sophia lying in the cool shade of the palm trees. The pool was surrounded by the families of white embassy officials and businessmen, waited on by uniformed black waiters. The whites and westernised black elite lived a separate existence from the native population and the club was regarded as one of the few places of civilised entertainment. Membership was strictly by referral and interview, a system set up by the British colonialists who built the club.

Sade waved as she noticed Marilyn sitting at the edge of the pool dangling her slim legs in the clear blue water. A Lebanese tried to impress her with his dive and Marilyn quickly stood up laughing at his belly flop.

Sade headed for the changing rooms, quickly slipping into her flimsy bikini.

'Sade! Your hair has grown even longer,' said Marilyn as Sade pulled up a deck chair. The sisters both had soft, short afro-hair.

Marilyn began to laugh.

'I remember that day when Sade was making *shakara* [show off] in school.' Marilyn's Chinese looking eyes sparkled as she spoke.

'Here we go again!' Sade sighed, relaxing back into the chair.

'The girls gave her such a beating,' Marilyn persisted.

'Was that the time that Sister Josephine expelled Sade and Queen?' asked Sophia.

'Yes,' Marilyn laughed, relating the story. 'Sade removed the ribbon holding up her hair and started throwing her hair back and forth. Just showing off. Just because the black girls are not allowed long hair. Queen became irritated by the display and called her a "cooked scone!" Instead of keeping quiet, Sade retorted saying she'd rather be cooked than burnt like charcoal. Since she offended the whole class, most of the girls joined Queen and gave her a good beating.'

Sophia and Marilyn laughed hysterically.

'Jealousy! As if it's my fault sister told them to cut their hair.' hissed Sade.

'But you don't have to torment them about it,' Marilyn laughed.

A group of Lebanese men arrived and sat next to the girls. Sophia nudged Sade.

'Don't look now,' she whispered.

'Isn't that the man renting your father's house–the one that owns a casino?'

Sade turned to find a strange Lebanese man winking at her. She blushed and quickly turned away.

'Now he will think I fancy him,' she scolded Sophia.

'I told you not to look,' Sophia smiled at the men, fluttering her long eyelashes.

'Remove your face,' Sade scolded.

'Don't mind her,' whispered Marilyn. 'She always fancies these Lebanese men.'

'Bloody gamblers and drunkards!' said Sade scorning them.

'There was one making eyes at us last week,' laughed Marilyn. 'Sophia kept asking me "Isn't he handsome? Isn't he handsome?" You know what work he did?' Marilyn asked Sade.

'What?'

'A chicken farmer!' Marilyn announced aloud.

'Shut up!' Sophia whispered. 'You want them to hear you?'

There was a moment of silence until Sade could hold back her curiosity no longer.

'I hear your brother is getting married?'

'Who told you?' demanded Sophia.

'My cousins, Taiwo and Kehinde. They've just returned from London and accidentally bumped into Clive who joined them on the flight from Lagos.'

'Well you're not supposed to know. If my mother finds out that Clive is already going around announcing this thing, she will have a heart attack.'

'Why?'

'Well Clive never mentioned this girl to anybody,' said Sophia angrily. 'He just arrived saying he was on his way to Umuahia to "knock on the door". We could not believe our ears. That's where he is now,' Sophia shrugged.

'Worst of all, this girl is so bush,' Marilyn sighed. 'She insisted on cooking for us, maybe to impress our Dad. When she served the food we saw one chicken's foot standing up in the soup, like this'. Marilyn sat up in her deck chair, opening up her hand to indicate what a cooked chicken's foot would look like.

'Yeah God!' shouted Sade as her friends hissed, flicking their fingers in disgust.

'Can you imagine?' asked Sophia frowning. 'And that's not all. Clive brought this stupid brother of hers to stay with us. One Emeka! Do you know he had the audacity to start chasing me. I was just lying on my bed minding my own business when he came into my room.'

'He came into your room?' Sade gasped.

'Yes now! I was looking at him.'

Sade and Marilyn fell about laughing.

'He even had the guts to sit on my bed. He said, "Sophia! There is something I want to talk to you about." I said, "Talk now!" He said, "Ah-hmm, You know I really like you? I would like you to be my girl-friend."'

'So did you agree?' Sade teased.

'You must be stupid. I told him to get out of my room and never venture near there again.'

They all fell about laughing.

'By the way,' Sade smiled, 'my cousins asked me to invite you to their celebration party tomorrow. They passed their A Levels and have been accepted at the University of Ibadan.'

'Yes!' shouted Sophia. 'I'm so happy. I've also been admitted in Ibadan to read Law. What are they reading?'

'Medicine. You know they have to take over their father's hospital.'

'I hope Dad will allow us to attend the party,' said Marilyn.

'Why not?' Sophia sounded puzzled. 'Clive will be back by then so he can escort us.'

'Taiwo said Clive's girlfriend is very handsome?'

The sister's laughed.

'Wait until you see her,' said Sophia.

'Is she big?' Sade persisted.

'No! She's small and black like a mosquito, with legs that resemble sticks.'

'And you need to see her head,' laughed Marilyn.

'God forbid I should have a head like that,' said Sophia flicking her fingers around her head.

'What's wrong with her head?'

'Nothing!' Sophia shrugged. 'Except that she has no hair. She wears a wig from the time that she takes her bath in the morning, to the time she goes to bed at night.'

'And you should see her shape!' Marilyn laughed.

'Which shape? She has no shape.' Sophia shrugged.

'And her teeth-eh! Her teeth come forward like this.' As Marilyn pushed forward her upper jaw, Sophia fell off her deck chair as it collapsed under her hysterical laughter.

Sade and Marilyn laughed until there were tears in their eyes. One of the Lebanese men rushed over to help.

'I can manage,' Sophia snapped. Aggressively she re-erected

her chair, the man retreating toward his teasing friends.

'This girl can't be as bad as you people are making out,' said Sade, rubbing the tears from her eyes.

'She's worse!' shouted Sophia lying back in her chair. 'Bush, black and ugly.'

'So what is Clive doing with her?' asked Sade.

'Isn't it money!' shouted Sophia. 'They say her father is a millionaire and has already built them a bungalow in Lagos. Of course her father knows that no man in his right senses will marry the girl without compensation.'

'Well! When Clive wants to do the thing…' Marilyn laughed.

'Which thing?' asked Sade.

'You know the thing now. At least it should be dark so he will not need to see her.'

'He won't even be able to find her!' said Sophia finishing off her glass of coke.

'So he will just tell her: "Smile!"' laughed Marilyn.

'You girls are too disgusting,' said Sade, struggling out of her chair and diving into the pool. She was devastated, swimming with a determined vengeance. A Lebanese man dived in after her.

'I win you,' he shouted as they turned at the far end.

Sade slowed to get rid of him.

'I am Mustafa,' he smiled, swimming alongside. 'And what is your name?'

She ignored him. As they approached the end of the pool, Sophia and Marilyn began to tease. Slowly she climbed out of the pool relaxing back into her deck chair.

'Let me buy you and your sisters a drink,' said the Lebanese man standing over her.

'We buy our own drinks,' Sade was objectionable.

'You can get me a coke,' Sophia told the man.

Sade shut her eyes. Clive! He was not married yet!

FIVE

ON THE EVENING of the twins party, Mrs Uwaifo wondered why Sade appeared so lethargic; perhaps she was ill. She lacked the usual excitement that a party created. At the last minute Sade made her way upstairs leaving her parents talking whilst listening to Beethoven. Quickly she slipped on her little black dress, and over that she wore one of her mother's caftans. Into a large handbag she placed a small bottle of her mother's perfume together with a small bottle of red food colouring. Filled with nervous excitement she made her way downstairs, her black patent shoes making an uncomfortable clanking noise on the wooden stairs.

'Are you ready now?' her father shouted at her. She nodded.

Justice Uwaifo stood up, adjusting his trousers. He walked towards the front door with his legs uncomfortably apart.

'Come on then!' he shouted at Sade.

'Bye Mum!' Timidly she followed her father, praying that he would not spot the diamante collar of her black dress.

'Bye luv! Have a good time.' Susan sounded dejected.

The driver rushed to open the Mercedes door as Justice Uwaifo approached, whilst Sade hurried around to the other side.

Sade felt nervous sitting in the back seat next to her father. A constant tension existed between them, and if Justice Uwaifo had loved her he had never shown it. Had he not been her father she would not have liked him very much, but as he was her father she felt obliged to love him.

'What is that in your hair?' he enquired looking at the diamante necklace, pinned in the form of a tiara.

'It's Mum's necklace.' Sade brought her hair forward to hide her shoulders.

'Ohhh! You look like a princess!' he smiled kindly. Then there was silence.

They approached Dr Samuel Uwaifo's house. *'This is a man's world!'* by James Brown blasted out at decibel range. The twins had returned with all the latest Black American Soul music, mostly expressing political and racial discontent. Television in Britain had made them very politically aware and they felt a part of the Black struggle against world-wide white domination. As the girls in London cried out for the Beatles, they cried out for Martin Luther King. His 'dream' was their hope of a 'new dawn'. For them, music was not merely entertaining but a means of creating awareness and spreading the message.

For Sade there was no message. She had never heard the word apartheid and knew nothing about racial segregation. She loved good music, whether classical, African highlife or Soul.

'Okay!' said her father abruptly as they pulled up outside the house. 'The driver will collect you at ten.'

Sade got out of the car.

'Bye Dad!' she said softly, shutting the door.

Brushing past the huge 'elephant ears' plant, she made her way across the veranda and into the lounge. It was full of chattering guests, each with a plate of jollof rice, *moin-moin* [bean cake] and chicken on their laps. Everyone between the ages of sixteen and twenty-five whose parents were of any consequence had been invited. Two housegirls carried around trays of food, whilst the houseboy distributed drinks.

The twins sat guard by the record player to stop anyone scratching or borrowing their records. When they saw Sade in a caftan they began to tease.

'Sade! Which one be this?' shouted Taiwo.

Sade hissed and scorned them as she made her way into the kitchen.

'Good Evening Auntie!' She smiled holding open the door ready for her return journey.

'Sade! How are you?' came her Aunt Miriam's usual singing insincerity.

'Fine Auntie. Is Uncle Sam at home?'

'No! He will be back later.'

That was all Sade needed to know. She headed straight for the bathroom, applying red food colouring to her lips. After smothering herself in perfume, she took off the caftan, stuffing it into her bag. With renewed confidence, she swaggered back into the lounge. As she entered she could see Clive's blue Volkswagen beetle pulling up in the drive-way. His 'handsome wife' sat next to him in the front, whilst Sophia and Marilyn were squashed up on either side of a man in the back.

Suddenly Taiwo came up behind her, placing his arm around her waist.

'Wow! International knock out!'

She had been concentrating so hard on what was going on outside that he startled her.

'I beg, leave me!' she snapped.

'You went to change?' he persisted. 'Isn't that the dress we bought you?'

'Do you like it?' she smiled flirtatiously.

'It's stunning!'

Sade soon realised that all the eyes in the room were focused on her. The other girls were mostly turned out in cheap, locally designed outfits. All except Idowu who wore an identical dress to her own.

'You bought the same dress for your sister?' she asked Taiwo.

'We bought in bulk.'

Noticing her enraged stare, Idowu came over to meet her. Although they were first cousins, Idowu bore no resemblance

40

to Sade. She was plump and sturdily built with dimpled cheeks and short afro hair.

'Sade! Nah wah-oh! I think your dress is shorter than my own!' Idowu smiled.

'It's not my dress that is shorter, it's you that is shorter.' Sade smiled maliciously. She turned to Taiwo. 'Why did you buy black for her? You should have known that the colour would not suit her.'

Idowu's smile slowly faded. Before she could respond, Sade pulled Taiwo onto the dance floor.

'Come on. Let's dance,' she insisted.

She could feel the female eyes of envy and the male eyes of lusty desire and she revelled in the attention.

Adjusting her position on the dance floor, Sade watched as Obi and Clive entered the room. Against Clive's bronze complexion, she appeared like a shadow. The frail looking creature hardly came up to Clive's shoulder and her upper jaw protruded in such a way that her front teeth were constantly on show. Obi's bright pink lipstick drew attention to the ugliness of her thick lips, and the straight haired wig made her look ridiculous. Timidly, she reached for Clive's hand, her lack of confidence contrasting sharply with his arrogant poise.

At the end of the record Sade went to meet Sophia. Taiwo followed. Of course Taiwo realised that his cousin Sade was the most beautiful 'chick' in the room, but to date a cousin was taboo.

Sophia looked enraged as they approached her, standing apart from her entourage with her hand on her hip.

'What's the matter?' Sade asked her.

Taiwo smiled at Sophia who shunned him, so he went to welcome Clive.

'It's that stupid Emeka. Because we were squashed in the back seat, he thinks he can use it as an excuse to start feeling my breast.'

Sade laughed.

'But don't you like him?' Sade teased, glancing at Emeka. He looked quite distinguished in his black suit, white shirt and tie. 'I'm sure you were enjoying it.'

'Come on shut up!' Sophia scolded, casting vicious looks in Emeka's direction. Emeka on the other hand smiled, his teeth brilliant white against his ebony skin. He poked his tongue out and Sophia hissed, eyeing him in disgust.

'But why are you making show for him? The man has sex appeal!'

'Which kind sex appeal?' Sophia snapped.

Taiwo returned, smiling at Sade.

'What's going on?' he asked.

'Nothing!' Sade laughed, turning to Sophia. 'You remember my cousin Taiwo?'

'Yes!' she responded, still glancing at Emeka.

'Can I get you something to drink?' asked Taiwo.

'Later!' Sophia responded.

'How about a dance then?' Taiwo persisted.

'Sure!'

Sophia went off with Taiwo and two young men approached Sade simultaneously. She pushed past them to Clive, now sitting in between Emeka and Obi.

'Congratulations!' she grinned. 'I heard you were getting married.'

'Thank-you!' he almost expected her to be genuine. 'This is Emeka, my brother in law.' Clive indicated and Emeka stood up to shake her hand. 'And this is my wife Obi.'

Obi smiled timidly. Sade shunned her and Clive put his arm around Obi as though to protect her.

'Would you give me the pleasure of this dance?' Emeka asked moving determinedly towards Sade. He could see she had already turned down two men, still waiting on the sidelines. Smothering her contempt, she agreed to dance with him.

'So you live in Lagos?' she asked.

'Yes. I have a four bedroom house there.'

'That's nice! I suppose your Daddy built it for you?'

Emeka gave a broad and arrogant grin.

'Yes! My father also built me a hospital.' He was sarcastic. Sade looked into his deep set eyes, the depth appearing to go beyond this world.

'You are a doctor, are you?'

'Yes. And what do you do?'

'I've just completed my O levels.'

'Really! And I thought you'd be around eighteen.'

'No! It's Sophia that's eighteen.'

Emeka laughed. At the end of each record he held onto her reluctant hand. Sade found this highly irritating, especially because of the mischievous grin that appeared to be fixed on his face. She cast flashing smiles at her many admirers, flirting wildly. By the fourth record her patience had worn out. Emeka performed a double spin in the middle of the dance floor which was the limit to her endurance. Leaving him bobbing energetically to the rhythm, she stormed off. Emeka stood still looking flabbergasted while Sade began to dance with Arthur Uku, a handsome architect's son.

She was the star of the party, swapping and changing partners but no-one could have realised that her soul was in torment. She watched Sophia and Marilyn who were obviously having a wonderful time. Everyone was dancing except 'Mosquito' who sat tightly on her prey.

Tired of all the charade, Sade went to sit next to Clive wriggling her slender leg and complaining of cramp. Her cheeks and jaw hurt from all the forced smiles. Suddenly Emeka was in the seat next to her. She looked up to see a tall dark stranger leaning against the wall opposite, undressing her with his eyes. He looked at least twenty-something with strong broad shoulders and his masculinity made her quiver. Their eyes met and a feeling of embarrassment came over her that her dress was too short. Taiwo left the room and Sophia came to sit down. Sade moved to join her.

43

'Sophia!' she tried to pull her dress down further whilst crossing her legs. 'Who is that man standing over there?'

'You like him?' It was her turn to tease.

'Why do you like annoying me? I ask you a simple question and you start talking rubbish.'

'Okay! Sorry, sorry sorry. Anyway, he has sex appeal!'

Sade sighed and turned away, the dark figure still watching her.

'It seems he must like you too,' said Sophia as she noticed the man's stare. 'You better keep away from him-oh. He's a dangerous character.'

'Dangerous how?' asked Sade eagerly.

'Just believe me.'

'I knew that was what you were going to say. I'm sure you don't even know him. Unless he's even your boyfriend.'

'Please!' shouted Sophia in disgust, the glint of fun now vanished from her face. 'Don't associate me with a murderer.'

'Eh!' Sade cried out. 'Who did he murder?'

'Don't tell anyone that I told you-oh! It was Beauty Oba that confided in me.'

'Who am I going to tell? You should know me better than that.'

Sade moved closer to listen.

'He calls himself Johnny Brown. I heard he comes from a very rich family, so he feels that he can behave how ever he feels. He has many girl-friends, but there was this fine girl living with him. Beauty told me he used to beat this girl until she would piss all over the house. When he had finished beating her he would push her out completely naked.'

'Ehhn!' Sade glanced in horror at the dark stranger.

'Don't look at him,' Sophia nudged her. 'Are you listening to me?'

Sade stared back into Sophia's Chinese looking eyes.

'Anyway!' Sophia continued to speak. 'When he impregnated this girl he refused to marry her. He said that she got pregnant

44

intentionally to force him into marriage. He used his own car to carry the girl to one back street doctor who aborted the child. He then dumped the girl outside her mother's house. Pain would not even allow the girl to stand up. When her mother found out what had happened she carried her to Dr Oba's house in the middle of the night. It was there that the girl died.'

'God!' Sade was filled with repulsion and disgust.

'Even before that incident he was known to have a terrible reputation. Many times he was seen coming from one juju man. People say that's where he carried the girl's blood with the foetus to go and do juju.'

'Chei! Please! I've heard enough.'

The dark imposing figure still watched her and as Idowu approached the man, Sade knew that she had a duty to warn her.

Sade's disturbed thoughts turned again to Clive. He was too much of a gentleman to refuse to marry her if she got pregnant.

By nine o' clock, Sade was depressed. Sophia was still dancing with Taiwo, Marilyn with Kehinde, Idowu with Johnny Brown and Obi had not left the arms of Clive. Noticing Clive's cigarettes on the floor by his chair, she remembered his craving. Ten minutes without a cigarette was his maximum. She returned to the seat in between Emeka and Clive, placing her bag by Clive's cigarettes. Clive stared at her objectionably.

'Sorry! I didn't know you were talking,' she said quickly picking up her bag together with his cigarettes.

'But it's okay!' Emeka insisted. 'Please sit down!'

Ignoring him, she walked off.

Using a side door, Sade made her way into the garden. Except for the dull light from the illuminated house the darkness was complete. Hiding under an alamanda tree, she waited. A cricket creaked and it suddenly occurred to her that snakes liked alamanda trees. Rapidly she moved onto the gravel drive-way, leaning against the side of Clive's car.

What if uncle arrives home? she thought. What excuse could she give him for standing about in the garden in a dress that came just a few inches below her navel? And supposing Clive came out with Obi? The girl stuck like a leech. Or supposing he didn't come out at all? Afterall, he could easily borrow a cigarette from Taiwo. She tried hard to calm herself singing along with the Supremes:

> '*Where did our love go?*
> *Don't you want me*
> *Don't you need me no more…*'

Her heart pounded with fury as she tried to think. What could she say to Clive? The words of the song were clouding her mind. All she knew was that she loved him and he had told her that he loved her. She had his letters to prove it. And wasn't true love supposed to last forever?

Suddenly the front door opened. Her heart skipped a beat as she crouched down. Predictably Clive came out. Standing up she tried to compose herself.

'Sade!' he shouted, startled by her appearance. 'What are you doing here?' His deep husky voice filled her with confusion.

'Shhh!' she whispered. 'Where are you going?'

'Some idiot stole my cigarettes. I'm going to buy some more.' He unlocked the car door and Sade jumped in.

'I'll come with you,' she said climbing over to the passenger seat.

'Why are you so nervous?'

'I'm not nervous. I just want some fresh air.'

Clive got into the driver's seat and set off. A cold emptiness entered her heart and she fell dumfounded. They approached the candle-lit road-side kiosk and she collapsed in tears.

'What's the matter?' he demanded, as he stopped the car.

Sade stared ahead in silence.

'Can't you tell me?' Clive asked, turning on the inside light in the car. After a moment's silence he got out of the car. She watched as he paid for the cigarettes, realising that she had lost control of the situation. Clive lit up a cigarette and returned to the car.

'Are you okay now?' he asked before starting the engine.

Sade nodded. Thinking of the dark, quiet road that led to her house, she asked to be taken home. The silence between them was acute as they drove down Uwaifo Road.

'Can you please stop for me to put this on?' she said, pulling her caftan from the bag.

'What is that?' he asked curiously.

'It's a caftan. If my father sees me in this mini he'll kill me.'

Clive laughed as he pulled up at the road-side, but stopped laughing when his packet of cigarettes fell onto the floor.

'I didn't know you smoked?'

'I don't. I'm the idiot that stole your cigarettes. Here!' she tossed them to him.

'So why did you take them?'

'To get you away from that "thing" you brought to the party.'

'What thing?'

Sade paused determined not to quarrel with him.

'Clive!' she pleaded, clutching her caftan. 'Why are you doing this to me? Why are you pretending that there has never been anything more than friendship between us? I kept all the letters you wrote me from university. Why should you write, saying that you loved me, then run off with the ugliest girl in Nigeria? Is it because her father's a millionaire? Do you see his millions when you look into her ugly face?'

Clive held on to the steering wheel as if it offered some kind of support.

'Didn't you tell me you loved me?' she persisted. 'Say something!' Sade began to cry again.

'I have to marry her.'

'What do you mean?'

'She's pregnant.'

Sade stared at him in shock and disbelief. With all her plans destroyed in an instance, she placed her head on her lap and cried. Clive sat in silence for a minute before turning to her in desperation.

'Sade! Please!'

He was annoyed at being forced into such a confrontation.

'Do you love her?' Sade eventually asked while wiping her tears in the caftan.

'We understand each other, and believe it or not she's a very nice person.'

'You stupid bastard,' she cried, getting out of the car and banging the door with all her might. She stormed off into the pitch darkness. Turning on the headlights, Clive drove after her begging her to stop. In her fury she turned into a bush road. He followed, driving past to block her advance. It would be disastrous for something to happen to the judge's daughter.

'Sade wait!' he shouted to no avail.

Left with no alternative, he abandoned the car and went chasing after her.

'Leave me alone!' she screamed.

Clive now grabbed her arm, trying to force her back into the car.

'What do you want me to do?' he demanded. 'Tell me. What do you want me to do?'

'You deceived me,' she cried in his arms.

'I did not deceive you. You know that I love you, but things don't always turn out as we want them to.'

Over come by forces stronger than reason they fondled and kissed in the darkness. The crickets and frogs persisted with their chorus and the fireflies sparkled in the bushes surrounding them. In the bosom of mother earth they became one flesh, their bodies swaying and dancing to the rhythm of the night.

When the magic was gone they were left with the cold cruel reality. They sat arm in arm on the car bonnet but suddenly their calm was shattered by an approaching car. Sade hid her face expecting the car to continue into the darkness, but when the driver pulled up along side them, she recognised the driver instantly.

'God!' she whispered as they stood up. 'It's Uncle Sam.'

And the woman at his side was not his beloved wife, Miriam.

'Sade?' Uncle Sam shouted. 'What are you doing here?'

'It was armed robbers, Uncle.'

'Armed robbers?' His deep probing voice filled her with confusion.

'Hey-woh! It has happened-oh!' shouted the strange bush woman at his side.

'Yes Uncle,' Sade fretted. 'We left the party to buy cigarettes and they waylaid us outside the kiosk. They ordered us to drive down this bush road before taking our money and disappearing into the bush.'

'Which bush?' demanded Uncle Sam to the clapping, hysterical excitement of the woman at his side.

'Down that way, Uncle.'

'This is very serious!' said Uncle Sam looking utterly confused. 'The two of you better go directly to the police station. I will go and inform your father to meet you there.'

Uncle Sam waited for them to drive off before speeding to report the incident to her already concerned parents.

'But why did you have to tell your Uncle that we were attacked by armed robbers?' asked Clive.

'It was the first thing that came into my head. And you were just standing there.'

'You know you can be very stupid,' Clive scolded. 'We can't get the police out, looking for armed robbers that don't exist.'

'They have nothing else to do,' Sade shrugged carelessly.

'I'm taking you home. I don't know what I'm going to tell

your parents, but I'm taking you home.'

Sade loved it when he became all masterful.

They arrived at Justice Uwaifo's house to find it deserted, except for Innocent who opened the door.

'Where Master?' demanded Clive.

'He go police station, Sah!'

'What of Madam?' asked Clive.

'He follow Master go police station, Sah.'

Leaving them in the lounge, Innocent returned to the kitchen.

'Look!' said Clive. 'Telephone the police station immediately and leave a message for your parents. Let them know you are back at home. When they return, tell them that I've gone to collect my sisters from the party. I better hurry before all hell breaks loose. I'll speak to you tomorrow. Okay?'

Clive kissed her lips and was gone.

SIX

AFTER LEAVING A message at the police station, Sade had a shower and got into bed. She tried hard to force sleep but when her raging father returned with his panic stricken wife, she realised that pretending to be asleep was not going to be the answer. Her name bellowed through the house as two police jeeps skidded to a halt on the gravel driveway. Still in her night-dress she made her way downstairs.

'Where have you been?' her father yelled at the top of his voice.

Sade was struck dumb. She wondered whether he was referring to before or after the alleged incident. Three of her uncles stormed into the lounge accompanied by the Chief of Police and she collapsed in tears.

'Can't you answer when you're spoken to?' her father persisted.

Predictably Mum came rushing to her aid.

'Stop your shouting,' she ordered placing an arm around Sade. She led her back upstairs. Justice Uwaifo followed, standing over the two women as they sat on Sade's bed.

'Were you hurt?' Susan fretted refusing to see past Sade's unscratched veneer.

'No,' Sade sniffled, her head lowered.

'What happened luv?' asked her mother.

'I can't remember.'

'What do you mean you can't remember?' Justice Uwaifo was shouting again. 'What were you doing in the bush with

Clive Udochi? Eh? And who did you tell that you were leaving the party? Armed robbers! Just talking rubbish! I'll be seeing that boy's father first thing in the morning.'

Sade collapsed on the bed sobbing desperately. Her mother stood up.

'Felix! That's enough! Can't you see the girl's in shock?'

She gently pushed her husband out of the room, closing the door behind her. She knew that once stirred her husband was like a bull after a red flag.

'Come on,' Sade heard her telling him at the other side of her door. 'We'll sort it out in the morning.'

How unfortunate, thought Sade, that Saturday night never ceased to be followed by Sunday morning. When her parents returned downstairs, she locked the bedroom door. Opening the balcony door, she listened to the muffled voices coming from the porch below her.

'Thank you very much,' concluded her father, dismissing the policemen. After a further conference, the chief of police left with her uncles. Sade's parents sat downstairs quarrelling into the early hours of the morning.

First thing in the morning, she was woken by her father who ordered her downstairs.

By the time Sade reached the study, her father had placed himself behind his large mahogany desk looking very officious. He was dressed in a black suit ready for church, both his elbows rested firmly on the desk before him. The only other available chair was occupied by her mother.

'Good morning!' she muttered, yawning and wiping her eyes.

'Good morning!' her parents responded.

From the tone of their voices she could tell this was going to be a more civilised conference than that of the night before.

'I'm sorry about last night,' she said, half expecting her father's immediate forgiveness.

He paused.

'What happened?' His manner was cool and controlled.

Sade was not fooled by these court-room tactics. She knew them all too well and they usually led up to a massive explosion. Noticing the Bible opened out before him she felt the need to be as truthful as possible in case he asked her to take an oath.

'I was not enjoying the party.' She tried hard to find a sense of direction. 'Clive said he was going to buy cigarettes, so I asked him to drop me home.'

'Umm-hm!' murmured her father, indicating that she should continue.

'Well, the car stopped in the bush and we got out. It was then Uncle Sam arrived with this woman, asking me what I was doing there. As a joke, I said armed robbers waylaid us.'

There was an irritating silence. Sade realised that her father was trying hard to maintain his composure because it was Sunday.

'What do you mean the car stopped?' he asked.

'It just stopped like that,' she shrugged, her eyes wandering aimlessly in panic.

'You are a bloody liar,' he said softly.

It was of course highly unusual for her father to swear on a Sunday. Nervously Sade cleaned her front teeth with her tongue.

'What were you doing in the bush with Clive Udochi?'

Sade stood silent wondering whether she had left the key to her bedroom in the lock. Her father had not beaten her for ages, but neither had she provoked him. As the rage took possession of his face she felt confident that she could race him upstairs. Then she recalled the last time that he had beaten her. And in broad daylight! It had been most unfortunate that she underestimated his athletic abilities as she sprinted off into the garden. It was not the beating that made her scream because he was too exhausted to do much damage when he caught her. It was just the shock of being caught.

And if it were not for the fact that she had skidded when trying to run zigzag through the bushes, he would never have caught her. He did not even consider his position as a High Court Judge. The servants were gossiping and giggling about it for weeks after.

'So there were no armed robbers?' asked her mother.

Before Sade could answer her father had cut in.

'Will you let me talk?' he shouted at Susan who pouted her disapproval. 'If you wanted to leave the party, why didn't you tell anyone? And why didn't you telephone for the driver to collect you?'

'The telephone was not working,' Sade's voice was quavery.

'You are a very stupid girl,' her father shouted. 'Do you hear me? A very stupid girl. Instead of reading your books you choose to be running around in the bush with men.'

Sade knew that the only way to reduce the severity of her sentence was to show deep remorse.

'It was not my fault,' she cried. 'It was Clive that asked me to follow him to buy cigarettes. I always get the blame for everything.'

'Did anything happen?' her father asked, suddenly realising that Clive might have taken advantage of her.

'Like what?' she sniffled.

'Did he touch you?'

She shook her head.

'From now on you keep away from that boy. You hear me?' Sade kept her head lowered.

'I said do you hear me?'

'Yes!' she cried.

Her parent's left for church and Sade rushed to the telephone.

'Sade!' It was Sophia's voice at the other end of the line. 'I was going to call you but I thought you would have gone to church. What happened last night?'

'Didn't Clive tell you?'

'No! He just suddenly insisted that he was travelling to Umuahia with Obi and her brother. They left early this morning.'

Sade could not believe or comprehend the words that flooded her mind. She was devastated.

'Sade!' she heard the voice on the other end of the line. 'Sade! Are you there?'

Sade replaced the receiver, collapsing in tears. Within seconds the telephone was ringing again. After composing herself, she answered.

'Sade! What happened–now?'

'We must have got cut off.'

'I mean last night.'

'Let me gist you when I see you. I hope you enjoyed the party?'

'I did. Except for that Emeka. He's so irritating. If it weren't for the fact that Clive works for his father, I would have slapped his face.'

'Is that where Obi met Clive?'

'No! Obi was Clive's course-mate at University. When they qualified, she asked the Eze to employ him in the Eze's legal practice.'

'Sophia, I have to go. I'll call you back later.'

Sade replaced the receiver and rushed upstairs. Locking herself up in her bedroom, she collapsed in unrestrained tears. Clive! How could he be so heartless? And supposing she became pregnant? She reached for the rosary on her dressing table and kneeling on the floor, she prayed.

'Hail Mary, full of grace. The Lord is with thee. Blessed art thou amongst women and blessed is the fruit of thy womb, Jesus. Holy Mary Mother of God, pray for us sinners, now and at the hour of our death. Amen.'

SEVEN

TAIWO AND KEHINDE arrived one afternoon accompanied by Sophia and Marilyn. Mrs Uwaifo was pleased to see them, hoping that they would lift Sade's spirit.

'Come and follow us to the market,' said Sophia casually. 'We're going to buy *Asbebi* (family uniform) for Clive's wedding. I hope you're going to join us?'

'Ah! You have to!' Taiwo told Sade. 'Or you will feel left out.'

'I'm not going to the wedding,' Sade sighed.

'Ah! Ah! What do you mean?' asked Sophia frowning in disapproval. 'Auntie! Aren't you coming to Clive's wedding?'

Mrs Uwaifo looked up from her novel.

'Of course we're coming.'

'You have to come,' Taiwo insisted.

It became obvious to Sade that an intimate relationship was developing between the twins and the sisters. She envied their happiness, wishing that she and Clive could have been amongst the happy couples.

'Go with them Sade,' her mother insisted. 'You can buy the material for us as well. Go and get my bag for me to give you money.'

'But I don't want to go,' Sade sighed.

'Don't be such a stick in the mud. Go on! Go and get my bag,' her mother persisted.

Reluctantly, Sade made her way upstairs returning with her mother's handbag. Susan handed her some money and she set off with the mischievous group. Driving down Uwaifo Road,

Taiwo made the Mercedes jerk in rhythm.

'A! A! A! A!' Sophia and Marilyn participated in the back seat.

Sade sighed. She was not in the mood for such foolery. On the main road, Taiwo manoeuvred into the fast moving traffic cutting in front of a taxi driver. The taxi driver now insisted on overtaking, forcing them off the tar towards a group of market women. Taiwo sounded the horn. Balancing heavy basins on their heads and their babies on their backs, the women jumped over the open drains into the bushy grass by the road side.

'God punish you!' one of the women shouted as the gari she carried spilt onto the mud pavement.

'God punish your father and your mother!' Sophia shouted back making gestures with her hand.

'You no fit look road?' Taiwo shouted.

'Idiot!' Marilyn added.

They all laughed except Sade.

'Sade! I've never seen you looking so miserable. What's the matter with you?' Sophia's voice was full of concern.

'It's just my father. He has been making my life a misery.'

'Why?' Sophia demanded.

'Because I left the party with Clive to buy cigarettes.'

'But Clive is like your brother. Or does he think that Clive is going to rape you?'

Sade felt hot with embarrassment as the car became her prison.

'But Dad said he caught you and Clive in the bush,' Taiwo teased ruthlessly.

'You should have asked him what he was doing in the bush,' Sade retorted.

'But I thought you said you went to buy cigarettes?' asked Marilyn.

'That's where we went.'

'Then from there you went where?' asked Kehinde.

'Please, you people are getting on my nerves.' Sade stared

57

out of the back seat window.

Taiwo slowed down as they drove past a funeral procession and a man in black aggressively held a framed photograph of the deceased to Sade's window. Persistently he raised and lowered the large photograph for all to see. In front of the procession a large golf umbrella bobbed up and down and excited children gathered the pennies that were being thrown.

When they arrived at the market, Sade was first out of the car. She hopped over the deep open drain at the roadside, watching as Sophia bounced a plank with her foot.

'I'm afraid-oh!' Sophia fretted looking down at the water, rubbish and green mould in the depths.

'Hmmmm! This place is smelling.' said Marilyn screwing up her nose and covering her mouth with her hand.

Taiwo jumped across before lovingly reaching out for Sophia's hand. Now Sophia walked daintily over the plank, followed by Kehinde and Marilyn.

'*Oyibo* [White person] pepper!' shouted a ragged little boy as they walked past his mother's stall. His calls drew the attention of other street children who gathered around, dancing and singing their taunts of the half-castes.

> '*Oyibo pepper*
> *If you eat-ee pepper*
> *You go yellow more more!...*'

Disregarding the insignificant beings they proceeded into the damp, smelly market. The wooden shacks were full of the most beautiful, imported fabrics and the traders eagerly called out to their potential customers.

'Fine girl!' one man shouted.

'Sisi! [trendy lady] Come buy,' shouted another holding out a roll of pink lace.

'How much?' Sophia demanded aggressively.

'For you?' the man hesitated to think. 'Bring five pounds!'

'Ehhn!' screeched Sophia. 'You think I be Oyibo?'

'You no want sell!' Taiwo told the man.

Sophia strutted off and the others followed.

'*Sisi!* How much you want to pay?' the trader shouted hopelessly.

'What of this one?' Marilyn asked picking up a beautiful red 'George' fabric.

'It's too bright. Can you imagine Mum wearing that?' Sophia asked. 'And Clive will not like it. I don't know why he had to rush off like that. He should have at least come to choose the material for his wedding.'

'Well, if he doesn't like it, that's his bad luck,' said Marilyn.

Sade twisted her lips and walked off to another stall.

'And we don't even know his size,' Sophia persisted. 'Anyway, I think Taiwo is about the same size. We can tell the tailor to sew two identical agbada robes.'

'What time are you going for your results tomorrow?' Sade asked, walking with Marilyn deeper into the market.

'As soon as school opens. I just hope they don't withhold the results again this year.'

'I'm so scared,' Sade sighed. 'I don't even want to see mine.'

'Well just pray,' Sophia intruded. 'I'm so glad that I've finished in that place.'

'I really envy you. I don't know how I can bear to stay there another two years,' said Sade.

'What of this one?' Sophia asked, reaching for a roll of purple brocade.

'Anything will look beautiful on you,' Taiwo smiled, his eyes sparkling flirtatiously.

After pricing it Sophia turned to Sade.

'What do you think?'

'It's nice.' Sade attempted a smile of encouragement.

She hated the fabric and hated the companionship of her friends and cousins. 'Take it!'

'Are you sure?' asked Sophia, unsure of her own instincts.

'It's beautiful,' Sade insisted. 'And it will suit the men as well as the women.

'Okay! Cut it,' Sophia ordered. The traders face lit up as he reached for the inch tape and scissors.

With Taiwo and Kehinde heavily overburdened with the fabric they returned to the car. Squatting at the back, a ragged madman hammered the mud off the mudguard with a huge crowbar.

'Chei!' Taiwo shouted apprehensively. 'Get out of there!'

The crazy man stared at them before proceeding with his mission.

'You no hear?' shouted Sophia. 'Commot there! Sha!'

The man looked up at them again. Sade and Marilyn prepared to run back into the market. A few children began to throw stones at the man.

'Craze man-oh! Ohewere! Ohewere!' the children teased.

'Look at these stupid children. They want to smash the car window.' Sophia looked apprehensive.

Ohewere picked up a massive stone and the bony children fled with the crazed man running after them. Quickly Kehinde unlocked the car doors and they all piled in giggling with excitement.

'That man!' panted Sophia as they speed off. 'He's always there. One day, one juju man came and rounded him up, together with all the other mad people in Benin. He flogged him sober.'

'Don't mind him,' laughed Marilyn.

'They should put him in a mental institution. Supposing he injures one of those children?' asked Taiwo sternly.

'Ah! The traders will kill him,' Sophia responded. 'There was one mad woman that killed a little girl. The traders gathered and beat her to death.'

'That's terrible!' observed Taiwo.

'You have become a proper Oyibo,' Sophia scolded. 'What was the alternative? Should they have left her to kill again? It's only because it was not your child that you can say that.'

'If the woman was mad, she needed treatment.' Taiwo sounded very defensive.

'And would you have paid for the treatment?' asked Sophia. 'We live in a society where people don't have sufficient money to buy food. So who can afford to keep her on medication for the rest of her life?'

'So where to?' demanded Kehinde, irritated by the argument building up.

'Let's go to the club,' said Marilyn.

Sade could not stand their companionship any longer. Taiwo and Kehinde's lusty looks and Sophia and Marilyn's flirtatious smiles made her feel more isolated than ever.

'Please take me home. I feel really sick,' she insisted.

After dropping Sade at home the happy couples set off for the club.

EIGHT

SIESTA WAS BORING. Unable to sleep, Sade lay in bed staring at the ceiling. Clive! She thought back to her moment of blissful happiness when they had become one flesh. Now she was left with a feeling of complete emptiness. Supposing she became pregnant? How could she tell her parents? How could she face the world? As the enormity of the situation overwhelmed her, there was a knock at the door.

'Who is it?' she demanded.

'Nah me Madam,' responded Innocent timidly.

'What do you want?'

'Nah your sister say make I come call you, Madam!'

'Which sister?'

'Sister Idowu, Madam.'

Sade rose from her bed, lackadaisically making her way downstairs. Idowu sat alone in the lounge.

'Sade!' she smiled, 'Taiwo told me you were sick. Are you okay now?' She sang her insincerity just like her mother.

'Yes! I was taking my siesta.'

Idowu stood up to leave.

'I was on my way to the village, so I said, let me just call and see how you are.'

'What are you going to do there?' Sade asked.

'To visit someone. I'll take a short cut through the bush.'

'I'll come with you,' said Sade walking with her towards the front door and into the garden.

The girls followed the leafy footpath through the dense

rubber plantation. The hot sun caused the dry rubber seeds to pop open above them, before crackling through the thick leaves to the ground. Sade loved the music of the forest and the wondrous stillness of its shade.

'So what happened between you and Clive on Saturday?' asked Idowu.

There was just no escape.

'Look! If you just want to annoy me, I better go back home.'

'Ah! Ah! Nah fight?' Idowu appeared genuinely surprised by Sade's response. 'Sorry-oh! I wont ask you again.'

The path came to an end in someone's back yard. A group of excited children gathered, dancing and singing in their nakedness.

'Oyibo Pepper
If you eat-ee pepper
You go yellow more more....'

'Get out!' Idowu scolded them.

She ordered one of the little boys to call his mother. Walking towards the house, Sade noticed a thatched mud hut, in a corner of the compound. It was obviously a shrine. The kitchen in the back yard consisted of four posts covered with zinc sheeting. Three building blocks at the centre of the covering formed a wood fire.

Idowu strutted confidently into the mud bungalow with Sade following. A child pushed past them opening the door to a dingy looking 'parlour'.

'Mama say make you sit down. He dey come,' said the child, his dusty body covered in a pair of ragged pants.

Idowu appeared quite at ease as she sat on one of the collapsible wooden chairs.

'Who did you say you were coming to visit?' Sade asked, surveying the room in disgust.

'My friend. She's a Priestess. Sit down now!'

'What kind of Priestess?'

'Priestess to Olokun.'

'Olokun?'

'Eh! Olokun! Have you never heard of Olokun? God of the sea, wealth and fertility.'

Sade had lived a separate existence to the local people and although she was aware that they had their own religious beliefs, she had never delved into them.

'I always thought you were crazy,' Sade scolded. 'But now I can see that you have completely lost control of your senses. How dare you bring me to such a place? Or you think I have nothing else to do at home? And don't think I'm not going to report you.'

'Did I tell you to come?' Idowu scorned her. 'Weren't you the one that insisted on following me?'

'You should have told me you were coming to a place like this.'

As she spoke the priestess entered the room. She wore a single white wrapper leaving her shoulders bare and her hair was plaited in black thread. Around her neck, wrist and ankle she wore coral beads and her cheeks were streaked with tribal marks.

'Evenin'-oh!' the priestess smiled exposing the gap between her front teeth. 'Sit down now!' she told Sade.

The priestess placed a low stool before Idowu, using native chalk to whiten the floor between them. Sade sat to watch as she handed Idowu a small white stone.

'My wealth! Am I dead,' Idowu asked touching her forehead and chest with the stone, placing it on the whitened patch. The Priestess picked up the stone, using it with cowries to throw divination.

'Eta! Enini!...' came the Priestesses high pitched incomprehensible phrases. 'Eta! Eta! Eto!' she shivered in trance. 'Hmmm! My pickin. Your brother don' come from overseas. They want to travel. Tell them make they no travel-oh! Hmmm! One woman dey jealous you well-well. He go fit kill you…'

So the priestess continued before coming to the work that needed to be done.

'Bring seven chicken…'

Sade scoffed. Idowu eyed her. She could picture Idowu walking down the road carrying seven chickens.

When the priestess had finished she pulled her stool before Sade and whitened the floor between them.

'No!' Sade protested.

'Let her consult the oracle for you,' advised Idowu.

Sade had become curious. The Priestess handed her the white stone.

'Use it to touch your head and chest.' said Idowu. 'Then you say, 'My wealth, am I dead?'

'My wealth.' Sade hesitated thinking how stupid she looked.

'Eh! Am I dead?' Idowu repeated.

Sade felt too pressurised to back out. She repeated the words before placing the stone on the whitened space. Again the priestess threw divination.

'You done pregnate!' declared the woman in a trance.

'The papa nah oyibo. You like am well-well, but he go left you. He go marry one woman from yonder.'

Sade twisted her lips in torment and rage. Obviously Idowu had told the Priestess something.

'Make you no vex. Go to the wedding. One man go propose marriage to you there. Accept. You go born man pickin. Trouble-oh! Hey! *Wahala!* [trouble] The wahala go beaucoup-oh! Hey! The wahala go beaucoup well well!…'

The priestess in trance sent shivers up and down Sade's spine and tears of confused emotions filled her eyes. She was determined not to collapse before this pagan woman.

'The thing you will do, be so:

Go to the wedding. Collect the kolanut. Bring am come! Bring pigeon, man and woman. Plus chicken–bring one.'

The consultation was over and Idowu handed the priestess some money.

Sade could have accounted for the fact that the priestess knew about the return of Taiwo and Kehinde because the whole of Benin knew. But she had never mentioned her love for Clive to anyone. Perhaps the woman had contacts in the police station. It must have been the talk of the town. Justice Uwaifo's daughter caught in the bush with an *oyibo* man!

'I can't believe you can be so gullible,' Sade scoffed as they walked back home.

'Who are you insulting?' demanded Idowu.

'I'm not insulting you. If I call a goat a goat, I would not expect the goat to feel insulted.'

'You are very stupid,' Idowu hissed. 'And I'm sure if the priestess said you're in love with a white man, it's true. I also know that man is Clive.'

'I didn't expect anything more intelligent from you.'

'Did he kiss you?' Idowu giggled. 'Was it sweet?'

Sade pouted, thinking of a response.

'Don't think I haven't heard everything about you and Johnny Brown.'

Sade strutted ahead down the bush path.

'Johnny Brown!' Idowu was on the defensive again. 'Heard what?'

'I heard everything. You don't need to pretend. It's common knowledge.'

'Common knowledge!' There was a look of panic on Idowu's face at the thought of that 'common knowledge' reaching her father. 'Who told you there was anything between me and Johnny Brown?'

Sade shrugged mischievously.

'Sade tell me now,' she pleaded. 'Okay! Just tell me what people have been saying!'

'I've already told you! I heard everything.'

'That he's my boyfriend?'

'That's just a small part of it.'

'And what else? Sade why are you behaving like this now? Tell me,' Idowu fretted.

'So is it true?' Sade asked.

'What?'

'That you and him have done the thing now?'

'Who told you this thing?' Idowu was now irate and Sade was revelling in her distress.

'Anyway!' Idowu mumbled, 'I don't see what's the big secret about you and Clive. I've known for a long time that you liked him. So why don't you just admit it.'

They both laughed.

'Look!' said Idowu. 'If you really want to take Clive from that girl, it's a simple matter. First you must make him madly in love with you. I will take you to collect something from the priestess which you will add to his soup.'

'Jesus Christ! He'd kill me!'

Both girls laughed.

'You need to get a photograph of him, together with his hair or nails. Take them to the priestess and you will see wonders.'

'How the hell can I get his hair or nails?'

'It can be any part of him. Blood is the most powerful but it could even be his sweat. The priestess will use the items to call his spirit. It may be that he is not even worth getting.'

'Not worth getting?'

'Yes. If his spirit tells the priestess that he does not intend to stay long in this world, then what's the point in getting him. Once the priestess has investigated him, there are many things you can do. You can do juju to make him hate his wife. You can make his wife barren or produce only female children. Or you can even kill her. It all depends on how far you are prepared to go.'

'What do you mean, how far I'm prepared to go?'

'Well, if the oracle asks you to sacrifice a cow, you will say it's too expensive.'

'So do you intend taking the chickens to the priestess?' Sade's tone was mocking again. 'You better not pass through my father's house or he will shoot you-oh.'

'Go and sit down,' Idowu scolded. 'If I had the money, I would certainly buy them for her to perform the sacrifice.'

'And what will she do with them?'

'It depends on the work. She might throw them into the sea.'

'But there is no sea in Benin. Maybe the woman wants to have a party.'

'Shut up! Isn't the river a part of the sea?'

There was a brief silence, both of them deep in thought.

'How did you come to know such a woman?' asked Sade.

'Well, you know at one time my mum was seriously sick.'

'The time your father flew her to London for treatment?'

'Yes. My father tried everything to cure her. Even the doctors in London could not find out the cause of her sickness. When she returned from London, still sick, Mama sent for the priestess to reveal all. After divination, she told them that a witch had set a trap and baited it for my mother's soul. Concealed in the bait at the bottom of a pot were knives and nails to kill her. My mother's dream-soul had entered the trap and managed to escape, but she was injured in the process and this was the cause of her illness.'

'And the priestess was able to cure her?'

'You've seen her now. She's better.'

The two girls walked in silence for a while both deep in thought.

'How does someone become a witch?' Sade asked, curious.

'They make human sacrifices to the god of the silk cotton tree.'

'God of the silk cotton tree?' Yet another god that Sade had never heard about.

'Yes! They say the god is huge, red in colour with straight hair. He comes out at night to waylay people passing, drinking their blood and eating them. After his night of feasting, he returns to his home in the underworld. As he goes down he wipes the blood off himself. That is why the soil under the tree is red.'

Sade looked into Idowu's dark eyes. The rubber plantation had suddenly lost its wondrous calm and its shade had turned to darkness. Sade did not want to believe but it was getting dark and she felt scared. Suddenly she jumped out in front of Idowu, growling to frighten her.

'I am the god of the silk cotton tree and I'm going to eat you up.'

'Get out!' Idowu scolded pushing her out of the way. 'What's wrong with you?'

'I'm going to drink your blood.' Sade growled.

'Sade behave yourself! Why do you like to take everything as a joke?'

Sade growled again and Idowu began to giggle. Idowu set off, running through the rubber trees. Sade chased after her and eventually caught her in Justice Uwaifo's compound.

NINE

AMIDST A GREAT deal of commotion and excitement a long convoy set off from the Udochi family house for Clive's wedding. Mr Udochi hired a minibus to convey family, friends and supporters all dressed in purple brocade to Umuahia. From the front passenger seat of her father's Mercedes, Sade watched Sophia and Taiwo kissing in the back seat of the minibus.

'Isn't that Sophia with Taiwo?' asked her father. Sade did not answer. 'So that is what Taiwo went to learn in England!'

'Brazen hussy!' huffed her mother.

'You better keep away from that girl,' Justice Uwaifo scolded Sade. 'Pass now!' he shouted at the driver.

The driver swerved aggressively in an attempt to overtake the minibus.

'You're a bloody fool!' Justice Uwaifo shouted as the driver almost crashed into an oncoming car. 'You no fit drive?'

The driver twisted his determined looking mouth, blinking in confusion. In frustration he put his hand on the horn and for the first time Taiwo realised that his uncle was behind them. He removed his arm from Sophia's shoulder.

'Commot for road now!' the driver shouted hopelessly at the mini bus driver.

Sade could see a car coming in the opposite direction but the driver pulled out, jamming his foot down on the accelerator.

'Wait!' she shouted to no avail. Quickly he cut in front of the minibus. With renewed confidence, he now sought to overtake all the other cars.

Sade closed her eyes in surrender. The forceful breeze passing through the open windows eventually forced the purple head tie off her head. Occasionally she looked out at the vivid greenness of the fast passing vegetation and the hopeless misery of the poverty stricken villagers. Her world was apart and above.

After about an hour of windy, tense silence, her father's voice intruded into her thoughts.

'Ho! That was quick.'

She opened her eyes expecting to be in the dreaded Umuahia.

'This is Onitsha! Look at the bridge! Ohhh! It's magnificent!' said Justice Uwaifo admiring the newly completed bridge. 'You know that bridge cost us £6,000,000,' he announced.

Sade looked down at the banks of the River Niger. They were jam packed with canoes and a mass of farmers hurriedly unloaded their yam harvest to sell in the nearby market.

'Well! This is the East proper!' said Justice Uwaifo at the other side of the bridge.

The convoy sliced through the oil palm plantations, the roads twisting and turning between the remote villages. They sped past the mud walled family compounds, each containing rectangular buildings with steep, thatched roofs. Close to the villages were the farms, covered in large soil mounds where yam had been planted. The occasional umbrella tree appeared to offer the crops an irrelevant shade.

After a couple of hours, they arrived in Umuahia. The convoy sped through the small hill town and eventually crunched to a halt in the Eze's gravel driveway. The newly completed 'palace' was the most impressive building in the town.

With a stretch of relief the entourage dismounted. The women boldly opened out their purple wrappers to re-tie them, resembling outsized butterflies weighed down by gold.

Under a tarpaulin cover on the front lawn, a group of Ibo women began to cheer, beating hard at their beaded calabashes, dancing and singing praises in Ibo. Waving white handkerchiefs and displaying beaming brilliant smiles of welcome, they approached, encircling the entourage.

A group of male drummers began to play and six young girls dressed in short wrappers began to dance. Energetically they hammered their feet at the earth, as though to awaken the gods. With bells on their ankles and heavy coral beads around their waists, the girls collapsed in sexual, hypnotic rhythm. Dark as night, their strong energetic bodies shone in the afternoon heat as they vibrated their shadowy forms. With heavy coral beads on their waists and cloth tied around their breasts they moved careless and regardless. Before the girls became exhausted a group of organised young men took control. In uniformed shorts and bells on their ankles they sprang and bounced like gazelles. Barefooted they danced to the rhythm of the drums.

Suddenly Clive appeared. He looked anxious as he hurried to meet his mother. Avoiding all eye contact with Sade, he collected his purple ashebi and hurried off to change.

The large crowd piled into the expensively decorated lounge. The setting was theatrically majestic. The Eze sat on his gold plated throne surrounded by his chiefs who appeared to be in mourning for their lost youth. Their mouths looked drawn down and their expressions solemn as people paid homage. Although the chiefs wore the traditional long shirts with wrappers and black bowler hats, the Eze was more modern. On his head he wore a golden crown and in his right hand he carried his staff of office.

'Money plenty-oh!' one of Clive's guests declared.

'Money make iron float,' Sophia responded. Sade followed Sophia, Marilyn and the twins.

'Are you going to prostrate?' Sophia whispered to Taiwo.

'Prostrate for what?' Taiwo responded, quickly leading the way to the back row where the group sat down.

'Look at that ceiling light,' Sophia whispered, looking up at the crystal chandelier.

'Nah chandelier they dey call am,' Taiwo jested.

'Eh! Mr Been-to!' Sophia retorted, offended by Taiwo's scoffing.

'I hope the thing doesn't fall down on somebody's head,' said Marilyn looking up apprehensively.

'Chei! What a waste of money!' Sophia hissed, rubbing her foot into the thick red carpet. 'They will have to change this one today!'

'And wall to wall! It must have cost a bomb.' Marilyn looked about in astonishment.

'Justice Uwaifo!' Sade heard Mr Udochi shout. 'Sir! Please! Over here!' Mr Udochi offered her parents the most comfortable front seats and they accepted.

In the hot clammy air the smell of fresh paint lingered, sickly and sweet. Servants distributed drinks and the guests chatted loudly. The Udochi family and friends now sat facing the Nzeogwu family and friends. Clive reappeared, now looking regal in his purple brocade. For the first time he looked towards Sade. Quickly he diverted his gaze, sitting down amongst his family members.

Emeka stood up to speak.

'Good afternoon ladies and gentlemen.'

'Look at his bowler hat.' Sophia nudged Sade next to her. Sophia and Marilyn bent their heads down to giggle. Sade knew that Sophia had never forgiven Emeka for taking advantage of the tight squeeze in the back of Clive's Volkswagen.

'The thing is too small for his big head,' Sophia giggled, peeping from behind the seat. 'And look at the feather sticking out of it.' Sophia held onto her nose and mouth to prevent the sound of laughter bursting forth.

'And his wrapper,' Marilyn giggled.

By the time they had regained their composure, Emeka had removed his bowler exposing his freshly scrapped scalp.

'Saccora head!' Sophia whispered insultingly.

Now Emeka was staring directly at them forcing them yet again beneath the seats in fits of giggles.

'Sade! Behave yourself!' Taiwo scolded.

'Me? What did I do?' she pouted.

Of course he would pick on her, he had too much to lose by scolding Sophia. The girls now sat quietly and Emeka started to speak.

'On behalf of the Nzeogwu family, I would like to welcome all of you to this great occasion. The Nzeogwu family is a very great family. A family highly respected in Umuahia and beyond. Today we are being visited by the Udochi family with a great intention. This intention will be unfolded to us shortly. We welcome all of you to witness this occasion according to the custom of this land. Eze Nzeogwu of Umuahia, my father...' Emeka directed the silent stares towards the throne and the Eze smiled with pride. '...is very happy to present the Udochi family with this small gift of kolanut, and also with the best imported gin, Guinness and Star beer, recognised as the king of beers in Nigeria. Emeka carried the gifts on a tray placing them before David Udochi, a senior member of Clive's family. 'You are all welcome.' He bowed courteously before returning to his seat.

After a lot of consultation due to the differences between Ibo and Bini customs David Udochi stood up to speak.

'I speak on behalf of the Udochi family and friends. We have seen the traditional gifts you have presented to us and we are happy to say that we feel well received by you the Nzeogwu family. We thank you for the gifts.'

Reluctantly, Sade joined in the applause as David Udochi sat down. The words of the priestess echoed in her head:

'You done pregnate! The papa nah oyibo. You like am well-

well but he go left you. He go marry one woman for yonder. Go to the wedding. One man go propose marriage to you there. Accept. Make you no vex. You go born man child.'

Sade looked around the large room. Clive!

'Trouble-oh! Hey! Wahala! The wahala go beaucoup-oh! The wahala go beaucoup well well! The thing you go do be this: collect kolanut. Bring am come...'

She watched as an elder from Clive's family held the kolanut in native prayer. The old man broke the kolanut into tiny bits and a servant offered it to the guests on a metal tray. The tray of kolanut came before her and she quickly took a small handful placing the pieces in her handbag.

'Chei! Straight into the carpet,' declared Sophia.

Sade looked up to find an elder pouring libation.

'Why can't the man do that outside?' Taiwo whispered in disgust.

With the first part of the ceremony completed the fat mamas from Clive's family stood up in jubilation songs. Slowly they clapped and danced, gyrating their large buttocks in the middle of the room. Filled with strength and confidence they opened out their wrappers as they danced. They symbolised womanhood, motherhood and unity. The powerful and indispensable link between God and man.

When the women eventually returned to their seats, Clive's family spokesman stood up.

'The head of the Udochi family has asked me to put forward their request. A few months ago, one of our children was playing around this area, when he saw a girl. This girl stole his heart and he reported home that he had found a partner.'

Sade put her head down behind the chairs.

'What's the matter?' asked Sophia, nudging her.

'Pain!' she cried, holding onto her side.

'You want me to take you out?' Sophia asked.

Sade shook her head.

'Today,' continued Clive's spokesman, 'we were lucky that

75

when we came here, we had not told you our mission, but you welcomed us. This is a pointer of more success to come. We have pleasure to make a request from you.'

The spokesman sat down to await the Nzeogwu family's permission. Emeka stood up to speak.

'You are not specific enough. You said you saw a girl? Who is the girl you saw?'

Sade thought how silly the whole game was becoming and sighed deeply.

'Well thank you very much.' Clive's spokesman continued. 'We saw many girls playing around here. But there was one in particular, who's name starts with Ooooo!'

The guests laughed and joked. Sade bit her lip in an attempt to control herself.

'But the rest of her name we do not know. But if we see her we will remember her.'

Emeka again stood up to speak.

'The Nzeogwu family have asked me to convey their sincere happiness for the wishes you have expressed and they have accepted your visit.'

He sat down. Calling their bluff.

'You are accepting just the visit?' asked Clive's spokesman.

'Yes! Just the visit!' Emeka replied. The congregation muttered.

'We thank God!' declared Sophia. 'They want to make *shakara* as if we are not doing them a favour taking their daughter. Who else will be stupid enough to marry a person looking like that.'

'Are they refusing the marriage?' asked Sade.

'Eh now! He said they will accept "just the visit". They should not have wasted our time dragging us here.' Sophia hissed.

'Well, thank you very much. Probably we will be able to give you more details.' continued Clive's spokesman, arranging for the requested crates of drinks to be placed before Obi's family.

'I present to you the following,' he declared loudly: 'Stout! Soft drinks! Star beer! Well-blended Schnapps! And kolanut! We wish you long life and prosperity!'

There was silence as Clive's spokesman sat down. Up jumped Emeka.

'The Nzeogwu family accepts your generosity and the beautiful things that you have presented to us. Our hearts are filled with joy, and the gifts are an indication of the great value you place on our daughter.'

The kolanut was passed to the eldest member of the Nzeogwu gathering for the traditional prayer before it was broken up and passed around. Again Sade placed some in her handbag.

'Don't you like it?' Sophia enquired.

'You know I have stomach pain,' Sade replied.

Libation was poured and people started to drink as the older women again broke out in song. Amid a great deal of cheering Obi was led into the room dressed in the latest and most expensive blue damask.

'Is this the girl you saw?' asked Emeka.

'She is the one!' shouted the Udochi family. Obi curtsied to greet them.

'Chei! Look at her ugly face!' hissed Sophia. A man sitting in front of her turned in disgust.

'Face front!' Sophia warned him. Obviously she knew the man who continued looking back at her. His pink lips parted in pretended shock.

'I say face front!' Sophia insisted, pushing the side of his scalp with her finger.

'Eh!' said the man. The girls began to giggle.

'...You think this is a joking matter?'

'Sophia!' Taiwo scolded in astonishment.

'Don't mind him,' hissed Sophia. 'He's a nonsense man!'

'You this girl!' the man warned wagging his finger. 'I will deal with you today!'

Throwing herself back in her seat and stretching out her legs, Sophia poked her tongue out and the man turned in disgust.

When the women were tired of dancing, Emeka again stood up to speak.

'The Nzeogwu family want to know who amongst you is taking our daughter.' He turned to Obi and handed her a calabash of palm wine. 'Obi! Stand up and show us the man.' Looking exceedingly coy, Obi approached Clive, knelt before him and handed him the wine which he drank. The crowd cheered and teased as he got up to sit with Obi between the families.

Clive's spokesman stood up yet again:

'Engineer Udochi has said he is the one marrying your daughter, Obi, to his first son, Barrister Clive.'

'Thank you!' Emeka shouted back. 'The Nzeogwu family is very happy to see this gentleman sitting next to Obi. Infact, men looking at his face will immediately identify him as a gentleman. His walk is elegant. His face is handsome. His speech is distinguished,' Emeka teased.

Clive smiled. As he looked into Obi's eyes she giggled in adoration.

'There is no doubt in my mind,' Emeka continued, 'and in the mind of the Nzeogwu family, that Clive is the right man for Obi. Clive! On behalf of the Nzeogwu family, we accept this marriage and may the good Lord bless it.'

Sade sat through the rest of the ceremony feeling as though her life was over. Yet the native priestess had offered her a ray of hope. She had collected the kolanut and all she needed was the blood, sweat or tears of the happy couple.

Darkness fell and the newly weds went outside to open the dance floor. Sade moved with the crowds.

'Let's sit there!' shouted Sophia heading for a table under the canopy.

It was all fun and merriment. Sade watched as her parents

sprayed the newly weds with pound notes. The bands played on. One after another, they competed for money. The lead singers called out to the rich distinguished members of the society, praising, teasing, beckoning and encouraging them to show their worth. The women laughed and teased, bending forward as they rocked and gyrated their large buttocks provocatively and the excited men responded. With arms held high they pushed forward their hips, dancing the dance of sexual union.

After eating, Sophia and Marilyn danced their way to spray the newly weds. They were indeed beautiful girls as men quickly acknowledged with pound notes. The girls danced and flirted, revelling in the attention.

Eager to protect their conquests, the twins hurried after them leaving Sade on her own. Justice and Mrs Uwaifo made their way indoors and Sade got up to spray the newly weds.

'Congratulations!' she smiled at Obi, placing a pound note on her sweaty forehead.

'Thank you!' Obi smiled timidly.

Sade took the same note to Clive's forehead using it to wipe the sweat. Opening her handbag she took out a few more notes to continue spraying. Two young girls collected the notes that floated to the ground but Sade made sure the sweaty one joined the kolanut in her handbag. Leaving Sophia and Marilyn on the dance floor she returned to her seat.

'Excuse me dance!' one man smiled at her.

She scorned him, putting up a wall of aggressive defiance. Emeka approached, smiling wickedly.

'Are you not dancing?' he shouted over the loud music.

She shunned him. Then she remembered that Clive was married to his sister. And that Clive worked at his father's legal practice in Lagos. And that Clive was a very good friend of Emeka's.

Emeka sat down on the metal chair next to her.

'So where did you disappear to that night of the party?' he

asked. 'I was looking for you everywhere.'

Sade eyed him maliciously.

'You know I really like you,' he persisted undeterred. 'That's why you're playing hard to get. When I first saw you in Benin,' Emeka smiled, shaking his head, 'you just blew my mind.'

Sade tried to ignore him but he wouldn't go away.

'You think you're too good for me! Don't you?' Emeka demanded.

Sade sighed deeply. He stared at her for a while before confidently relaxing his arm around the back of her chair. He grinned broadly, shaking hands with a friend who congratulated him on his latest conquest.

'I wish you could get to know me better,' he persisted. 'Why don't you come and visit me in Lagos? You know I have a four bedroom house in Ikoyi. Obi and Clive used to stay with me but now I'll be alone. Will you come?'

Sade glared at him under the light of the electricity bulb. He was dark as night but his teeth sparkled.

'You think that I am joking? I really mean it. I know a good thing when I see it, and I am sure you and I can get along very well. Will you come?' he asked confidently.

Sade scoffed. After filling his own glass, Emeka poured some brandy into her coke.

'What do you think you're doing?' she demanded.

'Try it. It's very nice.' He laughed mischievously.

Sade turned away in disgust. As she watched Obi arm in arm with Clive, her eyes filled up with tears. Deliberately she drank to get drunk. Perhaps then she could bear the pain. Emeka watched with a wicked smile and every time she placed the glass down, he topped it up with more brandy. She began to feel sick but still she gulped down more of the brandy and coke.

When eventually drunk, Sade started giggling inexplicably and flirting with her many admirers.

'A bird in hand is worth two birds in the bush,' said Emeka.

'That all depends on the bird in the bush,' she threw her head back as she laughed.

'Lets dance!' said Emeka pulling her to her feet. With his arm around her waist, she stumbled onto the dance floor. Drunkenly, she fell into his arms. She would have fallen into anyone's arms and Emeka happened to be in the right place at the wrong time for Sade.

'You know I really mean it about you coming to Lagos.' He tried to sound seductive whilst pulling her against his crutch. 'I'm sure your father will allow you to come.'

'Impossible,' Sade babbled drunkenly, leaning against him for support. He held up her chin, kissing her passionately in the darkness.

'I will be in Benin next week with Clive,' he said eventually releasing his grip. 'Can we meet then?'

'You want my father to kill me. He's just too strict.'

'So when can we meet?'

'We can't!'

'And what if I married you?' asked Emeka.

Sade recalled the words of the priestess: 'Go to the wedding. A man will propose marriage to you. Accept!'

How could the priestess have foreseen everything so clearly? Here was a man that she hardly knew, proposing to her! And supposing the priestess was right and she was pregnant? If she had a child out of wedlock her father would disown her and her mother would die of shame.

'Did you hear what I said?' asked Emeka. 'I'm serious. I will marry you and you can come to live with me in Lagos.'

Sade thought of being close to Clive and the idea began to sound attractive. After all, Emeka was a qualified doctor and the first son of the Eze.

'Did you hear me?' Emeka persisted.

'My father will never allow it. And I'm still too young to marry without his consent.'

'You let me handle your father,' said Emeka confidently. 'But if he consents, will you marry me?'

Clive was gone so what did it matter who she married, as long as he was from the Westernised Nigerian elite?

'I suppose so,' she shrugged.

'Do you mean it?' smiled Emeka, surprised at his good fortune.

'I wouldn't have said it if I didn't mean it.'

'Wow!' Emeka laughed. 'You've really made my day.'

Emeka's brother, Chukwuma came up to them, telling Emeka something in Ibo.

'Look after her,' Emeka told him jubilantly. He turned to Sade. 'I have to go to the family shrine with Clive and Obi.'

'To do what?'

'Just to collect the dowry and finalise the marriage. But don't worry, I'll be back very soon.'

With Chuks standing guard over her, Sade watched as the immediate family led Obi and Clive to the family shrine. A small boy pulled a goat along with them, which Sade guessed would be sacrificed to finalise the ceremony.

'I have to sit down,' she told Chukwuma who courteously showed her to a seat. In her drunken state, she put her head down on the table and fell asleep. She had not been asleep for very long when Taiwo woke her.

'Your father says he's ready to go.'

'Hmmm!' she murmured, her eyes half open. Kehinde and Sophia sat in front of her.

'You're drunk,' Sophia giggled, looking rather tipsy herself.

'You better go,' said Taiwo. 'Your father seems annoyed.'

Chukwuma and Taiwo walked her to the car. Her parents sat stone faced in the back. Taiwo opened the front passenger door and she staggered in. From her father's hostile mood and her mother's look of enquiry she could sense trouble. The driver drove through the dark, unlit streets to a nearby guest house. When Sade realised she had to share the room with her parents she knew she was in for a rough night. No sooner had they entered the hotel bedroom than they launched their attack. Words bombarded her drunken brain, the hot blood pounding at her eardrums. She was unaware that Emeka had already approached her father with his marriage proposal.

'You are a disgrace to the family,' scolded her father. 'Just acting like a drunken whore. One day it's Clive, next it's some Emeka.'

'I'm bloody pregnant!' she shouted at the top of her voice. She had only just missed her first period and was convinced that the prophecy would come to pass.

Her father suddenly sat down on the bed, remaining speechless whilst her mother broke down in tears.

'I'm bloody pregnant and I'm going to marry him,' she shouted realising that she now had the upper hand.

'Can't you keep your voice down?' whispered her mother.

'How can you be pregnant?' Justice Uwaifo asked.

It was as though the shock had subdued him.

'What do you mean, how can I be pregnant?' Sade scolded. 'How do people get pregnant?'

'Have you told Emeka?' he asked.

'No! And I'm not bloody going to. Not until we are married.'

Sade realised the sudden power that she possessed. Her father would have done anything to preserve his respectability.

'Anyway that's nothing to do with you,' she scolded her father. 'That's between me and Emeka. I've made up my mind and I'm going to marry him.'

'This girl has really grown wings!' her father stared in bewilderment.

Sade rushed to the bathroom where she was sick, supposedly confirming her parents' worst fears. After the Roman Catholic wedding the following day, Justice Uwaifo invited Emeka to Benin to discuss his proposal further.

TEN

JUSTICE AND MRS Uwaifo tried to make Sade see reason but their advice fell on deaf ears. In desperation they confided in Dr Samuel Uwaifo, who was head of the family. Dr Uwaifo turned up late one night and Sade was summoned. She felt a surge of apprehension as she sat down with the adults.

'I think I better come straight to the point,' said Uncle Sam. 'Now! You father has informed me of your wish to get married. He has also informed me that you believe yourself to be pregnant. This is a very serious matter. First of all, you know that you are too young to get married and from what I understand, you hardly know this…What's his name?'

'Emeka!' Sade responded with eyes downcast.

'Emeka! Secondly, I don't know if you know how a woman becomes pregnant, because I will be very surprised if you are not still a virgin.'

Sade twisted her lips in embarrassment.

'So when did you become pregnant?' asked Uncle Sam.

Sade fidgeted but didn't respond. 'Sade! I'm asking you a question.'

'I know how a woman gets pregnant and I don't appreciate being treated like a child,' she responded getting up to leave the room.

'What?' her father demanded standing up and quickly grabbing her arm. 'Who do you think you are talking to? Have you got no respect for your elders?'

Sade tried to pull away as her father slapped her again and

again. Susan jumped to her feet.

'Felix stop it!' she pleaded, grabbing his arm.

'I've taken enough of this nonsense!' shouted Felix, trying to hold on to Sade.

'Leave her alone!' Susan cried.

'You leave me alone!' Felix shouted. 'This girl is in need of a good beating! Remove your hand!'

Sade managed to break free but Uncle Sam caught her before she could run off.

'You are the one that has spoilt this girl!' Justice Uwaifo shouted at Susan.

'Felix!' Uncle Sam scolded. 'Just sit down! Let us all sit down and discuss this thing like civilised human beings.' He turned to Sade. 'Go and sit over there!' he ordered and she obeyed.

'Now!' said Uncle Sam. 'This is a very simple matter. First of all I need to take a urine sample to confirm that you are indeed pregnant.'

'I have already said all that!' shouted her father.

Uncle Sam held up his arm. 'Will you let me finish!' Once again he turned to Sade. 'If we find that you are indeed pregnant, all you need to do is come to the hospital and I personally will perform the operation. Nobody will ever know.'

Sade stared at the floor in silence.

'Well! Go and get a sample!' Uncle Sam demanded. 'Or you think I have nothing else to do? I'm a very busy man!'

'I'm not having an abortion.' Sade cried.

'Look! Sade!' Uncle Sam tried to sound reassuring. 'You don't need to be afraid. It's a very simple operation. In-fact it's a common D&C. It's just a scrape.'

'It's murder!' said Sade.

'This girl has definitely lost control of her senses!' Her father stared at her in rage.

'It's for the best, Sade!' cried Susan. 'Then you can do your A levels and go to University. When you've got your qualifications you can get married and have a family.'

'You're telling me to murder my baby?' Sade asked her mother who crumbled, blinking and stuttering before sobbing in her handkerchief.

'You're a very stupid girl,' scolded her father.

'Felix! Felix!' Uncle Sam protested. 'Leave her! If you are not prepared to let me handle this matter, I will get up and go!' Once again he turned to Sade. 'Nobody is telling you to murder your baby. Infact at this stage, there is no baby. It's just a foetus.'

'Then there's no problem,' Sade shrugged.

'Oh-ohh!' Uncle Sam, sighed in despair. 'But Sade, do you really love this man? A man you hardly know?'

'It's just petrol and fire love!' shouted her father. 'It ignites with a massive explosion, then there's nothing.'

Sade got up and made her way upstairs. She sat down on the bed listening to her parents quarrelling. Their voices were followed by the appeasing tone of Uncle Sam.

When Uncle Sam eventually left, her mother came upstairs to talk to her.

'Your father says you can get married as long as Emeka allows you to continue your education.'

Sade remained obstinate and unresponsive. Her mother left and she got into bed. Her mind was not at peace. She wondered whether Emeka would change his mind about marrying her. Afterall, he was drunk when he proposed to her.

The next day Idowu arrived to catch up on the gossip. The two girls sat in the shade of a mango tree talking and playing a game of Ayo.

'You know everything the priestess said came true,' said Sade, picking up four rubber seeds from one of twelve holes in the ground. 'I couldn't believe it when Emeka proposed to me at Clive's wedding.'

'You should not take these witch doctors' prophesies too seriously,' said Idowu, glancing apprehensively at Sade.

Sade glared at her.

'Weren't you the one that took me there in the first place?'

'Yes, but you can't believe everything they tell you.'

Sade stood up slipping on her cheap plastic slippers.

'Let's go to visit the Priest of Ogun, the god of iron.'

'Ogun! Why Ogun!' Idowu looked apprehensive.

'I want to compare their readings.'

'But I don't know him.'

'We can find out from the villagers where he stays,' Sade insisted.

'But Sade! You know there are many false prophets. They merely pretend to possess powers in order to take your money.'

'Come on Idowu. Hurry up before it gets dark.'

The sun was now below the horizon and the sky blood red. The beauty of the sun set was no miracle to Sade, she accepted it as she accepted the air that she breathed.

Idowu stood up brushing the dust off her skirt and they walked to the end of the garden. There they joined the path which led them through the rubber plantation to a nearby village. On getting to the village Idowu asked the priestess to Olokun, god of the sea, where they could find the priest to Ogun, god of iron. The priestess directed them down another bush path to a river. They were to follow the river bank which would bring them to another village.

'Let's leave it till tomorrow,' Idowu fretted. 'Look! It's already getting dark and we don't know this man.'

'Come on!' Sade insisted. 'The woman said it's not far.'

Idowu reluctantly followed after her.

'I just hope that priestess will not feel jealous that we are going to consult someone else.' said Sade.

'Why should she be jealous? Our gods are not jealous gods. If you want to worship all or just one it makes no difference.'

'Did you give her the money for the chickens?' Sade smiled.

'Where will I get such money from? You know my father is

strongly against these things.'

They walked along the banks of a sluggish river, watching the tiny silver fishes swimming about in the shallow, clear water. Not far from the river bank a tree was covered in white orchids and Sade hurried over to gather them. She knew her mother would have loved to have them in the garden.

'Get them on the way back,' Idowu fretted.

'Look!' said Sade suddenly heading off into a cleared circle. The circle was surrounded by large mud huts with thatched roofs of palm leaves.

'No!' shouted Idowu. 'Get away from there.'

'Come and see!'

Sade peeped into one of the shrines. Large carvings of a man and woman with grotesque looking genitals rested on the mud floor and the walls were adorned with red cloth. The body of a dead dog lay before them.

'God Ohhhh!' Sade shouted. 'Juju servers. You need to see this man's prick. It resembles a horse's head.'

'Sade come out!'

'Why?'

'Because it's sacred. You will be cursed.'

Idowu crossed her arms over her chest, looking uncertain.

'That must be the shrine to Ogun, god of iron. You said they sacrifice dogs to Ogun, didn't you?'

'Sade! I don't like what you are doing-oh! If you don't come out, I will go and leave you.'

'Hey!' Sade shouted, completely preoccupied with her find. 'This must be the shrine to Olokun, god of the sea. It's so beautiful. Come and see Idowu. Look how they brought white sand and chalk to put on the ground, and even a clay pot of water. The priestess must have done some work here. There's a dead chicken.'

'I'm going!' shouted Idowu walking off. Sade knew that she was bluffing.

Looking into another shrine, she met the terrible image of

the devil himself. Dumfounded she stared in horror at the large horned figure carrying a twin headed spear. She did not need to confirm that it was the shrine of devil worshippers. Oil and blood flowed down from its body to the ground, and a dead goat hung from its neck. Trembling uncontrollably, she dropped the wild orchids, slowly walking backwards out of the circle. Idowu laughed, thinking Sade was acting the fool as usual. Suddenly, Sade turned, sprinting for home. Panicking, Idowu ran after her. The tree branches acted as whips, lashing out at the two girls and scratching their eager legs. Lightning struck, followed by the roar of thunder.

'Wait for me!' Idowu cried but there was no stopping Sade. Discarding her broken slippers, Sade ran faster than she had ever run in her life. In her father's garden she collapsed to the ground, breathless. Idowu followed in closely behind her, supporting her large breasts in her hands as she also collapsed.

'I'm dead-oh!' Sade cried, holding her side with the stitch. 'I've been struck by lightning. I'm going to have a heart attack.'

'Shut up!' Idowu scolded. 'Didn't I tell you not to go into the circle?'

'Aren't you the one that took me there in the first place?' Sade shouted back.

'What do you mean? Isn't it you that said I should go with you to find a witch doctor?'

'Is the devil a witch doctor?'

'Who sent you there? When I was begging you to come out would you listen to me? I said, "Sade! Come out! It's sacred ground." You said, "Hey! Come and look at this ones prick-oh!" I said, "Sade! Come out!" You said, "Hey! juju servers!" I think you've seen the juju servers you were looking for? Then you dare to tell me that I took you to meet the devil. You always like blaming other people for the trouble you cause. No wonder Clive dumped you to marry another woman.'

'You bitch!' Sade stood up furious that Idowu dared to use her misfortune to insult her.

'But it's true…' shouted Idowu.

Idowu was silenced as Sade picked up a large stone. She stared at Sade apprehensively knowing she was furious enough to throw it.

'Talk again–now!' dared Sade, poised to throw the stone.

Suddenly, the heavens opened and the rain poured down.

'God saved you today!' said Sade hurrying indoors. Her parents were out, so she was able to lock Idowu out in the pouring rain.

ELEVEN

SADE WOKE UP in a cold sweat, her heart racing wildly. In a nightmare, she had seen the horrific image of the devil, a huge goat with human features. Turning towards the wardrobe she saw an enormous snake creeping out and crawling towards her. She screamed in terror and her mother came rushing in. Mrs Uwaifo flicked the switch for light but there was no light. The god of thunder and lightening had once again defeated man.

'It's a snake!' Sade screamed.

Her father rushed in, holding his pyjama trousers up.

'It's a snake in the wardrobe!' Sade persisted, now kneeling up in bed and pointing towards the wardrobe.

Justice Uwaifo turned quickly to look in the wardrobe. There was no snake.

'It's fever!' Susan fretted, whilst feeling Sade's forehead. 'I'll get the Aspros.' Mrs Uwaifo made her way downstairs to fetch a glass of water, whilst Justice Uwaifo watched over her. This was one of the few occasions that Sade appreciated her father's company. Soon every crease in the bedding had turned into live, slithering creatures.

'Kneel down and pray!' Justice Uwaifo ordered.

Sade knelt down besides her father.

'In the name of the Father and of the Son and of the Holy Ghost.' he began, making the sign of the cross.

'There's a snake on your foot!' she jumped away from him.

'I said kneel down! And close your eyes!'

Sade obeyed, joining in the recital of the Lord's Prayer. She felt the presence of her mother who came into the room with a bush lantern. After reciting the Hail Mary, she opened her eyes and the snakes had mysteriously disappeared.

'They've gone!' she cried, swallowing two Aspro tablets.

'Come on! Get into bed,' said Susan. 'Will you be allright now?'

She wanted to tell her mother about the shrine field and confess her sins to Almighty God, but the stern look on her father's face prevented her from doing so. Her mother kissed her forehead.

'Call me if you need me. Okay?' Susan attempted to sound reassuring.

Her parents left the room and again the snakes returned. Jumping out of bed, she discovered that the floor was alive with snakes. Holding her cheeks in horror, she made her way into her parents' bedroom.

'Snakes!' she cried. 'They're everywhere!'

Her mother got out of bed and re-lit the lantern. It seemed that the devil did not like the light. Again the snakes disappeared.

'Come on!' said her mother, leading her back into her own bedroom.

Leaving the bush lamp burning on the dressing table, Susan got into bed with Sade. Sade could not sleep. She was afraid the devil might blow the lamp over and set the house ablaze.

Immediately after breakfast Sade set off on the short walk to her cousin's house. Uncle Samuel had gone to the hospital but Auntie Miriam was having breakfast.

Sade made her way upstairs. She found Idowu lying on Taiwo's bed, still in her wrapper and night-dress. Idowu scorned Sade.

'I need to talk to you?' Sade whispered, sitting down beside her.

'You need to talk to who? When you locked me outside in

the rain yesterday, you didn't know you would need to talk to me. Please don't bother me.' Idowu hissed and got up.

'Taiwo!' she yelled, banging on the bathroom door. 'Hurry up! What are you doing in there?'

Sade came after her.

'I'm sorry about last night.'

Taiwo came out watching as Sade followed Idowu in to the bathroom, locking the door behind them.

'Ah! Ah!' shouted Idowu. 'What kind of nonsense is this? Won't you let me take my bath?'

'What's wrong with you people?' shouted Taiwo from the other side of the door.

Sade began to cry, leaning against the door.

'The devil sent snakes to meet me last night.'

Idowu stared at her.

'I swear. It's true. I was wide awake and found my bed, my bedroom floor, everywhere completely covered with snakes.

Idowu removed her wrapper and stripped off her night-dress.

'Did you tell your father?' she asked, climbing into the bath.

'Of course! When I saw the snakes I began to scream.'

Idowu knelt before a large bucket of water, using a small bowl to pour the water over her body.

'You told him about the shrine field?'

'Of course not. Just that I was seeing snakes.'

'What did he say?'

'He asked me to pray with him. My Mum said it was fever.'

Idowu scrubbed herself with a soapy, native sponge, and climbed out of the bath.

'This one pass me-oh!' she declared, drying her body before wrapping herself in the towel. 'Should we tell my mum?'

'No! She will tell your Dad and he will report me.'

'So what do we do?' asked Idowu.

'I don't know. I think I'm going to die. I think my soul will go to hell.'

'Sade! You like talking rubbish,' Idowu scolded.

She opened the bathroom door to find Taiwo with a big grin on his face.

'I heard everything-oh!' he teased.

'Poke noser! God punish you,' scolded Idowu, hissing as she walked past him.

'God punish who?' Taiwo shouted after her. 'God hammer your head!'

The two girls locked themselves in Idowu's bedroom.

'We have to see my friend,' said Idowu, quickly getting dressed.

'The priestess?'

'Yes now! She's the only one that can advise us.'

The two girls set off.

'Do you think I've been cursed?' asked Sade as they walked down the road.

'Anything is possible! I warned you not to enter that shrine field. Anyway, the priestess will reveal everything. I hope you have money to pay her?'

'I better run into the house and collect my pocket money.'

'How much have you got?'

'Five pounds. It's the money they sprayed me with at Clive's wedding.'

'Is your Mum at home?' asked Idowu as they approached the house.

'No! She has gone out with Auntie Omo to buy ashebi for the native wedding. Emeka is coming next week to "knock on the door."'

Idowu scoffed.

'Wait for me! Let me run upstairs and get the money.'

In her bedroom, Sade collected a small brown envelope. It contained a black and white photograph of Clive and his bride, the sweaty pound note, kolanut, and five pounds. She hurried back downstairs to find Idowu sitting on a step touching the 'touch me not' plant. Idowu appeared so involved with her quarrel with the leaves that she had forgotten Sade's plight.

'Let's go!' Sade insisted, setting off through the garden.

Idowu hurried after her. They joined the footpath through the rubber trees, soon arriving at the priestess' compound.

The priestess led them down the dull corridor to her parlour. As usual, she threw divination and went into a trance.

'...Aaaaa! My pickin! The ting whey you do, no good. You enter the place of spirits.' Sade twisted her mouth like a naughty child. 'The trouble too plenty. Make you careful well well-oh! Make you careful-oh! Hey! The man whey go marry you. He like you too much. He like you-oh!' the priestess laughed as she continued. 'He no fit see the bad thing you do. But he no go stay long. Be careful-oh! You must be very careful! The father of your child strong well, well. He no go marry you unless the wife die-finish. The thing you go do-be so. Bring goat-oh! Yam-oh! If you want to make the woman born woman pickin, or make the pickin die-finish, bring dog-oh! Chicken-oh! Eh-hen! If you want make the man marry you, bring pigeon, one man, one woman. You go pray for river make Olokun protect you.'

The priestess came out of the trance to a brief silence. She looked as though she had been woken up from a deep sleep. As though her body had been possessed and she was retaking possession of it.

Sade took the things out of the envelope.

'This money I use–collect their sweat.' Sade handed it to the priestess.

'That's very good,' the priestess responded.

'I want the man. Whatever it takes.'

'You go get am,' the priestess assured her.

'How much to buy everything?' Sade asked.

The woman calculated it to five pounds, exactly the amount Sade possessed. She handed the priestess the money, without hesitation.

That evening at sun down, Sade and Idowu lined up with seven other girls to be initiated into the cult of Olokun. They were dressed in a single strip of white cloth and their skin coated in chalk. Each carried a chicken as they followed the priestess through the bush. A few women who had already been initiated joined the procession, together with two strong men who tapped at metal gongs.

When they arrived at the river, weights were attached to the chickens' legs. The men waded into the water where they sunk the chickens in the tide. The women began to sing praises to the god in Edo. They prayed that no evil should befall on them. They prayed that the girls would be blessed with wealth and many children.

One at a time the girls went into the water. Standing on the river bank, Sade watched Idowu apprehensively making her way into the water. One of the men grabbed Idowu, tilting her backwards until she was completely submerged. When released, Idowu appeared possessed. Hysterically, she tossed about, like a fish in shallow water. The older women hurried into the river. They grabbed hold of Idowu and another girl who seemed intent on drowning themselves.

Sade felt the strong arms of the priestess around her shoulders .

'No!' Sade protested. 'I don't want to go in.'

The spirit of Olokun descended on her heavy and emotive. She began to cry uncontrollably as the priestess led her into the water. One of the men grabbed her firmly, holding her under until she appeared to lose consciousness. Protected only by the strong arms of the initiated, she tossed and turned, possessed by Olokun.

TWELVE

ON THE APPOINTED afternoon, Emeka arrived at Justice Uwaifo's house with his entourage to 'knock at the door'. Feeling unable to cope with the sudden reality of the situation, Sade fled upstairs. From the landing she strained to listen. She prayed that her father would not be stupid enough to confront Emeka about her supposed pregnancy. The muffled voices coming from the lounge made no sense. Time seemed to drag. Suddenly her father was standing at the bottom of the stairs.

'Sade!'

In a fit of panic, she ran into her bedroom.

'Sade!' he called again.

'Yes Daddy!'

'Come downstairs!' He always sounded charmingly authoritative in front of important visitors.

Nervously, she obeyed. In the lounge she found Clive who had accompanied Emeka. His face was void of expression.

'Sit down!' her father instructed.

All the eyes in the room were focused on her. The three elderly chiefs that had accompanied Emeka appeared besotted by her beauty.

'Dr Nzeogwu has come to ask for your hand in marriage. Do you consent?' asked her father.

'Yes!' she responded, trying to avoid all eye contact.

'Well!' Justice Uwaifo sounded despondent. 'You all know that I am against this marriage. If my daughter had been five years older, I would have gladly given my consent. But I still feel that Sade is too young.'

Sitting on the edge of her seat, Sade sighed in frustration. She glanced at her father warily.

'Anyway!' Justice Uwaifo continued. 'I know Emeka is well educated and from a highly respectable family. I understand that he is financially secure and is indeed, a very eligible bachelor. Emeka has given me an assurance that he will get Sade into a good school in Lagos so that she can complete her education. On that condition alone, I am reluctantly giving my consent to this marriage...'

Before Sade knew what was happening the traditional ceremonies were over and her father was leading her down the aisle of the overcrowded Roman Catholic Church. Her beautiful white dress had been flown in from London, as were the pink dresses of the six brides maids and six flower girls. The six page boys and the tiny ring bearer wore black suits and white shirts.

Emeka looked back at her from the altar. He wore black tails and white gloves and in his hand he carried a black toper hat. On his right hand side stood Clive, Emeka's best man.

Sade was struck with panic. It was not meant to be this way. The wedding of her dreams was turning into a nightmare. Before she had time to think the white priest beckoned her. He summoned her to take her place for the first reading. She climbed the stairs to the pulpit, her veil hiding the tears that rolled down her face. Trying hard to compose herself, she stared at the red and yellow flowers adorning the church. The god of the sun had laid hold on them. They had become magical, inspirational and uplifting. They no longer resembled the product of mother earth. Looking down at the faces of eager anticipation, she realised that Olokun, goddess of the sea, had laid hold on them. The women's elaborately constructed blue headties had formed waves. Up on the arch above she saw the sad face of the Lord, Jesus Christ. His last words echoed in her head.

'My God, My God, why hast thou forsaken me?'

Jesus Christ. The human sacrifice to save man from his terrible sin. Was Jesus the son of Osanobua, God Almighty? Was his African name Olokun? Or was he the son of a powerful white God? Trembling in confusion she looked down at the Bible and began to read:

'Judge not, that ye be not judged. For with what judgement ye judge, ye shall be judged: and with what measure ye mete, it shall be measured to you again...'

The priest stood up to stop her. It was the wrong chapter. As he shuffled through the pages of the Bible, she glanced down at the stern face of her father. The priest pointed out the relevant page.

'A reading from the book of Ruth, Chapter 1. Verse 15 to 20.'

Her voice betrayed her innermost feelings and her white laced hands trembled as they rested on the large bible. Sade realised that her whole body was trembling. She felt faint and wanted to pull out. But supposing she was pregnant? Although she refused to be tested, she had missed her first period. She had to be strong.

'And she said, Behold, thy sister-in-law is gone back unto her people, and unto her gods, return thou after thy sister in law.'

Was there a message for her Sade in the reading? Who was her sister-in-law? Obi? She looked down at Clive's attentive face and stuttered as she tried to recollect herself.

'And Ruth said, entreat me not to leave thee or to return from following after thee, for whither thou goest, I will go, and where thou lodgest, I will lodge, thy people shall be my people and thy God my God. Where thou diest, will I die, and there will I be buried:'

She looked down at Clive knowing that he was a part of her very soul and no matter where they roamed, in spirit they were united forever.

'The Lord do so to me and more also, if ought but death part thee and me. And she said unto them, call me not Naomi, call me Mara, for the Almighty hath dealt very bitterly with me. This is the word of the Lord.'

As though hypnotised, Sade performed the necessary acts to solemnise the marriage. After the ceremony she found herself walking out of the church arm in arm with her husband, Emeka. The cameras flashed again and again and soon the people were swarming around her, hugging and kissing and making her weak. The local children pushed and shoved to get a glimpse of the *oyibo* bride.

'What have I done?' she cried as her mother kissed her cheeks.

The Eze quickly stepped in.

'This is a happy occasion, not one for tears!'

'Ah! Ah!' declared Mama Emeka, surveying Sade objectively. Sade surveyed her too. She surveyed the heavy gold and coral around the older woman's fat neck and the huge blue head-tie on her head. She surveyed her powerful looking arms, right down to the clenched fist.

'Emeka!' his mother shouted. 'Emeka! Come take your wife!'

Abandoning his teasing friends, Emeka came over.

'Where is the driver?' asked the Eze. 'You better go straight to the reception and we'll meet you there.'

Emeka led his mourning wife to the awaiting Mercedes.

'Let's go!' he ordered the driver. He put his arm around Sade. 'You don't need to cry. You'll have no regrets about marrying me. I'll really take good care of you.'

They approached Justice Uwaifo's compound and a group of Bini girls in straight wrappers and coral-covered hair sang praises. The driver pulled up outside the canopy and the Mercedes with the bridesmaids pulled up behind them.

Idowu jumped out and rushed to help Sade with the train on the dress. They walked past the rows of metal chairs to the high table which had been set up on stage.

'I hope I have a dress like yours when I get married,' sighed Idowu.

'You can have this one,' Sade responded, struggling to climb the stairs to the stage.

It was the groom that mattered and Sade had the wrong groom.

The high table was covered with a white damask cloth and there were flowers creeping down to a massive wedding cake beneath it. Six white bridges linked six smaller cakes to the main four tier wedding cake. The main cake possessed a water fountain between the first and second layer and at the highest point rested the figures of perfection: a white bride and groom.

'The cake is fantastic!' said Emeka as they sat down. 'Who made it?'

'An American woman my mother knows,' Sade was dismissive.

'Testing! Testing! Testing!' shouted the lead singer of the police band. 'Testing! Testing! Testing! Wan! twoo! Teree! For!'

The microphone squealed and Sade waved her white fan violently.

'I told my father not to get the police band,' she told Idowu.

'Leave them! They are just warming up.' Idowu responded.

Soon the compound was bursting with life. The chief of police waved and shouted excitedly at the other dignitaries as Justice Uwaifo shouted at his wife and servants. One of the dogs chased after a page boy, biting his new trousers and Justice Uwaifo ordered Innocent to lock up all the dogs in the boysquarters. From the high table, Sade watched as Innocent approached the excited dog. He made funny kissing, sucking noises. Suddenly he grabbed its neck. The dog broke free and bit his hand. The guests moved away as Innocent kicked it. It yelped, then fled into the garden.

'Be very careful!' shouted Uncle Sam. 'That dog could have rabies! I've noticed it's acting in a most peculiar way.'

Sade twisted her mouth in outrage. She knew the dog didn't have rabies. It had been inoculated.

'Indeed!' shouted another one of her uncles. Her interfering uncles were everywhere, all thirty-five of them. In their elaborate white agbadas, they looked twice their normal sizes. They approached the high table in strong daunting groups, their arrogant waddling high-heeled wives following behind them. Now the family hierarchy was very much in evidence, the senior members of the family shouting orders at their juniors. Sade looked down on them and could sense trouble. A storm brewing!

'But you should be on the high table!' Auntie Miriam shouted at Uncle Sam.

'Of course! As head of the family, you must be on the high table,' another uncle insisted.

Mrs Uwaifo had arranged the high table in the English way, for the bride and groom, parents of the bride and groom, chief bridesmaid and best man.

'Idowu! Come down from there!' Samuel Uwaifo ordered.

Eyes averted in fear, Idowu jumped off the stage.

Uncle Sam turned to Sade. 'Where's your father?'

'I think he's in the house,' she responded respectfully.

'Innocent!' Uncle Sam yelled.

Innocent cowered as he approached.

'Take another chair up there for my wife,' he ordered, leading Auntie Miriam up the steps. Chief Dr and Mrs Samuel Uwaifo now sat proudly on the high table from where they looked down on the less important beings.

'Well, if that's the case,' mumbled Emeka to Sade, 'the Eze's brother should also be on the high table, and there are some VIPs that came all the way from Umuahia. They have to be on the high table.'

'For God's sake!' Sade sighed.

'What is that?' asked the Eze, who was sitting next to her.

Emeka stretched over to respond.

'I said there are some VIPs you invited, who should be on the high table.'

'Indeed!' the Eze nodded. 'Or they will feel slighted.'

Emeka gave orders to Clive, who rushed off to consult Justice Uwaifo. He returned moments later walking three steps behind Justice Uwaifo. Emeka went to meet them.

'What's the problem?' Justice Uwaifo asked Emeka.

'The Eze has said that he came with many dignitaries who will feel slighted if they are not placed on the high table,' Emeka responded respectfully.

After a great deal of commotion the VIPs were identified, replacing the bride's entourage on the high table.

Now the canopy was thronged with guests and all the seats occupied. Still people kept arriving, invited and uninvited. Smiling, laughing and gossiping they stood around the open sides of the covering. Eventually Clive took the microphone.

'Your Excellencies! Igwe! Eze! High Chiefs! Chiefs! Ladies and Gentlemen! May I start by wishing you all a very warm welcome to this happy occasion. This is a particularly delightful day for me, due to my close relationship with the families of the bride and the groom. As most of you here are aware, I married my dear wife from the Nzeogwu family. So I can assure Sade, that she could not have married into a better family. Not wanting to waste too much of your time, I will now hand you over to the father of the beautiful bride, Justice Uwaifo.'

As food and drinks were distributed, Sade returned to her hypnotic state. Occasionally she felt conscious of the applause as her father made his speech. When he had finished, her uncles hogged the microphone, proferring endless advice on every possible topic: The importance of bearing sons! How a wife can avoid a beating! How a woman should behave in the matrimonial home! There was no subject left untouched.

The over heated guests fanned themselves violently with their programmes and anything else they could lay their hands on. After Emeka had made his speech the Eze decided it was his turn. He did not stand like everyone else. The microphone was brought to him.

'Today! Is a very great day! Today, my first son has become a real man. He has taken a wife. The day my son Emeka returned from England as a qualified doctor was indeed one of the proudest moments of my life. But today he has made me even prouder. I was not happy when he told me he wanted to marry a Bini girl. I always expected my first son to marry an Ibo girl. But looking at Sade, I don't think that there is any Ibo girl that can compete with her. Emeka has found a very beautiful bride, from a highly respected family. A young girl without blemish. And I must say that I am very impressed. As a sign of my happiness, I am going to give the newly weds the deeds to the four bedroom house that I built in Lagos.' The guests cheered very loudly.

'What remains now is for them to fill the rooms with my grandsons.' Everyone laughed and joked. 'I wish them a long and happy married life.'

The guests continued to cheer as Emeka and Sade got up to thank the Eze. When the noise eventually died down Clive again took the microphone.

'As time is very short we must move on to the cutting of the cake. May I request that the bride and groom please come down to cut the cake.'

Emeka and Clive helped Sade off the stage, the bridesmaids long displaced.

'The cutting of the wedding cake is a very important part of the programme,' announced Clive. 'Because it is the first thing that the newly weds are going to do together.'

The guests laughed and joked as the couple stood before the cake.

'Emeka! Let me warn you. It is not something to be rushed. You must take it slowly and carefully.'

'Emeka! Repeat after him!' shouted Auntie Miriam from the

high table.

'Slowly and carefully!' Emeka repeated giving Sade the glad eye. Sade went hot with embarrassment and felt faint.

'Sade! Please take the knife,' said Clive.

He realised that Sade did not appreciate his jokes. She picked up the knife, frowning in disapproval.

'Smile please!' the photographer requested.

'Emeka! Guide her from the top,' Auntie Miriam shouted again.

The guests laughed hysterically.

'Sade! Remember that the man must always be on the top,' Uncle Sam laughed.

'Now after three you may cut the cake,' ordered Clive. 'One! Two! Three!'

Sade rushed the knife through the cake and hurriedly removed her hand from under Emeka's. She tried to return to her seat.

'Won't you feed your husband?' shouted Auntie Miriam.

Sade felt herself going giddy. The tiny stars encircled her and her world turned black.

When she came round she found herself in Clive's arms. Her mother was fanning her hysterically.

'Let her have space!' Uncle Sam shouted as the guests crowded around.

'Come on! Get her into the house!' Susan ordered Clive.

Emeka tried to take her from Clive.

'I'm allright now!' she insisted pulling away from the men.

They led her into the lounge where she flung the veil off her head, collapsing in tears.

Her wedding day had turned out to be the worst day of her life.

'You're okay now!' said Uncle Sam, placing an arm of reassurance on her shoulder. 'It's too much excitement,' he told Emeka.

Susan sniffled in her handkerchief. 'Well she can't travel tonight. It's all been too much for her. You'd better stay here tonight. You can go to Lagos tomorrow.'

'We'll be driving back to Lagos tomorrow.' Clive put his arm around Obi as he spoke. 'If you want, you can come with us or there's a flight in the afternoon.'

'There's no rush, is there?' said Justice Uwaifo. He turned to Susan. 'Ask the boy to make the beds for them.'

'Thank you very much, Sir.' Emeka responded. 'We'll leave tomorrow.'

Sade sighed in relief.

THIRTEEN

SADE KNEW THAT she was going to like Lagos. She felt exhilarated by the zest for life. It was almost dark but the streets were jam-packed with cars, bicycles, motor bikes and mammy-wagons, their drivers cursing and blaring their horns impatiently. Excitedly they manoeuvred through the traffic. Child beggars and street sellers leaped about pressing their wares against the car window. Highlife and soul music blasted out from the record shops as vendors competed for business. It was like a fun fair, wonderfully exciting.

'This is the area I live,' said Emeka arrogantly.

The taxi driver sped through Ikoyi and Sade realised that this was the most exclusive part of Lagos. The old colonial houses were now occupied by white expatriates. The driver pulled up in front of the gates to Emeka's beautiful four bedroom house.

'Blow the horn!' ordered Emeka.

The driver obeyed. A ferocious looking alsatian came running towards them. Barking and growling, it jumped up at the wrought iron gates. Mohammed, the Hausa night-watch man, ran through the garden, his long white robe billowing in the wind.

'Hold am-oh!' the frightened taxi driver shouted, rolling up his window as Mohammed opened the gates. Sade followed his example as the huge dog ran out, jumping up at the windows and scratching the paintwork with its claws. Mohammed, a slight old man, smiled and bowed with dignity.

'*Sanu!*' he greeted, his teeth yellow from eating too many

kolanuts. The dog skidded towards the back of the car, growling and biting the tires. It ran back to the front, jumping up at the driver's window. Its long tongue hung out of its mouth and its saliva cascaded down.

'Master!' The taxi driver shook his head and turned to face Emeka. 'I no go fit enter! Look the teeth!'

'Enter!' shouted Emeka. 'He no go bite you.'

'As I see dis dog, Sah, he go fit chop person,' the driver protested.

'I say enter!' Emeka gestured in frustration. 'Or you want us to get down on the road?'

The driver hesitated. He looked out at the wild beast and shook his head. Suddenly he put his foot down on the accelerator, speeding down the driveway. The dog took off after them, growling whilst trying to bite the tyres. The driver skidded to a halt, almost hitting Emeka's brand new Mercedes parked under the red bougainvillaea covered porch.

'Ah Ah! Craze dey your head?' scolded Emeka. 'You want to jam my Mercedes?' He got out of the taxi. 'Lucky!' he yelled at the dog. 'Come here!' The dog wagged its tail, delighted to see its master. 'Mallam! [Mister] You no dey feed dis dog?' he grabbed Lucky's collar.

'I feed am Sah!'

Mohammed considered it a waste of good meat giving it to the dog and always ate half himself.

'Come and hold it.' Emeka ordered Mohammed who quickly approached with its chain. The dog began to struggle as he attached the chain to its collar. Mohammed pulled the dog away from the car.

'Get down now!' Emeka told Sade.

With an eye on the dog, she got out of the car. It growled and Mohammed hit its nose with the leather handle of the dog chain.

'Get the suitcases out of the boot,' Emeka ordered the taxi driver.

The driver glanced back at the dog.

'Master! I no fit.' he responded.

'Give me the key.'

The driver took the keys out of the ignition and Emeka snatched them from his hand. As he unlocked the boot, the houseboy came to meet them.

'Welcome Sah! Welcome Ma!' Bunmi bobbed up and down, rushing to collect the suitcases from the boot.

'Take those things upstairs!' Emeka ordered him.

'Yes Sah!'

Once paid, the taxi driver eagerly drove off.

'Do you like my car?' Emeka asked Sade. 'My father ordered it straight from Germany.'

'It's beautiful,' she grinned, feeling like an intruder on his property.

Emeka showed her into the lounge-dining room. Two Persian rugs covered the terrazzo floor and all the furniture was imported and new.

'Please sit down.' said Emeka turning on the air-conditioner.

She sat on the sofa and Emeka lounged down besides her.

'Would you like a drink?'

'Maybe a coke!' she responded, feeling very vulnerable in his territory.

'Bunmi!' he yelled.

The boy hurried in.

'Get a coke for Madam and a beer for me!'

Bunmi returned to the kitchen.

'What would you like to eat?' asked Emeka. He confidently put his arm around Sade's shoulder. 'Bunmi can prepare something. I have an excellent cook, but unfortunately it's his day off. You'll meet him tomorrow. He was trained by an Englishman working at the University of Ibadan.'

'I'm not hungry.' Sade got up and made her way towards the radiogram. 'Is it allright if I put on a record?'

'You don't need to ask.' He followed, opening up a low

cabinet to reveal his large collection. 'What do you like, soul? reggae? highlife? Excuse me for just a moment.'

Sade sighed in relief as he headed off into an adjacent toilet. Flicking through the records, Sade pulled one out by Miriam Makeba. She put it on. In order to avoid Emeka's advances, she sat on a chair. Shutting her eyes, she tried to cope with the situation. She recalled her mother's tears at Benin Airport and her father's serious face as he wished them 'all the best!'. She thought of the theatrical performance that had been her wedding. She could no longer recall the promises she made, but the words 'love, honour and obey' echoed from her subconscious.

Emeka returned and lounged back in the sofa.

'Darling! Come and sit here,' he tapped the seat next to him.

Sade smiled coyly but ignored his request.

'Bring the drinks over here,' he ordered as Bunmi came into the room.

Bunmi placed the tray on the coffee table in front of Emeka.

'Just leave them there. You can lock up and go.'

'Yes Sah! Good night Sah! Good night Madam!' Bunmi bowed before leaving the room.

'Are you feeling shy?' asked Emeka, opening the bottle of coke. 'Then let me come to you.' He grabbed a glass, making his way towards Sade. After filling the glass, he sat on the arm of her chair. 'You are so beautiful,' he smiled, placing his arm firmly around her shoulders.

Quickly she moved forward and picked up the glass of coke from the stool.

'Does Clive live near here?' she asked sipping her drink.

'Yes! My father built them a bungalow immediately behind us.'

'Let's go and see them. They should be back from Benin by now.'

'They won't! It's a four hour drive.'

He took the glass from her hand, placing it back on the

110

stool. Sade jumped to her feet.

'I'm exhausted! Show me the bedroom.'

He led her upstairs to the master bedroom, where her suitcases rested on the tiled floor.

'I'm coming!' Emeka's voice was full of anticipation. 'I forgot to turn off the player.'

When he had gone, Sade shut the door but could not find the key to lock it. After unpacking, she changed and got into bed. Shutting her eyes, she pretended to be asleep. Emeka returned, strutting confidently into the room. He stripped down to his white underpants and climbed in beside her.

'Darling!' he moved close, kissing her shoulder and rubbing her leg.

'Keep away from me!' she cried, jumping out of the bed in panic.

Emeka sat up in bed.

'Darling! You don't need to be afraid!' He got out of bed to console her.

Running past, she headed for the closest bedroom, locking herself in. Collapsing on the bed she sobbed desperately. How could she allow herself to be violated by a man she didn't love.

'Sade!' called Emeka, tapping at the door. 'Believe me, it doesn't matter! I understand.'

After all, he thought, she was bound to be afraid of him, being only a young and innocent virgin.

FOURTEEN

Sade slept little all night, but was waken by the dog barking to children's screams. Jumping out of bed, she rushed to the bedroom window. A few excited school children ran past the garden. Suddenly, she realised how drastically her life had changed. One day she was a schoolgirl and the next, a doctor's wife and mistress of a large house. There was a tap at her door.

'Darling!' Emeka called.

She did not respond.

'I'm off to work. I'll see you later.'

From the bedroom window she watched Emeka drive off.

After her morning routine, she made her way downstairs. In the lounge a strange man came to meet her.

'Good morning Madam! You are very welcome!' he bowed.

'Good morning! Who are you?'

'I am Godpower. Madam!'

'Godpower?'

'Yes Madam. I am the cook.'

'Ohhh! Master said you cook very well.'

'Yes madam. One *oyibo* train me.'

'That's very good.'

'Madam, What you go take for breakfast?'

'Bring tea and cornflakes.'

'Yes Madam. What of lunch Madam?'

'Anything!'

'Make I cook rice?'

'Yes! That's fine!'

'Yes madam! I go send Bunmi go market.' Godpower was obviously trying to exhibit his authority over the common houseboy.

'Master give you money?'

'Yes madam!'

Godpower returned to the kitchen whilst Bunmi came to lay the table.

'Good morning Madam!'

'Morning! You know where Master's sister lives?'

'He dey stay for back yard, Madam.'

'Later on you will take me there.'

After breakfast Bunmi led Sade through the garden towards Clive's house. Spotting them, the dog jumped to its feet, barking and growling. It approached with such a speed that it skidded as it drew back about four feet away. Sade froze to the spot as Mohammed came running up with the dog-chain.

'Good morning Madam!' he bowed respectfully before chasing after Lucky.

Once Lucky was tied up, they continued through the garden. It was in full bloom and well developed like most of the old colonial gardens. Bunmi led her behind the dingy looking boys' quarters, through a small garden, to an unfinished bungalow. Clive had indeed come cheap. Perhaps he was looking at the long term advantages of working for the Eze. Bunmi led her up a few steps to the front porch. Sade banged on the door and a shabbily dressed housegirl opened it.

'Good morning Ma!' the girl curtsied.

'Good morning! Where your madam?' asked Sade, looking past the girl, into the lounge.

The walls were unpainted, the floor untilled concrete and the furniture constructed of cheap cane.

'Madam go work.'

'What of Master?'

'He go work.'

Sade returned home feeling wonderfully powerful. Clive's livelihood obviously depended on the goodwill of the Eze, and being married to the Eze's first son offered her tremendous influence. When Emeka returned in the afternoon he looked exhausted.

'How was your day?' he asked, lounging into the sofa.

'Boring!' she sighed. 'I went to see Obi, but she was at work.'

'I'll have to make arrangements for you to start school,' he put his head back and shut his eyes.

'You look as if you've had a hard day.'

'Believe me, I'm exhausted.'

Bunmi came to inform them that the food was served and Emeka jumped to his feet.

'Let's go and eat!' he said.

'I've eaten.'

'At least come and sit with me.'

He pulled her up. The dog began to bark as a car pulled up in the driveway. Sade listened to the crunching footsteps and muffled voices, identifying them as Clive and Obi. Bunmi showed them in and they sat down at the table.

'Godpower!' Obi yelled. 'Bring two more plates.' She smiled at Sade. 'I haven't had time to cook and that housegirl is very useless.'

Sade grinned as she studied Obi's dark face. She was covered in patchy blemishes and her forehead was too long. It appeared to fold over itself, leaving a lump above her eye brows. She thought of Clive and Obi making love and felt sick inside.

'How are you finding Lagos?' Obi asked her.

'Boring!'

'Oh no! Lagos might be many things, but not boring.' Obi laughed. She turned to her brother. 'Why not take her to Ikoyi Club or the Federal Palace? She'll enjoy the casino there.'

'After church tomorrow, we can drive to Badagry beach.' Emeka responded.

'That sounds nice.' Sade turned to Clive. 'Would you like to come?'

'Of course they're coming,' insisted Emeka.

The Roman Catholic Church mass the following morning was long, hot and boring. Once it was over, the group set off on the long drive to Badagry. At the beach, Emeka drove over the fine white sand, parking under a coconut tree. The group struggled through the sand dunes and hired one of the many thatched huts. A ragged little boy supplied them with canvas deck chairs and they all relaxed under the mid-day heat. Suddenly, Emeka stood up and began to strip off his clothes.

'Come on! Let's go for a swim.'

Clive and Obi were happy to oblige. Obi stripped off her European style dress. Underneath she wore a bikini. Sade looked at her frail dark body, her pregnancy now obvious.

'I will have to take off my wig.' Obi sounded apprehensive.

'Take it off now!' Clive shrugged carelessly.

Slowly Obi pulled it off. She had lost an inch of hair all around her hair line and what was left had been tightly weaved flat on her head. Although Obi was not smiling, still her front teeth protruded from under her upper lip.

'What I would do to have hair like yours,' said Obi, noticing Sade's stare. Sade threw herself back in her deck chair and closed her eyes.

'Darling!' said Emeka rubbing her arm. 'What's the matter? Let's go and swim.'

Sade realised his ploy. He thought he could see her naked.

'I don't feel like swimming.' she responded.

'Why now!' asked Obi.

'Darling, don't be like that.'

Sade sighed. 'Will you stop calling me darling.'

'Ah Ah! Why shouldn't I call you darling?' Emeka teased. Clive and Obi burst out laughing.

'Come on! Let's swim.' Emeka persisted.

'God! I've told you I don't want to swim,' she snapped.

'Maybe later–yeah?' Emeka sounded hurt.

Awkwardly he followed Clive and Obi down the sandy beach to the surf. Sade watched, as he dived into the waves, his white underpants clinging to his firm backside. At least Clive was civilised enough to purchase a proper pair of swimming trunks. The group swam out to sea and Sade thought how wonderful it could have been, playing amongst the waves, arm in arm with Clive. From the sand dunes she watched the fishermen pushing their canoes out and over the barrage. They cast their nets. Singing, they hauled in their silver catch. Squabbling market women arrived and filled their large enamel basins before scattering into oblivion.

In the bright sunshine, Sade fell asleep. She was waken by shouting.

'Sharks! Sharks! Come out of the water!'

She sprang to her feet looking anxiously out to sea. The herd of creatures on the horizon filled her with horror.

'Clive!' she screamed, rushing down the sand. 'Sharks!'

Emeka was first out of the water. Clive and Obi were too far out to hear her calls.

'Oh my God!' she cried, trembling in shock.

Emeka joined in the panic stricken chorus.

'Swim out and call them!' Sade ordered him.

He stood still, scratching his head in confusion. The water ran down Emeka's legs from his wet, sand filled, underpants.

'Go on!' Sade insisted.

He walked into the shallow surf, where he continued his calls. Obi noticed her brothers frantic waves and the couple returned to shore.

'Didn't you see the sharks?' asked Sade. 'We've been calling you for ages.'

'Those were no sharks!' laughed Clive. 'They were dolphins.'

'Dolphins? How do you know they are dolphins?' Sade demanded.

'Because sharks don't jump over the water like that,' Clive

explained. 'I want to walk down to the slave fort. Does anyone want to come?' Clive climbed into his shorts as he spoke.

'I'm too tired.' Obi whined, relaxing in one of the deck chairs.

'I'll come!' Sade responded, eager to be alone with Clive.

'Okay! Let's go!' said Emeka. 'Obi can look after the things.'

Clumsily, Emeka hopped into his shorts and snatched up his shirt. Walking along the beach, he attempted to hold his wife's hand but she pulled away.

The three walked parallel to the huge thudding waves of the Atlantic. Occasionally they stopped to watch the crabs that rode the surf. Between the two men, Sade felt protected and powerful. She recalled the sacrifices she had made to the goddess of the sea. Licking her salty lips, she felt confident that Clive would return to her.

'That's the slave fort!' said Clive.

He pointed to a daunting looking building, surrounded by thatched shacks-the homes of fishermen and the wretched poor. They approached the fort, and a shabbily dressed man offered to show them around. They followed him down the empty stone built corridors and past a solid iron door. A ramp hurried them to a dull cellar filled with the stench of excrement. The old iron slave chains lay harmlessly around the room. Sade picked up a heavy, iron, neck clasp.

'Try it on,' she insisted, opening it up for Emeka.

Eager to please, he put his neck into the clasp and got stuck. Sade burst into hysterical laughter as the guide struggled to free him. She pictured Emeka driving home with the heavy chains around his neck. When the irons were removed, Emeka stormed out of the dingy room. Clive and the guide hurried after him. Still laughing, Sade looked through a hatch at the end of the dungeon. It was through here that countless Africans were led into slavery. Kings and commoners together, dehumanised, herded and whipped into line, to board the awaiting European ships.

Suddenly, the heavy iron door was slammed shut. Surrounded by darkness, Sade rushed to the door and tried to push it open.

'Clive!' she shouted. 'Clive!'

There was no reply. All she could hear was the sound of the ocean waves, voice of Olokun, goddess of the sea. Leaning against the stone wall, she tried to compose herself. Had Emeka and Clive gone or were they playing a trick on her?

'Emeka!' she screamed to no avail.

She recalled his panic stricken face, trapped in chains. Was this his revenge? The smell of the filth made her feel sick and the heat made her feel faint. She began to scream and bang on the door hysterically. Her mind became clouded with images of the past. She could see the terrified faces of the slaves, men, women and children. They surrounded her, screaming in terror and begging to be allowed to return to the tranquillity of their villages. They pleaded for somebody to save them from the alien white invaders. Alas! The whips came down. Babies were ripped from their mother's breasts and discarded in the sea. Weeping and wailing the people went forth. They were pushed and shoved through the hatch to be forever orphaned from mother Africa.

Sade covered her ears with her hands and shutting her eyes tightly crouched down on the floor. Emeka opened the door.

'Vengeance is sweet!' Clive laughed aloud.

The light and air hit her face and she rushed out of the dungeon and down the beach. The laughing of the men blended with the voice of Olokun. Emeka ran after her.

'You bastard!' she screamed as he caught her arm. 'I hate you. I should never have married you. Take me home!'

'Come on!' said laughed. 'It was just a joke. Can't you take a joke?'

She stormed off to the car. Soon, she was joined by the rest of the group. Emeka drove them home in silence.

FIFTEEN

SADE WAS SITTING in the lounge, applying red nail varnish to her long finger nails, when Clive walked in.

'Is Emeka ready?' he asked slumping into one of the upholstered chairs.

'He's been called to the hospital. Where's your wife? Isn't she coming to the party?'

'She's not feeling well.'

'What a pity.' Sade sounded sarcastic.

'Before I forget, Sophia asked me to give you this letter.' Clive handed her a sealed pink envelope.

Placing her feet up on the sofa, Sade began to read.

Dear Sade,

How are you doing? Sorry I didn't write earlier, but things have been so hectic in Ibadan. How is that your husband? On a better note, how are you enjoying Lagos? I will be coming to Lagos before Christmas, so we can all travel to Benin together for the holidays.

I am still dating Taiwo but we are having a lot of problems. He keeps suspecting Kehinde of chasing me. By the way don't mention it to Marilyn. Kehinde is always so nice to me and treats me like a sister. However when Taiwo sees us together he gets annoyed and retaliates by chatting up this Indian medical student...

While Sade was reading, Clive poured himself a drink from

the cabinet and turned on the record player. He dismissed the house staff and locked the front door. It was the first time they had been alone since the escapade in the bush.

'So how is married life?' Clive asked, resuming his seat.

'What kind of question is that?'

'Well, it seems obvious that you don't love Emeka, so I wonder why you married him?'

'Well, believe it or not, he's a very nice person,' she sneered.

'You treat him like shit. You should have stayed in Benin.'

'I would have gladly stayed in Benin, had you not made it impossible for me to do so.'

'What do you mean?'

Sade was certain that she was in the early stages of pregnancy.

'You know exactly what I mean so stop pretending ignorance.'

Clive laughed.

'You think it's funny, do you?' she scolded. 'Let me tell you something that will really make you laugh. My marriage has never been consummated, yet I find myself pregnant.'

'What?' Clive flew off his seat. 'So what are you trying to say? That I am the father?'

'No! It was the immaculate conception.'

'Shit! I can't believe it. Have you said anything to Emeka?'

'I was waiting for you to tell him.'

'Listen to me!' Clive sat down beside her. 'I'll take you to Benin for the week-end. One of my friend's is a doctor.'

'Get away from me!' cried Sade, standing up. 'Why didn't you take Obi to your friend?'

'You are married to Emeka.'

Clive stood up and moved quickly towards her. His hands grasped her shoulders. 'Look! You just told me that your marriage has not been consummated. Don't you think that Emeka will realise you are pregnant? The moment he touches you, he'll know. And what are you going to tell him?'

Sade began to sob bitterly and Clive circled her in his arms.

'Believe me I never intended to hurt you. I'll do everything I can to help you. Just tell Emeka that you want to go home for the weekend. I'll make all the necessary arrangements.'

'I'm not having an abortion!' Sade broke free from his grasp.

'You have no choice,' Clive shouted in frustration.

'Don't you dare raise your voice to me! If it wasn't for you, I wouldn't be in this mess. You used me like a whore, then buggered off to Umuahia, leaving me to face the music.'

'Who was it that took my cigarettes? You lured me out of that party.'

Sade lashed out at him, her fingers leaving three red lines down his cheek. Clive stared at her, his eyes tense with rage.

'You just wait!' she warned. 'You think you can sweet talk me into aborting my child? Well you can't!'

Heading for the drinks cabinet, she grabbed a bottle of brandy and took a swig.

'Sade! This isn't getting us anywhere. Just tell me what you want me to do?'

Clive sat down, looking utterly dejected.

'Divorce her!' said Sade, sitting down beside him. 'I love you and I know that you love me. And I want this child more than anything.'

'You better get one thing clear.' Clive spoke without sentiment. 'No matter what happens, I will never divorce Obi. If it were not for her, I would not be a barrister today. She paid my fees and even fed me whilst I was at university. She's a good person, and so is Emeka.'

'You will pay!' Sade jumped to her feet. 'You will watch your son growing up in Emeka's house and bearing Emeka's name.'

'Once Emeka comes home, I'm going to talk to him.'

'You do that! But before you do, consider the consequence! Your child will be identified as Barrister Clive Udochi's bastard. And as for you! You will be an outcast in the Eze's family. Obi, I'm sure will stand by you, but will she appear so attractive without her father's money?'

'How can you understand anything? My father never drove about in a Mercedes, or had houses to collect rents from. I have had to struggle and suffer for everything. I wasn't born with a silver spoon in my mouth.'

'And neither was I! But I don't go about jealously exploiting others. Now I can see that you never loved me. You just used me.'

'You know that's not true.'

'You used me! Just like you're using Obi.'

A car approached the house and the dog began to bark. Knowing that her eyes would be red, Sade fled upstairs. In the bathroom, she washed her face with cold water. Worried that Clive would expose her, she stood on the landing to listen.

'The man was Ibo,' Emeka shouted. 'Those political party thugs poured petrol over him and set him alight. It's Akintola and the Nigerian National Alliance stirring up all this hatred for us Ibos. Have you heard their electoral appeal? What Ibo domination are they talking about? Akintola should have been put in jail a long time ago. And does he seriously think with all his unpopularity he can win these November elections? Even his own people don't want him. The Yorubas certainly do not want him.'

Sade sighed. Same old boring politics. Returning to her bedroom, she examined her eyes in the mirror. Suddenly she realised that she was developing a pot belly. Had she eaten too much, or was her pregnancy beginning to show?

'Sade!' Emeka called.

He was on his way upstairs. Sade went to the bedroom door. Emeka was looking very upset.

'I hope you won't mind if we stay home tonight.' He hardly looked at her as he spoke.

Whilst he was in the shower, Sade went back downstairs.

'Are you okay now?' Clive asked.

She nodded, trying to avoid his penetrating stare.

122

'What's wrong with Emeka?' she asked, sitting down next to him.

'He just lost a patient,' Clive got up. 'I better get going. Just tell him I'll see him tomorrow.'

Sade saw him to the door.

'Clive! Promise me you won't say anything to him,' Sade reached for his arm.

'Just get rid of it!' Clive spoke quietly but he sounded aggressive.

He walked away from her, disappearing into the African darkness. Sade locked up and went back upstairs. As usual she locked herself in the spare bedroom. Taking off her dress, she stared at her reflection in the mirror. She was developing a bulge, or was she? She put on her night-dress and got into bed. The priestess had been right, Clive would never leave Obi. Unable to sleep, she knew that she had to consummate her marriage. The hours dragged by, until she realised it was 2 a.m She decided to pretend she was having a nightmare, to lure him into her bed. She filled her lungs with air, but exhaled rapidly. Jumping out of bed she rushed to unlock the bedroom door before returning to bed. Her first scream got no response so she went into a screaming fit. Emeka came running in, holding his wrapper at his groin.

'What happened?' asked Emeka, anxiously fumbling for the light switch. 'What's the matter?'

'There was a man!' she screamed, pretending to be in utter panic and distress.

'Where?' Emeka pulled away.

'Here! He was going to kill me. Don't leave me. Please don't leave me!'

'Let me check the house.' he whispered.

'No! No! He'll kill you! Don't leave me!'

'I am coming!' he snapped, pulling away aggressively whilst still clutching his wrapper. 'Let me check the house.' He crept to the landing. 'Who's there?' he shouted, deepening his voice.

Sade smothered her laughs in the pillow. He returned, pushing a chair up against the wardrobe. She peeped from the pillow, to see him pull out a shot-gun. He pointed it at her and she screamed.

'Shut up!' he whispered turning off the light. Sade jumped out of bed to follow him downstairs.

'Stay here!' he ordered.

'I can't! I'm too afraid.'

Slowly, he made his way down the terrazzo staircase with Sade close behind him.

'There's nobody!' he said, having checked every room.

Emeka put his arm around her and they returned upstairs.

'You must have had a nightmare,' he said, leading her into the master bedroom.

'But it was so real,' she whimpered, sitting down on the bed.

'It's okay now.'

He sat down next to her, pushing her back as he kissed her. Sade felt that she had successfully entrapped herself. She thought of Clive's warning. Surely Emeka would discover her pregnant the moment that he touched her. She tried to push him aside but he was determined not to let her go. He was licensed 'to have and to hold', and he was not prepared to forfeit that right another day.

'I need to tell you something,' she pleaded.

Stiffling her protest with a kiss, he discarded his wrapper and took of the forbidden fruit.

SIXTEEN

CHRISTMAS APPROACHED AND Sade ordered the gardener to cut down one of the many fern trees in the garden. After a lot of commotion, Godpower and the gardener managed to get the tree into the house, erecting it in the corner of the lounge.

'What happened to your eye?' Sade asked, as Godpower sadly rubbed a sore eye.

'Nah Apollo eye Madam!'

Sade was relieved that it wasn't anything more serious than conjunctivitis blamed on the Apollo moon landing. She thought it was an injury from the Christmas tree.

'Help me hang these cards,' she ordered, handing Godpower a pack of drawing pins, some string and a bundle of Christmas cards.

Whilst Godpower carried out her instructions, she got the gardener to hang lights and trimmings on the tree.

'He fine well well-oh!' said the gardener, staring in wonder as she turned on the flickering lights.

'You can go now!' she told them, turning on the record player.

The angelic voices of children singing Christmas carols pervaded the air. Filled with contentment, Sade gently rubbing her bulging belly. This was sure to be the best Christmas ever. Taiwo and Kehinde would be in Benin with Sophia and Marilyn, and she would be with Clive-and Emeka. When Christmas was over, the masqueraders and juju dancers would take to the streets, dancing and whipping in the new year.

Emeka returned from the post office to find Sade lying down on the sofa.

'Wow!' he looked delighted. 'You've really been working hard. I didn't realise we had received so many cards,' he laughed, kissing her forehead. 'And would you believe we had another six today.' He handed her the opened envelopes containing Christmas cards. 'There's also a letter there from your father.'

Her father never wrote. Such trivialities were always left to her mother. Anxiously, she sat up and opened the sealed envelope. Pulling out the letter, she began to read.

Dear Sade,

It is with great regret that I must inform you of the violent and senseless death of your cousin, Taiwo.

Surely she had not read properly. She looked again at the name and cried out in horror. Her chest tightened in anxiety.

'What's the matter?' Emeka asked.

'It's Taiwo! He, he's dead!' she sobbed.

'Taiwo! I'm so sorry!' Emeka sat beside her, trying to console her.

With difficulty she read through the rest of the letter.

He was shot in Ibadan by political party thugs and will be brought home for burial on the 10th of December 1965.

Your mother is very concerned by the State of Emergency in the Western Region. It would appear that murder, looting and arson have become the order of the day. I would advise you and Emeka to return home as soon as possible, until the political tensions have eased.

There could be no consoling her. Taiwo so young and handsome. Dead! Why? What did he know about politics? Her father's letter had taken two weeks to arrive, so she knew that Taiwo would already be six feet under the heavy earth.

'I have to go home,' she cried.

'When is the burial?'

'He must have been buried but I have to be with the family.'

'Try and calm yourself. Your father should not have given you such news, knowing you are pregnant.'

'But we must leave Lagos. It's not safe here. Just a few weeks ago, you were the one saying a man had been brought to hospital after being set alight. We can stay in Benin until the new year, by then I'm sure things will be calmer.'

'We'll discuss it some other time. Just try and calm down.'

He could not tell her that they were expected to spend Christmas in Umuahia. He always travelled home for Christmas and this year was to be no exception. For days he evaded any discussion about the topic, but when Obi and Clive joined the mass exodus from Lagos, Sade demanded to know when they would travel.

'I've purchased our air tickets. We leave for Umuahia tomorrow morning,' Emeka told her over dinner.

'Umuahia? What the hell are you talking about?' Sade was in a state of confusion. 'You know I'm expected in Benin. I've just lost my cousin.'

'He's been buried, hasn't he?'

'I can't believe you are doing this to me. If you had told me earlier, I could have travelled with Clive and Obi.'

Emeka stared down at his plate of eba and okra soup.

'I want some money,' Sade demanded. 'I'm leaving for Benin on the first flight tomorrow.'

'You're not going anywhere!' Emeka stared at her in defiant authority.

'What?'

'I said you're not going anywhere!'

Standing up, she felt her hands tighten on the table cloth. Without thinking, she quickly pulled the cloth sending the plate of food over him. The china shattered on the floor and he rose to a near upright position. The soup hung down like slime from his outstretched arms.

'What the hell is this?' He stared at Sade, his face overcome with confusion.

Sade made her way upstairs. On the landing, she found a vase of freshly picked lilies. Grabbing the vase, she sent them flying down the stairs.

'Bastard!' she screamed, kicking the soil out of a pot plant on the landing.

In despair, she locked herself in the master bedroom. Lying on the bed she cried in temper. She could hear Emeka giving orders to Godpower, followed by the sound of china being swept up. The hours went by and the silence became irritating. Sade could not bear it. Taking all Emeka's clothes out of the wardrobe, she flung them all over the landing. She then snatched the china figure of the virgin Mary and smashed it on the landing. The unborn kicked within her and she returned to the room, locking the door. Sitting on the bed, she tried to quell the raging fire in her soul. Suddenly the door handle was pushed down.

'Sade! Open the door!' Emeka demanded.

Godpower had obviously gone home because Emeka never gave the housestaff any indication that there were problems with his marriage.

'Sade, I want to take something,' he demanded angrily. 'Come on open this door.'

He kicked at the solid wood, making her jump off the bed.

'I hope you know when I abort this child it will be on your head,' she responded.

'Don't open the door then. Stay there!'

She had not intended to open the door anyway, but what right did he have to order her not to open it? It wasn't up to him. The deadening silence made her room seem like a prison cell. The overpowering smell from the Queen of the Night plant, growing up the wall outside, made her feel sick. She shut the louvre windows, turning on the air-conditioner, but the smell persisted. Such a vindictive plant. Tomorrow she would have it chopped down.

Early the following morning, Sade was waken by the sound of knocking. It was still dark.

'Darling!' Emeka called, 'Darling! wake up!' His voice was pleading. 'You know we have to travel today! Just open the door, let's talk.'

'Get lost!' she responded, covering her ears with the pillow.

'Come on open this door!' yelled Emeka. 'I've taken enough of this rubbish.'

He banged and pleaded, but Sade was determined to stay locked up until the house staff arrived. Eventually he gave up and she went back to sleep.

Sade was woken by a crunching sound on the gravel driveway. She jumped out of bed and rushed to the window to see Emeka driving off. The alarm clock indicated that it was already nine o' clock. Had Emeka gone to Umuahia without her? Had he left her in Lagos with no money? He wouldn't dare! Quickly she had a shower, got dressed and went downstairs.

'Good morning Madam!' Godpower bowed slightly.

'Good morning!'

Breakfast of cornflakes and toast awaited her.

'Master tell you where he dey go?' she asked, sitting at the table.

'No, Madam.'

Godpower returned to the kitchen. As she ate, she could hear the boys giggling.

'If to say nah my wife,' laughed Godpower in what he believed to be a low tone. 'I for beat am. He just scatter everyting,' he hissed.

'Master no vex?' asked Bunmi, who had missed all the excitement the night before.

'Ah! Master vex well well-oh!'

Sade dropped her spoon into the half finished bowl of cornflakes.

'Bunmi!' she yelled.

Bunmi appeared very quickly, now straight faced.

'What were you saying in the kitchen?' Her voice was frighteningly calm.

'Ma?'

'I say wetin you dey talk for kitchen? You tink say I no dey hear? You go commot dis house today-today!' Her hand landed with a thud on the table.

'Hey madam!' Bunmi pleaded. 'Nah beg, I dey beg you. Make you no vex.'

'Go pack!'

Bunmi fell to his knees.

'See as I dey beg you, Madam. No be me dey coo-coo talk am. Nah Godpower talk am.'

'Godpower!' Sade yelled.

Godpower hurried in, wiping his hands on a tea towel.

'Ma!' He glanced at his comrade.

'Wetin you dey talk for kitchen? The two of you, go pack. Begin go.'

'Hey Madam!' Godpower placed his hand on his head in despair. 'Make God punish dis my mouth. I beg you, Madam.'

The both pleaded desperately. Sade thought about the trouble she was already in. She knew that if she sacked them they would go to beg Emeka. If he re-employed them it would be terribly humiliating for her.

'The two of you are very lucky today. Get out!' she shouted. They scampered.

Breakfast passed and lunch before Emeka returned home. Without speaking to Sade, he went straight upstairs, removing the keys from every door. Sade found him in the master bedroom, taking his siesta.

'Where have you been?' she asked.

Folding her arms she lent against the wardrobe. He ignored her and continued to stare at the ceiling.

'I need money to travel,' she demanded.

He glared at her.

'If I had known you were like this, I would never have married you,' he responded, fidgeting in temper.

Sade laughed. 'How I wish you hadn't. But we can always get divorced.'

He scorned her.

'I want some money.'

'I have already told you, my family are expecting us in Umuahia.'

'And I have already told you that my family are expecting us in Benin. Or do you think it's only your family that counts?'

'I am the man! I feed you. I clothe you. I take my responsibilities. You are married into my family. You bear my family name. Did Obi refuse to spend Christmas with Clive's family? Don't you think that she too would have preferred being with her own sisters and brothers in Umuahia?'

Sade decided to try a change of tactics.

'Darling please!' she sat on the bed. 'Just this year. You know that I've just lost my cousin.'

'I'm telling you for the last time,' said Emeka. 'I will not go to Benin.'

'And I am telling you for the last time,' said Sade jumping off the bed, 'I will not go to Umuahia, and neither will I spend another night in your bed.'

She stormed towards the wardrobe, snatching all her dresses off the hangers.

'And don't you dare lay one finger on me ever again.'

She packed her things back into the spare bedroom.

SEVENTEEN

ON CHRISTMAS DAY, Emeka appeared to be the only Ibo person left in Lagos. All his friends had gone to celebrate Christmas in the East. On New Year's eve, he insisted that Sade accompanied him to midnight mass. The Church was filled beyond capacity with elegantly attired men and women, dressed in their traditional outfits. There was a sombre mood. The talk was of nothing but the corrupt politicians, and the chaos in the country. People were in fear of what the new year had in store for them.

'Let us pray!' the Nigerian priest cried out in the candlelit darkness. 'Let us pray that the Lord will look mercifully upon us, and grant us a peaceful new year. Guide our people O Lord! Guide our leaders! And guide our country! So that we may be free of the corruption and tribalism that is destroying us...'

Within a few weeks it appeared that their prayers had been answered. An almost bloodless military coup, by Ibo officers, resulted in an end to the corruption and vote-rigging of the politicians.

Fifteen minutes before midnight, on the 16th of January, 1966, Emeka sat downstairs listening to the radio. His hero, General Ironsi, announced that the armed forces had been asked to form an interim military government and he was invested with authority as head of the Federal Military Government. Emeka was jubilant. An Ibo man now ruled Nigeria. He always believed that the Ibos were intellectually superior and therefore worthy of high position.

The following day, he went with Sade to visit an army friend, Captain Boniface Ifeajuna. He was a tall, stocky man of dark complexion. His living room was crowded with excited Ibo soldiers.

'Doctor!' Boniface called out in delight, rushing to meet them.

'Captain!' Emeka responded as they slapped hands, flicking their fingers in warm friendship.

Boniface turned to Sade, shaking her hand politely. They sat down, and Boniface shouted at a houseboy, to bring in some drinks.

Nothing could take the conversation away from the military coup.

'Akintola!' said Boniface, the chair cushion bulging down under his weight. 'He thought he was infallible! Yet even his own private arsenal could not save him.'

'Private arsenal?' Emeka asked. 'Did he have a private arsenal?'

'Of course he did!' Boniface sounded authoritative. 'And instead of surrendering peacefully when the army came, he decided to fight. He killed four of our men but we made him pay. When we got him-eh! We really suffered him, before finishing him off.'

Sade was silent. She felt intimidated by their loud, aggressive mannerisms, yet held the soldiers in contempt. It was the illiterates that joined the army. The less intelligent, who had failed in school. They were mostly from low class backgrounds.

After about an hour she pinched Emeka who sat next to her. He jumped slightly and looked back at her.

'Let's go!' she whispered.

'Just have some patience!' Emeka responded.

Sitting on the edge of his chair, he continued his debate with the men.

One of the soldiers sitting next to Sade noticed her impatience.

'You want to go?' he asked her.

His face was lean and his eyes bulged out of their sockets.

'I'm feeling tired,' Sade responded, rolling her eyes in despair.

'Is that your husband?' he pointed with his lips at Emeka.

'No! He's my brother.' Sade was being sarcastic.

'So what's your name?' the soldier sounded full of glee.

'Sade!'

'I am Joseph!'

Sade grinned contemptuously.

'Do you live close by?' asked Joseph.

'Ikoyi.'

'That's a very nice area. You're still at school?'

'Yes!'

The soldier obviously believed she looked too young to be married with a child on the way. Sade had worn a very loose dress, which effectively concealed her pregnancy.

'Are you on the telephone?' he asked, reaching into his pocket for a pen.

'Yes! But my father will be annoyed if you call.'

Emeka who had been engrossed in conversation, suddenly turned, watching Sade suspiciously.

'Let me give you my number,' the soldier quickly wrote it down on a scrap of paper and handed it to Sade.

'What's that?' demanded Emeka.

'What's what?' Sade responded, casting a look of scorn at Emeka.

'I hope you don't mind my talking to your sister?' The soldier's voice was pleading.

'My sister?' Emeka was furious. 'Let's go!' he stood up abruptly and headed for the front door.

Sade followed.

'Ah! Ah! What's up?' asked Boniface leaping from his seat.

134

'We'll talk tomorrow,' responded Emeka.

The men shook hands and they set off. At the junction, Emeka aggressively snatched the paper from Sade's hand.

'You must be stupid!' he told her, looking at the name and number on the paper before flinging it out of the window. 'And why should you tell that man that I am your brother?' His eyes moved about erratically as he turned onto the main road. 'I'll have to report this matter to your father.'

They arrived at home to find Clive waiting in the lounge. He had just arrived from Benin with Obi and their new baby daughter.

'Congratulations!' said Sade giving him a kiss on his cheek.

By now Clive knew that Sade's uttered words rarely reflected her innermost feelings. He was also aware that she was mocking him.

'Don't worry!' Emeka joked. 'The next one will be a boy. What of Obi? I hope there were no complications.'

'None at all. A doctor I know delivered the baby at home.'

Sade scoffed. She wanted to ask if it was the same doctor he had recommended to abort her child. She was longing to see the baby and hoped it would give her some indication of what her own baby would look like. The three walked the short distance past the boys' quarters to Clive's bungalow. The housegirl opened the door. Obi sat in the lounge, breast feeding the infant.

'I think she looks like you,' Sade told Obi, looking down at the new-born. With her face all screwed up, the baby looked rather ugly.

'That's why she's so beautiful.' Obi laughed.

Obi obviously had something wrong with her eyes, as well as her head.

'Have you named her?' asked Sade.

'Sarah! It means princess.' Obi smiled in contentment.

Such a beautiful name, thought Sade, for such an ugly little creature. Gently she rubbed her own belly and sat beside

Clive. Her child could never turn out to look like that.

'When are you due?' Obi asked, as Sade sat down next to Clive.

'When I see it.'

Obi looked at Emeka for a more definite answer.

'I've been telling her to go and register at a maternity clinic, but she refused.' Emeka complained. 'She won't even allow me, her husband, to examine her.'

'Why not?' asked Obi.

'My grandmother delivered twelve babies without anybody messing about with her.'

Clive called the housegirl ordering her to supply them with drinks. Sade knew that he was trying to protect her and himself by changing the subject.

'But you have to be examined,' Obi persisted. 'The child could be dead inside you.'

Sade got up. 'Did your own child die inside you?' she snapped.

'But what's your problem?' asked Obi.

'The fact of the matter, is that you need to go and register at the maternity clinic,' shouted Emeka.

Sade walked towards the front door.

'Ah! Ah!' Obi sounded flabbergasted.

'Don't mind her!' Emeka was dismissive.

Sade went back home.

EIGHTEEN

EMEKA RETURNED HOME to find Sade and Obi sitting in the lounge. Five months had gone by since Christmas, and Sade was huge with child. Flirtatiously, she reached for his hand. He accepted the invitation, kissing her lips before sitting down beside her. Leaning against him, she looked into his eyes. Her mood was of girlish gaiety.

'Darling, I'm bored sick! Let's go shopping for the baby.'

'But you don't even know when it's due.' Obi frowned as she spoke.

'Will you please tell your sister to stop interfering.' Sade told Emeka.

'Leave her alone!' Emeka scolded Obi. 'If she wants to go shopping, there's nothing wrong with that.'

Emeka went upstairs to his safe where he collected some money.

'I'll come with you.' Obi insisted, as they were about to set off.

She climbed into the back seat with Mercy and Sarah. Emeka took them to Kingsway, the most exclusive department store in Lagos. Arrogantly, he led the way into the cool air-conditioned interior. The store was full of smartly dressed white women who appeared to have little else to do in life but browse and exchange gossip. Emeka led the way up an escalator to the baby department. The imported goods were being sold at exorbitant prices.

Sade chose a cot, a pram and a highchair.

'Why not leave the high chair until the baby is born?' Obi asked jealously. 'Look at Sarah, she's almost three months now, but she doesn't need a high chair.'

Ignoring Obi, Sade went to choose baby clothes and Obi followed.

'Why are you buying everything in blue?' asked Obi.

'For a boy of course. Pink for a girl and blue a boy.' Sade fluttered her eyelashes at Emeka.

'You can never be so sure!' Obi frowned in disapproval. 'I made the same mistake.'

Sarah began to scream and Obi took the feeding bottle out of her bag. She shook it hard before handing it to Mercy.

'You better take some things in white,' Obi nagged.

Ignoring her, Sade took the things she wanted to the counter. Without asking, Obi picked up two dresses for Sarah, placing them with Sade's shopping. Emeka paid for the items and Obi took Sarah from Mercy.

'Take the things to the car,' Obi ordered the girl.

'All I need now is a painter,' said Sade, as Emeka set off for home.

'For what?' demanded Obi.

'To decorate the baby's room.'

'But Emeka just decorated the whole house before you arrived.' Obi's voice sounded aggressive.

'I want the babies' bedroom blue.'

'But the baby should sleep with you. Sarah sleeps with me and Clive.'

'I think our baby should have his own room. Emeka! What do you think?'

'Anything you want, darling,' he replied, his voice full of adoration.

Gently he placed one arm over her belly. Sade pushed it away.

'It's okay! You think I'll have an accident?' he smiled.

They arrived back to find Clive waiting in the lounge.

'Where have you been?' he asked Obi, annoyed that his meal was unprepared.

'We went to buy things for the baby,' Sade informed him.

Clive dragged hard at his cigarette.

'It looks as if you've bought the whole shop,' he told Emeka, as the baby-nurse carried everything past him, on her way upstairs.

'You know what these women are like. If you don't give them what they want it's trouble,' said Emeka arrogantly.

He sat down beside Sade, holding her hand. The baby nurse completed her task and Obi passed Sarah back to her.

'Dance now!' she ordered Mercy as Sarah screamed unreasonably.

Still panting, having carried the shopping upstairs, Mercy began to rock Sarah back and forth.

'Have you fed her?' Clive asked Obi.

'Yes! I don't know what's wrong with her.'

'Maybe she needs changing,' Sade suggested.

'You haven't changed her?' Clive scolded Obi.

'Take her home and bath her before I come,' Obi ordered Mercy.

There was a knock at the door and Godpower opened it. Chukwuma, one of Emeka's brothers, walked in.

'Ah! Ah! Chuks!' Emeka stood up to greet him.

Chuks appeared to be in a great deal of distress.

'What happened!' demanded Obi, also getting up.

Chukwuma acknowledged Clive and Sade, before sitting down.

'As you see me here,' said Chukwuma, looking down in despair. 'I am lucky to have escaped with my life. Those barbaric Hausas! All over the North, we Ibos are being slaughtered like goats.'

'I've been reading about the disturbances, but I thought the police had the situation under control,' said Emeka.

'The police!' Chukwuma hissed in disgust, 'The police are actively participating in the killings. I've seen it with my own eyes. Even the army, sent in to save us, are just standing aside, watching. Of course they were Northerners, so would not dare open fire on their own people.'

'What is the point of all this?' asked Obi, standing next to Emeka. 'Why Ibos? What have we done for goodness sake?'

'It's political!' Chukwuma responded. 'In the university where I lecture, the expatriates and Northern lecturers have been inciting the students to riot. One student informed me, that they had been advised of the need of a counter-coup, to restore political power to the North. Otherwise we Southerners will enslave them.'

'Is that so?' Emeka droned.

'This is what is happening.' said Chukwuma. 'I was saved by a friend. He is a Southerner, but speaks Hausa like a Hausa man. When the students began to riot, he hid me in his house. We thought things would calm down, but instead the problem is spreading all over the North. The Northerners have decided to eradicate us from their land, men, women and children. I was informed that gangs of political thugs are being transported around the *sabon garis* [strangers' quarters] all over the Northern cities. Their job is to slaughter the residents, before looting their property and setting fire to the houses. In Sokoto, a group of Southerners had gathered in a church to pray. Those Hausas cordoned off the church, pouring petrol over it before setting it alight. At the Kano railway station some Southerners where waiting for a train, to bring them back down to the South. There a mob set on them, killing and maiming them with machetes, before looting their property.'

'Is that so!' Emeka droned again.

'So we are not welcomed in the North!' said Obi, 'But they think they can share in the riches from our land!'

'This is terrible!' said Clive. 'So what are they after?'

'Secession!' Chukwuma answered.

'They should go their way!' shouted Obi making gestures with her arms. 'We have carried those illiterates for too long. Look how backward they are. They don't want to learn. All they know how to do is herd cattle and sit on prayer mats reciting the Koran.'

From where she was sitting, Sade looked out onto the driveway. Pouring water out of a plastic kettle, Mohammed washed his feet, ears and mouth. Invoking Allah, he bobbed up and down on his prayer mat.

'Then they say we want to dominate them?' shouted Emeka, 'If they educated themselves, who can dominate them?'

'Really the British are to blame for Nigeria's problems.' said Clive. 'They should never have created Nigeria as one country. The Northerners are completely different to us Southerners. Their religion is different, their language is different, their traditions and customs are different and even the food they eat is different.'

'It will be better if they go their way!' shouted Obi. 'What do we need them for? We have the most fertile land, whilst their land is turning into a desert. We have the oil! We have highly educated people, that can build and develop our land. In fact, they are holding us back. Let them go their way!'

After dinner, Obi ordered the houseboy to make up one of the guest bedrooms for Chukwuma. The group discussion went on for hours. Eventually Sade abandoned them and went to bed.

NINETEEN

EVERYDAY EMEKA DROVE Chukwuma from one friend to another in search of a job. After a few weeks of rejection Chukwuma's frustration was obvious. He became bad tempered and sacked the Hausa night watchman without good reason.

'They're barbaric!' he announced. 'You never know when they might turn against you.'

Soon afterwards the dog was found dead in the garden and it was assumed that Mohammed had poisoned it.

Within a few weeks, Chukwuma decided that he had to return to his job in Zaria.

'How can you return?' Emeka shouted at him over the dinner table. 'Have you forgotten how you arrived here? And don't you read the papers? Ibos are still fleeing from the North. It's not just one hundred or two hundred people that have been slaughtered. It's over five hundred thousand! Can you even imagine such a pile of corpses? Five hundred thousand! Or were those people not human beings?'

Sade looked up at Emeka. She sighed, pushing away her plate of rice and beef stew. Surely it was not in good taste to talk about corpses over dinner.

'But brother,' Chukwuma insisted, 'if I do not return to my position in the University, someone else will be appointed. Things have started to calm down.'

'Calm down!' Emeka shouted. 'What has calmed down? The people who stirred up the trouble in the first place, have any of them been punished? What about your property that was looted? Have you received any form of compensation? So what have you been working for all these years? And the children that are now orphans, who is feeding them? I don't want to hear any more nonsense about you returning to the North. For the time being you can work with Clive at the Eze's legal practice.'

'Brother! You know that private practice does not pay. If Nigeria is to remain intact we must forgive and forget. Even Ojukwu, our leader, is pleading with us to return to our jobs. We have to regard the killings as a sacrifice we must make for one Nigeria.'

'Chukwuma!' Emeka got up. 'You do what ever you want to do! But don't forget that I am your elder brother. If you leave my house to get killed in the North, the Eze will hold me responsible.'

Emeka abandoned his meal, leaving Sade and Chukwuma at the table. Sade glanced up at Chukwuma. The brothers were like two peas in a pod, not only physically alike but also in temperament. Sade was glad that Chukwuma had arrived when he did, because the stress he caused diverted the attention away from her pregnancy.

'Wait a few more weeks,' she pleaded with Chukwuma. 'We will all be so worried if you go back now.'

Luckily there was no need for Emeka to speak to his brother again. Six a.m. one morning, there was a loud knock on the front door. Somebody was shouting. Fearing thieves, Chukwuma and Emeka went to the door together. There they found a panic stricken Captain Boniface Ifeajuna, in his bloodied uniform. Hearing the sound of gun fire, Sade jumped out of bed, rushing downstairs.

'What's happening?' asked Emeka, his voice filled with panic.

'It's a coup! I need civilian clothes,' Boniface cried.

He almost fell through the front door in his rush to enter.

Chukwuma quickly locked the door and they hurried upstairs to the master bedroom.

'We must return to the East!' said Boniface sitting down on the bed. 'The Hausa soldiers are killing all Ibos.' He spoke with haste, his voice creating panic.

Sade stood by the bedroom door trembling in shock. A sudden pain shot through her abdomen, but she was determined to find out what was happening.

'Yesterday,' Boniface panted, 'A friend of mine escaped from Abeokuta barracks, where the Northerners had staged a mutiny. He telephoned me to say that one Hausa captain led a group of troops into the officers mess at 11 p.m. and shot dead three Ibo officers. Then they besieged the barracks, disarming all Southerners and seizing the armoury. After arming all the Northerners they sounded the call for action, rousing the whole garrison from its sleep. They lined up on the parade ground where the Southerners were singled out and locked up in the guard room. Then they went around making house to house searches for those not present. My friend was at home when a fellow soldier came to warn him. He had the sense to go into hiding. Later he heard that all the soldiers of Eastern origin placed in the guard room were brought out and shot.'

'It's genocide!' proclaimed Emeka.

'I assumed that the mutineers would eventually be rounded up and shot.' Boniface looked up at Emeka, his face covered in blood and tears. 'Little did I know that this was just the first stage of a highly organised coup. This morning the Northerners started rounding up all Easterners in the barracks here in Lagos. I was able to warn a few friends and six of us managed to escape. Unfortunately we were caught at a road block. They tied our arms behind our backs with wire and started whipping us ruthlessly. See my back.' Boniface showed them the deep wounds from the wire filled horsewhips. 'It's only God that saved me. I'm sure my friends are dead! I was just lucky that they had not tied my wrists securely. When I broke free, I ran for dear life.'

With elbows resting on his knees, Boniface squeezed his eyes with both hands and cried. The room was filled with a tense and deadly silence.

'All of us have to get back to the East,' said Boniface. 'If we are caught here, we'll all be killed.'

'But Emeka and Chukwuma are civilian,' Sade protested.

'Believe me!' insisted Boniface. 'It's not just soldiers they are killing. They are killing all Ibos.'

'But why?' asked Sade.

'It's because of Ironsi. The Northerners refuse to accept an Ibo man as their leader. Because we staged the last coup, they believe we want to dominate them. All over the barracks the Hausas are shouting Araba! Araba! Araba!'

'What is Araba?' Sade puzzled.

'Secession!' Boniface replied.

'Let them go in peace.' Emeka sounded utterly despondent.

'What do we do now?' asked Chukwuma.

'There are road blocks everywhere,' Boniface still sounded terrified.

'Then we have no choice but to stay put for the time being. We must wait for news. Go and take a bath,' Emeka ordered Boniface. 'Then let me treat those wounds.'

While Boniface bathed, Chukwuma burnt the Nigerian army uniform behind the house. In the boys' quarters he discovered that the Yoruba house staff had fled. Obviously they did not wish to be associated with an Ibo household. Chukwuma went to inform Obi and Clive about the coup and they returned with him to the house. The worry now was that the vindictive Mohammed would bring soldiers to arrest them.

For hours the group sat in the living room listening to the radio. Emeka fiddled with the tuning knob. From the BBC World Service he tuned into the local radio stations and back again.

For Sade the stress was too much and Emeka realised that she had gone into what he believed to be premature labour. Still she refused to be examined. In frustration Emeka abandoned her to the care of Obi.

In her bedroom, Sade rolled from side to side on the large double bed. Obi did the little she could to attend to her but was obviously more interested in the discussion going on downstairs. By evening Sade was weak, delirious with pain and drenched with perspiration.

'I'm going to die!' she cried as Emeka came in to check on her.

From the intervals between the contractions, Emeka knew that she was about to give birth. He sent Obi to collect boiling water from the kitchen and began to sterilise his equipment. Sade screamed, doubling up in agony as the child tore through her. Placing his equipment on the bedside table, he pulled away her sheet. Sade gave an almighty push and within minutes the baby was resting in Emeka's capable hands.

'It's dead!' she cried looking down at the lifeless form.

Hitching herself up, she stared at the child in panic. Emeka cleaned its nose and blew into its mouth, whilst pressing at its tiny rib-cage. The baby coughed, then taking a deep breath, began to scream. Quickly cutting the cord, he passed the child to Sade.

'We have a son!' Emeka cried, proudly kissing Sade's forehead. 'Ironsi! We will call him Ironsi.'

Obi appeared to be equally jubilant.

'You're so lucky! To have a boy, first time. I'm just hoping my next one will be a boy.'

Sade looked at Obi's bulging belly. She must have become pregnant within weeks of Sarah's birth.

'I can't believe this is happening!' Emeka sounded despondent. 'Unfortunately we must leave for Umuahia tomorrow. Once the curfew is lifted we will set off for Benin. It's best if we travel together incase of trouble. Mercy will remain in Lagos to keep an eye on the houses. We must get Boniface to the East as quickly as possible. If he is caught he will certainly be shot.'

'But we are putting ourselves at risk by travelling with Boniface,' said Sade.

'You are as much at risk travelling with me, as with him.' Emeka responded. 'If he travels alone, the chances of him being caught will certainly be greater. He will have to pose as our driver. Chukwuma can act as driver to Clive and Obi. That way we will look like two families returning home. If we are questioned by soldiers, we must tell them that we are all from Benin.'

Sade could not comprehend the situation she found herself in and cried unconsolably.

'Don't worry!' Obi tried to reassure her. 'God will deliver us from these forces of darkness!'

TWENTY

BONIFACE DROVE DOWN the virtually deserted streets of Lagos. An unnerving calm hung over the city and the tension in the Mercedes was acute. Slowly, they approached the first checkpoint. A thick bamboo branch had been placed on two empty oil drums either side of the road. A tall soldier dressed in green and brown jungle camouflage uniform stood in the middle of the road pointing his FAL carbine directly at the car. From his belt hung pouches of magazines and a bowie knife. His dozen or so comrades, identically dressed, moved about aggressively at the roadside.

'Halt!' the soldier yelled, his finger on the trigger.

'They look like Hausas!' Emeka announced.

Boniface pulled up and Emeka wound down his back seat window.

'Come down!' the soldier yelled.

They all obeyed.

Holding tightly onto her newborn, Sade noticed two bodies in a trench at the road side. The driver of another car was being beaten ruthlessly with the *koboko* [horse whip]. Sadistically the soldiers revelled in the evil lust of power.

'You are Ibo?' a soldier shouted at Emeka.

'I am not Ibo. I am from Benin,' Emeka looked panic stricken.

'Nah Ibo!' shouted a comrade. 'Kill dem! You Ibo people want to master us. You kill our leaders. We will kill you.'

'Believe me! We are from Benin,' Emeka insisted.

A thin old man attempted to ride past on his bicycle and was kicked off.

'Craze dey your head?' the soldier shouted at him, giving him a taste of the whip. The old man collapsed but was dragged to his feet. His punishment was to carry his bike high above his head and run up and down the road. The soldier returned to Emeka.

'Open boot!'

Boniface handed the keys to Emeka who quickly obeyed.

'Where you dey go?' the soldier demanded.

'I am a doctor…'

'Shut up! Who ask you whether you be doctor? You think I no fit do doctor?' The aggression in the soldier's voice was frightening. 'I say where you dey go, you tell me you be doctor. I go pepper you today!'

The soldier moved towards Sade and her newborn.

'Where you dey go!' he shouted at her.

'Benin.'

'For what?'

'We are going home.'

The soldier laughed. 'Shree shree shree shree!'

He was making fun of the way she spoke.

'You want to talk oyibo for me? You nah Bini?' asked the soldier.

'Yes!'

'Talk your language.'

Sade had never had the opportunity to learn her father's language. She was taught in English at school and her father had never encouraged her to learn the native tongue. English was the language of the educated elite.

'I say talk!' demanded the soldier.

'I no dey speak Bini.'

'I no dey speak Bini,' the soldier mimicked in jest. His comrades crowded around laughing at the novelty. The soldier moved towards the front of the Mercedes.

'We dey commandeer dis motor!' he banged on the bonnet with his hand. 'Where key?'

Without any dispute, Emeka handed over the keys to his treasured possession. They all watched helplessly as it was driven away.

'You can go!' one of the soldiers shouted at them.

Fearfully, they all climbed into Clive's Volkswagen. Sade and her new-born were given the luxury of the front passenger seat while Obi sat on Emeka's lap, next to Boniface and Chukwuma in the back. Sarah cried relentlessly as she was passed from one person to another.

'We can't continue like this,' Clive insisted. 'The engine is already overheating.'

'We better turn round and go back to Lagos.' Emeka responded. 'I have to recover my car. Those illiterate bastards think that because they hold a gun, they can hold the country to ransom.'

'You better forget about your car,' warned Boniface. 'Or are you forgetting that you are an Ibo man? We were lucky to have escaped that checkpoint with our lives. We can't risk going back.'

With the babies crying, Clive continued to head for Benin. Within a short time, they were at another checkpoint. Clive pulled up cautiously as an armed soldier waved them to stop.

'Good morning!' Clive sounded confident.

'Where are you going?' asked the soldier.

'I'm returning with my family to Benin.'

The soldier studied the faces in the back then noticed Clive's cigarettes on the dashboard.

'Bring cigar!' he ordered.

Clive handed over the packet, also giving him a small 'dash', before they were allowed to continue.

'We can't carry on like this,' Sade cried. 'They are trying to pinpoint Ibos. We weren't caught at the first checkpoint or this one, but what about the next one or the one after that?'

'So what do you propose?' asked Emeka impatiently.

'I don't know!' she cried. 'You should have left us in Lagos.'

'Sade! You're making things ten times worse than they already are,' Clive rebuked.

They continued in silence.

The soldiers at the other check points appeared less hostile, perhaps because of the '*oyibo*' couple in the front seat. Occasionally they stopped, allowing the engine to cool. With the bonnet left open they proceeded along the narrow pot-holed roads.

When eventually they arrived at the Mid-West, the dreaded checkpoints became less frequent. On reaching Benin the relief was enormous. Clive drove straight to his family house where he left Obi and Sarah.

With the three men in the back seat and Sade beside him, Clive set off again. He appeared anxious as he pulled up in Justice Uwaifo's driveway. They all dismounted and Mrs Uwaifo rushed out to meet them. Seeing Sade with the new born baby, she broke down in tears.

'Let me have her,' she cried, reaching for the baby.

'It's a him,' Sade informed her.

Justice Uwaifo came out onto the porch.

'Ohhh!' he declared, shocked at their unexpected arrival.

'Look!' cried Susan, showing him the baby. 'You have a grandson.'

Justice Uwaifo beamed as he looked down at the baby in Susan's arms.

'And what a handsome fellow he is,' he said proudly. 'Come inside! Come inside! We tried to telephone you when we heard about the coup.'

'We've been worried sick,' added Susan, wiping the tears from her eyes.

They all sat down and Innocent supplied them with drinks.

'It's been terrible, Sir!' Emeka told Justice Uwaifo. 'We had intended to continue our journey to Umuahia, but the soldiers commandeered my Mercedes.'

'Ohhhh! But you should have remained in Lagos until things calmed down,' Justice Uwaifo responded.

'We would have done so, Sir, but the soldiers are killing all Ibos. To make matters worse, I had employed a Hausa guard who we feared would betray us.'

'Well, there's plenty of room here! You are all welcome to stay for as long as you want.'

'That's very kind of you, Sir,' Emeka responded. 'But it is of the utmost imperative that Captain Ifeajuna gets back to the East immediately. If he is caught he will certainly be shot for desertion.'

'Ah Yes!' Justice Uwaifo appeared to suddenly realise the seriousness of their situation.

'I hope when things calm down I will be able to retrieve my Mercedes.' said Emeka.

'Well, from the reports I've been getting, you might as well forget about your car,' said Justice Uwaifo. 'I understand the Northerners are commandeering cars, trains and even aeroplanes to convey their people back to the North. They have decided they want secession. What I would suggest is that you stay here tonight and my driver can take you all to Umuahia in the morning.'

'I'm not going to Umuahia,' Sade informed them, returning her father's stare.

'You will go where your husband tells you to go,' Justice Uwaifo ordered.

Sade got up and made her way upstairs. Her bedroom was exactly as she had left it. She heard gentle footsteps on the stairs and knew that they belonged to her mother.

'I'm not going,' she insisted, as her mother entered the room. Mrs Uwaifo rocked Saul to and fro in an attempt to stop his screaming.

'Come on, pull yourself together.'

'He wouldn't even allow me to come home when Taiwo

died, or for Christmas. Now he is using me and the baby as a shield to get back to the East. I'm not going!' Sade sobbed desperately. She knew that her mother could not bare to see her in distress and expected her to crumble at this display.

'We told you not to marry him, but you always knew best.' Her mother sounded firm and Sade thought how thick skinned she had become since she had been away.

'I was bloody pregnant, wasn't I?'

'Well you should have kept your legs crossed.'

'I'm not going to Umuahia. I'd rather be dead!'

Sade glanced at her mother who was now blinking and close to tears.

'Stop making such a fuss! You won't be in Umuahia long. And I'm sure his parents are longing to see their grandchild.'

'There's just one problem.' Sade sighed deeply preparing to deliver the final blow. 'It's not Emeka's child. It's Clive's child.'

Mrs Uwaifo stumbled and looked faint. Sade jumped off the bed grabbing Saul from her arms. As her mother fumbled for the stool, she screamed for help.

'If you want to kill me, you're going about it the right way,' said her mother, sitting down.

'I didn't mean it!'

Sade was sickened at the thought of anything happening to her mother.

'Sit down and shut up!'

Sade obeyed.

'Does Emeka know?'

'No.'

'Then I never want to hear another word about it. Emeka is your husband and this is his child. Do you understand what I'm saying?'

Sade nodded. The bedroom door was flung open and Justice Uwaifo barged in.

'What is all this shouting about?' he demanded.

'Nothing!' Susan responded. 'I just had a funny turn.'

To Sade's relief, her mother's 'funny turn' melted her father's stance and he agreed that it was unreasonable to subject mother and child to another long journey so soon after childbirth. Justice Uwaifo decided that Emeka should remain in Benin, whilst Chukwuma and Boniface continued on their journey the following morning.

TWENTY-ONE

IT WAS THREE a.m. and Sade was at her wits' end. She felt sure that the baby would drive her insane. If only she had known what motherhood was all about. Emeka was asleep in the guest bedroom and she couldn't get the baby to stop screaming. Perhaps the long journey had given him heat stroke. Or perhaps there was something seriously wrong with him. Perhaps the hole in his teat wasn't big enough? She bit at the teat making the hole larger, sticking the bottle back in his mouth. The baby began to choke.

'What on earth do you think you're doing?' scolded her mother, coming up behind her. Susan had been woken up by the baby's screaming. 'Give him here,' she demanded taking the child from Sade.

Sade watched as her mother placed him against her shoulder to bring up his wind.

'Orrrr! Poor little thing,' Susan cooed.

She turned to Sade. 'You don't know how lucky you are. He's so precious!'

There was a look of sadness in her eyes, as she remembered the times she too had nursed her own sons. Too soon taken from her to be buried in unmarked graves.

When Saul eventually fell asleep, Mrs Uwaifo shut the bedroom door and sat next to Sade.

'It was the night of the twins' party, wasn't it?' she asked quietly.

Sade nodded, eyes down cast in embarrassment.

'The filthy scum. Taking advantage of you like that! He ought to be bloody shot.'

'It wasn't his fault. I love him.'

'Don't talk such bollocks! Of course it was his bloody fault. You were still at school. If your father found out, he'd bloody kill him.'

'You're not going to tell him, are you?'

'Of course not. If this gets out, well! I don't know what will happen.'

'I don't know what to do!'

'Well for a start you better learn to control yourself. That bastard has had his fun and you're left to pick up the pieces. Does Clive know it's his child?'

Sade nodded her response.

'He's filth! How can he look Emeka in the face? You better make it very clear to him, this child belongs to Emeka. And I never want to hear any different. Not ever!'

The following afternoon, the Udochi family came to visit. Walking through the door, Mrs Udochi reached for Saul, who was sleeping in Mrs Uwaifo's arms. Cradling the newborn, she sat down.

'He really is a beaut!' laughed Mrs Udochi.

Sophia and Marilyn sat on the arms of her chair looking down the child.

'Thank God he didn't take after Emeka,' Sophia jested.

Everyone laughed except Sade, Clive and Mrs Uwaifo. Mrs Uwaifo stared at Clive, who averted his eyes, looking very uncomfortable.

'Have you decided on a name?' Mrs Udochi asked Sade.

'I like the name Saul but Emeka has named him Ironsi.'

'Aren't you going to name your grandson?' Mrs Udochi asked Justice Uwaifo.

'Of course! I have named him *Kosoko*.'

'Kosoko?' Mrs Udochi repeated. 'What does that mean?'

'There is no hoe!'

'There is no hoe?' she puzzled.

'Yes! There is no hoe to dig a grave.'

Mrs Udochi laughed. She looked at Mrs Uwaifo who turned away. How could she explain the pain of losing a child, only to be told that it had been reborn in her grandchild?

'When do you travel to the East?' Clive asked Emeka.

Sade realised that he was trying to change the topic.

'As soon as possible,' Emeka replied.

'It appears that the North is determined to secede,' Clive's voice lacked the usual confidence.

'That would be impossible!' said Justice Uwaifo. 'The Northerners are not united. And what about us in the South? The Yorubas will be unwilling to unite with the Ibos, so such action can only result in outright civil war.'

Sade sighed in frustration. Why couldn't anyone speak of anything but war and politics? Sophia came to sit on the arm of her chair.

'Let's go outside,' she whispered to Sade.

The two girls set off towards the front porch and Marilyn stood up to join them.

'We're coming!' Sophia snapped, anxious to have Sade to herself. 'Have you seen Kehinde?' Sophia asked as they walked into the garden.

'No! He's the only person that has not been to see the baby.'

'It's all my fault,' Sophia began to cry. 'If it were not for me, Taiwo would still be alive today.'

'What are you talking about?' Sade stopped and leant against the flame of the forest tree.

'It was my fault they killed him.'

'What do you mean?'

'Didn't anyone tell you what happened?'

'My father wrote, saying he was killed by political party thugs.'

'Yes, but I was there. We were driving through Ibadan on

our way to a party. Taiwo and Kehinde were in the front seats and I was in the back. We were stopped by some thugs. They had blocked the road with a plank, covered in nails. Kehinde tried to reverse, thinking they were armed robbers. It was an ambush. A car pulled up behind us, blocking our way. Kehinde asked them what they wanted. They asked him which political party he belonged to. What could he say? He was not a member of any political party. Seeing that they were Yoruba, he said he was with the NNA (Nigerian National Alliance), which was Akintola's party. They said we should get out of the car or they would smash the windows. We had no alternative. When we got out, one of the men bought out a pistol and ordered me into the bush. I knew they were going to rape me. I refused to move. I said it was better for them to shoot me.' Sophia broke down in tears. 'When I started fighting with them, Taiwo came to my rescue and they shot him dead. Kehinde and I were lucky. Another car pulled up behind us and the driver fired two shots. The thugs fled but it was too late for Taiwo. We rushed him to the hospital, but he was dead on arrival. Kehinde will never forgive me. And I will never forgive myself,' Sophia sobbed.

Sade placed her arm on her shoulder but could not find words of consolation. She too needed to be consoled.

'Sometimes I think I should have let them rape me,' said Sophia in despair.

'You shouldn't say things like that.'

'I feel guilty about surviving. Before Taiwo's death, Kehinde and I had become very close. Now he won't even talk to me. Anytime I go to his house, he sends a message that he's out. But I know he's there. I love him Sade.'

'Isn't he dating Marilyn?'

'That is nothing serious. Please talk to him for me.'

Marilyn called from the porch as the family prepared to leave. The two girls made their way back to the house. Mrs Udochi handed Saul over to Sade, and they left.

Sade joined her parents and Emeka in the lounge. They listened to the news on the radio. A certain Lieutenant Colonel Yakubu Gowon declared himself Supreme Commander of the armed forces and Head of the National Military Government of Nigeria.

'I thought they wanted to secede?' asked Emeka.

'I told you that would be impossible. The British would never allow it.' Justice Uwaifo sounded confident.

'But it's not up to the British. We are no longer their colony.'

'Hold on!' Justice Uwaifo raised his arm and the family sat in silence.

'I now come to the most difficult but most important part of this statement,' Gowon continued. 'I am doing it conscious of the great disappointment and heartbreak it will cause all true and sincere lovers of Nigeria and of Nigerian unity both at home and abroad, especially our brothers in the Commonwealth…'

Saul began to scream and Justice Uwaifo cast angry glances at Sade and her mother. Sade got up and rocked the child in a vain attempt to silence him.

'…As a result of recent events and of the previous similar ones, I have come to strongly believe that we cannot honestly and sincerely continue in this wise, as the basis for trust and confidence in our unitary system of Government has been unable to stand the test of time. I have already remarked on the issue in question. Suffice it to say that putting all considerations to the test, political, economic as well as social, the basis for unity is not there.'

'Oh God!' shouted Justice Uwaifo over Saul's screams. 'Can't I hear the news?'

'Why not take him upstairs?' suggested Emeka.

Sade scorned him and made her way to the kitchen. She hated the restrictions motherhood placed on her. At least being at home meant an endless supply of friends and relatives to hand the baby to.

'Innocent! Wash your hands and prepare a bottle of milk,' she ordered, rocking Saul.

Innocent took a clean bottle out of the sterilising unit. Having filled the bottle with water he put in six scoops of powdered milk, spilling it all around the base of the milk bottle.

'Madam! You want baby nurse?' he asked.

Sade wondered why she had not thought of it herself.

'You know somebody?'

'Yes Madam! My sister dey look for work.'

'Your sister dey for Benin?'

'Yes Ma!'

'Okay! Bring her tomorrow morning.'

Sade returned to the lounge, holding a bottle up to Saul's mouth. The news was over.

'I've asked Innocent to bring a baby nurse for Saul,' she announced.

'But we will soon be travelling to Umuahia,' Emeka responded.

'She can stay here with my mother until we return to Lagos.'

'But things are so uncertain,' Emeka protested. 'We don't even know what is going on.'

'You are not the one that has to stay up all night,' Sade told him impatiently. 'I've asked Innocent to bring the girl, and if I like her, I'll take her.'

The following morning Patience arrived. She was a short pretty girl, her hair parted into many pig-tails. Her rounded figure was accentuated by the tight bodice of her ragged dress and her plastic slippers had been repaired many times. The ordeal of being interviewed made Patience extremely nervous. She was trembling and close to tears.

'Where are you from?' demanded Emeka, lounging back into the upholstered chair.

'Owerri Sah!' she replied, her voice quiet and weak.

'You are Ibo?' Emeka confirmed.

'Yes Sah!'

'*Kedu?* [How are you?]' Emeka was becoming enthusiastic.

'*Odinma* [fine], Sah!'

'How many years you reach?' asked Justice Uwaifo.

'Thirteen Sah!'

Mrs Uwaifo leant over and whispered to Sade, 'I wouldn't have her. She's too pretty. The next thing you know, she'll be in his bed.' She indicated that she was referring to Emeka.

'That would be a relief,' Sade whispered back, before turning to the girl. 'You go follow us go Lagos?'

'Yes Madam!'

'For where you work before?' asked Mrs Uwaifo.

'I work for one *Oyibo*, Madam!'

'Why you leave?' Susan persisted.

'The Madam travel go London.'

Sade looked at Emeka who appeared to be undressing the girl with his eyes.

'So what do you say?' she demanded.

'You want her?' Emeka glanced at Sade.

'Yes!'

'Then have her,' he shrugged, still admiring the girls figure.

Sade went upstairs to her bedroom where she collected two old dresses and a pair of shoes. Her mother collected soap, Dettol, and a sponge. Once bathed Patience started work under the close supervision of Mrs Uwaifo.

TWENTY-TWO

SADE RECOVERED FROM Saul's birth within a remarkably short time and being back amongst her relatives lifted her spirits. One afternoon, whilst Emeka and Clive were out drinking she set off for her cousin's house. On getting there she found Kehinde sitting alone in the lounge looking lonely and depressed.

'Congratulations! My father told me about the baby,' said Kehinde. He attempted to look delighted but his eyes remained downcast.

'And you didn't bother to come to see him?' Sade half-scolded.

'I'm sorry.' Kehinde's voice was weak. He was obviously still in deep mourning. 'Let me tell Idowu you're around.' He left the room, a sad and reclusive fellow.

When Idowu arrived she found Sade wiping the tears from her cheeks.

'Is Kehinde always like that?' she asked as Idowu sat down.

'Since Taiwo's death! That's how he's been behaving,' Idowu replied sadly. 'He just sits on his own refusing to talk to anyone. Sade, I feel so guilty. You know the Priestess warned us. I keep thinking perhaps if I had performed the sacrifice, or if I had warned him, he would be alive today.'

'You can't blame yourself,' said Sade, wiping the tears from her eyes. 'They had to travel.'

'Yes! But if I had warned them, maybe they would have been more careful.'

'It wouldn't have made any difference. They would have laughed at you.'

'That's what I keep telling myself. I know that Taiwo would have teased me ruthlessly. You know he heard us talking about the snakes in your bed. He said we were both ignorant and stupid. He said it was coincidental that you started hallucinating after the visit to the shrine field. That it was all psychological.'

'Well, to me who witnessed it, the snakes were as real as you are now.'

'He said there was no scientific evidence to prove the existence of a spirit world.'

'Neither is there scientific evidence to prove the existence of God,' said Sade. 'Yet the greatest scientists in the world believe in God.'

'And if there was no spirit, how do people die?' Idowu was in obvious agreement. 'If life was purely physical, then people should live for ever.'

'Idowu! Please come with me to find the priest of Ogun.'

'You haven't learnt your lesson?' Idowu tittered as she recalled their previous attempt to find the priest.

'I need to go.'

'Why?'

'Just to satisfy my curiosity.'

'But I'm scared.'

'Please! Come with me. Emeka might decide that we should travel to Umuahia at any time.'

Reluctantly, Idowu agreed and they set off along the familiar route. When they got to the village, some children directed them to the back yard of a mud house. The priest stood by a sacred fire. His hair had been plaited with black thread so that it stood erect at his forehead and his middle-aged face was scarred with deep tribal marks. A tight coral necklace formed a noose above his Adam's apple. Over his torso he wore a vest of cowries and a long skirt made from strips of handwoven cloth hung down from his waist. In the shrine behind him was an altar with wooden carvings of a female and a male figure.

Idowu greeted the priest as they approached but he did not respond. He simply stared into space with flaming red eyes. 'Perhaps he's been smoking Indian hemp,' Sade whispered.

Idowu nudged her sharply. Suddenly, his wife called them away, leading them to a wooden bench. She explained to Idowu that the priest was in a trance, asking them to sit down and wait.

'Should we leave it?' asked Idowu, as the woman left.

'No!' Sade responded, watching the priest. 'We've come this far so we might as well wait.'

'You know when the priest is possessed like that, they can pass iron rods through their tongues or even under their eyeballs. They say that they don't feel a thing.'

'Have you seen them do it?'

'Yes, during an Ogun festival. It was very terrible. But there was no blood.'

The two girls watched an assistant disrobe the priest.

'Go now!' his wife shouted to them.

They approached. A young boy supplied them with stools. The three sat in a triangular shape as the priest threw kola for divination. Three pieces faced up and one down. The god was displeased and the cause could only be established by breaking and throwing more kola. The priest prophesied in Edo and Idowu translated his chilling words into English.

'Blood surrounds you.' she called out after the priest. 'You may not survive. Your husband may not survive. Your child may not survive. Leave your father's house. There is a curse on your father's house. No male child shall survive in your father's house. A woman has cursed your father and your mother's offspring. Her son shall inherit your father's house. The work to be done is this: Bring one yam and a male dog for sacrifice.'

'Who cursed my father's house?' Sade demanded.

The consultation was over with no more questions

answered. Idowu stood up, kneeling respectfully to greet the priest. Sade handed him a shilling and they left.

'Do you believe him?' Sade asked Idowu, walking through the now darkening forest.

'Yes!'

'But why?'

'You know that your mother was cursed with an Abiku child?'

'What?' Sade was shocked.

'Didn't anyone tell you?'

'No!'

Idowu looked awkward and embarrassed.

'I'm only telling you so that you can save your son, but if you tell anyone that I told you! I swear I will never speak to you again.'

'I promise. Just tell me.'

Sade was desperate to hear this terrible secret.

'Remember your brother, Malomo?' asked Idowu. Sade nodded her response and Idowu continued. 'Malomo means: 'Don't go any more'. Your mother had already lost one child when Malomo was born. On the seventh day of his birth, Mama called a native priest to determine where the child had come from, who the child was in a previous life, and how he had died. The priest warned them that the child was Abiku. He asked them to perform certain rituals but your mother said she had never heard anything so ridiculous in all her life. When the child died, against your mother's wishes, Mama called the native priest to mark the body. He said when the child returned, he would bear that mark. Your mother eventually became pregnant again and the baby was born with that very mark. I saw it myself. Your mother said it was witchcraft and refused to make any sacrifices to his spirit companions. The priest named the child Durojayi which means "Wait and enjoy this world". Your Mum insisted on calling him David. As David grew, he kept on telling people about his spirit companions. Your mother brushed it off. She said that most small children have imaginary friends. When David would eat, he would also offer food to his spirit companions. He was four when he returned to the spirit world.'

'My mother is still too upset to mention the death of her sons. You know I was there when David threw himself into the club swimming pool and drowned.'

'That's how Abiku children behave. The spirits tempt such children to throw themselves into water or do things that may result in their return to the spirit world. You know as we are talking now, so they play wonderful games with their spirit companions. They actually prefer their spirit companions to their human playmates, so when their spirit companions call them back to the spirit world, they gladly go.'

'If Saul is an Abiku child, what can I do to make him stay?'

'The spirits usually request the child to return between the ages of four and ten. No matter how attached the child is to its mother, it cannot resist the call of the spirits. If Saul is the reincarnation of your dead brother, he should have a small scar on his body. The one incised on the body of your brother. I will check for you. The native priest will be able to prevent his return to the spirit world. He will prepare iron anklets with native medicine. The spirits may threaten at first, but when they realise that magic is at work they will leave him alone. In the mean time you have to spoil him. As he grows up, give him anything he wants or he will threaten to die.'

Sade sighed in despair.

'Anyway, what does all this have to do with the woman who has cursed my father's house?'

'Well you know before your father went to study in London, he already had a wife with two children?'

'What?' shouted Sade. She stopped and stared at Idowu in disbelief. How could it be true when her father was such a strict disciplinarian, condemning promiscuity in others?

'Believe me, it's true.' Idowu shrugged. 'One of your brothers came to our house searching for his father.'

'My brother!' Sade was disgusted. 'And he didn't know his father's house?'

'That's what I'm trying to tell you. Your father disowned them. He must have been ashamed of them. Their mother was illiterate, so they were brought up like village children. The only way their mother could retaliate was with juju. She said your mother must have bewitched him or used her god to take him. So she confessed that she had cursed your mother and your father with Abiku sons.'

Sade sat down on a tree stump.

'I wish I had not gone to the priest. How can I hide such a thing from my mother?' she cried.

'You promised me you would not tell anyone.' Idowu looked down at her in panic.

'I'll keep my promise.'

The two girls went into the house. They found Patience in the lounge, rocking Saul. Mrs Uwaifo was trying hard to concentrate on her latest novel. Sade collected Saul from Patience and they went upstairs.

'On what part of the body was the incision made?' asked Sade, undressing the child in her bedroom.

'His left shoulder.'

Sade lifted the night-dress to find a small birthmark as Idowu had predicted.

'You see! What did I tell you?' Idowu appeared disturbed.

'What shall I do?'

'First of all perform the sacrifice, then travel immediately to Umuahia. Later on you can return to Lagos.'

'But how can I get the things for the sacrifice?'

'If you want, I can buy the yam. You bring one of your dogs and we can meet behind the house tomorrow.'

'I can't sacrifice the pets!' Sade was shocked that Idowu could suggest such a thing.

'Well, it's up to you, but as far as I am concerned it's better to sacrifice the dog than to risk losing your child.'

Sade looked down at the birthmark on Saul's shoulder. Surely birth marks were just skin defects? But supposing it was true that Saul was an Abiku child and that her father's house was cursed? She knew she would only have peace of mind by performing the sacrifice. The girls arranged to meet the following day in the rubber plantation.

TWENTY-THREE

IN THE COOLNESS of the afternoon, Sade sat on the porch watching the dogs play. She was trying to decide which of the dogs to take for the sacrifice. Rex, an old black dog, had been a childhood companion. She watched him sniffing the gravel. It was out of the question. She couldn't betray his trust. Perhaps she could take Lady, or maybe Peugeot. Peugeot was fully grown and her mother's favourite. It would have to be one of the three puppies. Suddenly Emeka approached.

'So, Madam!' he said pulling up one of the cane chairs and sitting down. 'When will you be ready to travel?'

'When ever you're ready.'

He laughed in disbelief. 'Then how about tomorrow morning?'

'Fine!'

Emeka looked puzzled. There had to be a catch.

'So I can tell your father?'

'Do what ever you want to do.' She got up and walked into the garden.

Emeka jumped up and hurried after her.

'Where are you going?' he asked.

'Just for a walk.'

He attempted to hold her hand but she pushed him away. Emeka smiled mischievously. Irritated by his presence, she made her way back into the house. He followed and they sat with her parents in the lounge. Saul lay fast asleep in her mother's arms and seeing him reminded her of the meeting she had arranged with Idowu.

'I'm going to take my siesta,' she announced making her way upstairs. Surely Emeka would not bother her for at least two hours. Once in her bedroom she locked the door. Quietly she opened the balcony door and went out. Pulling up her dress, she stretched her right leg over the railings. As she got her left leg over she saw Clive's car approaching and the dogs began to bark. She had to make a dash for it. The stone inlaid walls formed a ladder which she quickly climbed down. Unfortunately Emeka had come onto the porch to meet Clive.

'What's going on?' he asked, as Sade jumped to the ground.

The dogs barked as Clive approached with a big smile on his face.

'Did you see what she was doing?' Emeka asked him before turning again to Sade. 'And where were you going that you should need to climb down the wall?'

Sade began to walk off but Emeka grabbed her arm.

'Get off!' she shouted, trying to pull away.

The sudden outburst brought her parents out.

'Ah Ah!' declared her father. 'Sade? I thought you went to take your siesta?'

'I caught her climbing down this wall,' Emeka announced proudly.

'No-ooh!' Justice Uwaifo examined the evidence. 'It's not possible! How can anybody climb down this wall?'

Sade sighed, tamping in fury.

'Will you tell him to get his hands off me?' she told her father. 'I'm not a thief.'

'I want to know where you were going, that you should need to climb down the wall?' demanded Emeka.

'I was going for a walk. I am sick and tired of you following me about like a dog,' she shouted, abruptly pulling away.

Clive broke out in uncontrollable bouts of laughter.

'I don't know what you've got to laugh about!' Mrs Uwaifo

scolded. She rocked Saul vehemently as he screamed in her arms.

Clive looked embarrassed.

'Let's go inside,' said Justice Uwaifo.

Sade attempted to walk into the garden but Emeka again catching her arm. She pulled away violently.

'Leave her!' insisted her father. 'I've noticed she's been acting very strangely since she delivered. You know childbirth can affect some women that way. Let's just watch her.'

Emeka and Clive followed her parents into the lounge.

In the rubber plantation, Sade found Idowu hiding behind one of the trees. In her hands she carried a huge yam.

'What kept you?' Idowu demanded. 'Look! It's already getting dark.'

'It's that bloody Emeka.'

'Where's the dog?'

Sade whistled and all the dogs ran towards them.

'Here boy!' she whistled. 'Here boy! Come here Whisky.'

The trusting dog approached, wagging its tail in excitement. She picked it up and it wriggled about in her hands. Emeka called from the garden. In fits of laughter, the girls ran through the rubber trees.

They found the priest sitting on a stool outside his shrine.

'Come!' he ordered, standing up to meet them.

Apprehensively, they approached the shrine. The priest seized the puppy from Sade's arms and tied it to a stick. With its mouth tied the dog whimpered whilst struggling to break free.

'Kneel down!' he ordered Sade, before taking the yam from Idowu.

He cut the yam and used it for divination. When he threw the kola, it was the most favourable answer. Two faces up and two down. The priest shouted for another man to help with the prayer.

'I go call "Ogun", you say "Yah!" the priest told the girls.

'Ogun!' he shouted facing Sade with his arms outstretched.

'Yah!' Sade and Idowu chorused a feeble response.

The helper on the other hand shouted out with commitment and power.

The priest turned to face his shrine.

'Ogun!'

'Yah!'

The priest turned to the side.

'Ogun!'

'Yah!'

The priest now turned to face the sunset.

'Ogun!'

'Yah!'

'Ogun god of Iron! We praise you.' The priest rang an iron bell in his shrine and the dog fell silent for a moment before resuming its struggle.

'…Ogun son of Oduduwa we praise you.

Ogun that washes with blood! We praise you.

Sade is not dear, but Ogun is dear.

Do not let her be destroyed!'

'Let it be so, oh god of iron,' shouted out the helper.

'Let Sade give life to many children!'

'Let it be so, oh god of iron.'

'Let nobody curse her or her children.'

'Let it be so, oh god of iron.'

'Let Sade have wealth!'

'Let it be so, oh god of iron.'

'Let Sade live to worship Ogun oh!'

'Let it be so, oh god of iron.'

'As the snake creeps about, unhurt by the thorny bush, let it be so, that there will be no obstacles on your path. May you conquer all your obstacles. The god of iron will help you to conquer all your problems,' continued the priest.

'Let it be so, oh god of iron!' came the final chorus of Idowu and the helper.

The helper grabbed the fighting dog shouting for a young boy to help. He tied a large stick tightly to the dog's neck at the point where the neck joined its head. With the boy holding onto the dog's hind legs the priest grabbed a machete from the altar. With a single stroke the dog's head was severed and Sade collapsed in tears. The priest spilt the blood over the idols before anointing her head, arms and legs. He placed the body of the dog in a small altar of stones in front of a sacred peregun tree. The helper took up the talking drums, echoing their message into infinity.

> *Please do not behead me.*
> *I implore you*
> *Do not behead me as you beheaded Oye and Kitibe*
> *Do not behead me...*

The young boy took up an iron bell which he began to tap rhythmically. Hearing this, the women in the house approached, dancing around them as they clapped and sang in Edo. The priest insisted that Sade and Idowu join in the dancing. The gods were attracted to music, dance and wine. In the centre of the human circle, the girls danced. Filling his mouth with palm wine, the priest blew it out, before the girls. Overcome by the hypnotic, repetitive beat, Sade surrendered herself. A moment came when the dance became possession. Lost in the rhythm, she spun around and around, in oneness with the eternal universe.

TWENTY-FOUR

SADE FELT APPREHENSIVE as the driver pulled up in the Eze's driveway. When the driver set off on the return journey to Benin, she knew that she was completely at Emeka's mercy.

'Ah-hhh! Welcome! Welcome!' shouted Mama Emeka as they approached the porch. She flung her hefty arms around Sade's neck. 'My child!' she cried taking Saul from Sade. 'Look my pickin!' she showed Saul to Mama Obi, her junior wife.

'Chuks! What of Boniface?' Emeka shouted, as Chukwuma rushed out to greet them. He was followed by all eleven of Emeka's brothers and sisters.

'He's in the barracks,' Chukwuma replied.

Emeka laughed as two little girls grabbed his hands.

'Ezinma! Kechi!' he called in delight.

'I hope you haven't forgotten me?' a tall dark girl asked Sade. 'I was at your wedding,' Frances told her.

Sade wondered how anyone could expect her to remember anything from that fateful day.

'This is Kennedy,' Emeka indicated grabbing a seventeen-year-old by the back of his neck. 'And this is Truman. And this rat here is Jude.'

It occurred to Sade that the Eze obviously had some kind of infatuation with the American presidency.

'How old are you?' she asked Jude, trying to be friendly.

'Eleven!' he smiled proudly.

'I am Nixon.' a seven-year-old albino child announced.

'Who asked you?' laughed Bogart, his seventeen-year-old brother. He gave Nixon a knock on the head and Nixon squealed, screwing up his face.

'She will know them all,' shouted Mama Emeka. 'Come inside.'

Mama Emeka led the way into the lounge where the Eze sat on his gold plated throne. Emeka prostrated before him.

'You have to kneel down,' Francis whispered to Sade, leading her before the Eze.

Sade knew that her mother had never knelt down before any African ruler, and saw no reason why she should. Anxious not to offend, she curtsied slightly.

'You are welcome!' said the Eze, reaching to shake her hand. His voice was croaked. 'How are your parents?'

'They're fine.'

Mama Emeka showed the Eze his new grandson.

'What a handsome boy!' the Eze smiled. 'Please sit down. Sit down!'

Baby, the Eze's junior wife, came in and knelt before her master. She was a very attractive, fair skinned woman. The age gap between them was so great that Baby looked more like a daughter than a wife.

'What will you take?' the Eze asked Emeka.

'Beer!' he replied, turning to Sade. 'You'll have fanta?'

Politely, she nodded her consent.

'And bring pepper soup,' Mama Emeka ordered Baby, who subserviently left the room.

Emeka explained to the Eze the situation they had left in Lagos. The Eze pondered.

'You can see, all my children are home now.' The Eze sounded melancholy. 'In fact, Kennedy, Bogart and Truman were almost killed by soldiers in Ibadan. I will never send my children to school outside the East again. I would rather send them to England. It's a terrible situation we're in. The country has disintegrated.' The Eze shook his head sadly.

'Well, it will be better for us if the country can divide peacefully,' said Emeka.

'I don't think that is possible. With the oil in the south, the Northerners have too much to lose by allowing the Country to divide.'

Baby returned from the kitchen with a tray of drinks. Behind her appeared a housegirl, carrying a tray covered with bowls of pepper soup. Baby knelt down to serve the Eze. She then served Mama Emeka, Emeka and Mama Obi. The family hierarchy was plainly in evidence. The housegirl eventually served Sade who was now the most junior wife.

Looking down at the contents in her bowl, Sade was able to recognise part of an animal's ear.

'What meat is this?' she whispered, nudging Emeka next to her.

'Goat,' he replied.

Her mother never cooked the head of any animal, except to feed the dogs. Anxious not to offend, she took a sip of the soup which sent her into a state of panic. Her face reddened and her eyes filled with tears.

'Too much pepper!' shouted Mama Emeka, as Sade began to cough.

Emeka handed her a glass of fanta which she quickly gulped down. The smaller children tried to hide their giggles.

'Nixon! Jude! Kechi! Ezinma! Get out of here,' the Eze ordered. The children scampered.

'I'd better change Saul,' Sade told Emeka as she went to collect Saul from Mama Emeka.

Emeka led the way upstairs. Frances followed to remove her belongings from his room.

'What of your children?' Emeka asked Frances, as they walked up the terrazzo staircase.

'Their father would not let me take them. We'll talk later.' Frances obviously did not wish to discuss her personal problems in front of Sade. 'Now that everyone is home, this house is just not big enough.'

'How many bedrooms are there?' Sade asked her.

'Seven! But the Eze and Emeka are the only ones lucky enough to have their own rooms.' Frances teased her brother.

'The Eze's wives all have their own rooms,' Emeka reminded her.

'But they have to share with the smaller children.'

'So! Now I will be sharing with my wife and child. Won't I?' Emeka pushed open his bedroom door and walked in. Sade followed. She glanced in horror at the single bed covered with a quilted bedspread. Looking out of the long louvre windows, she could see a girl pounding yam in the back yard.

'This room appears to get smaller every time I visit.' Emeka sighed. 'They'll have to bring a cot for the baby.'

Frances opened a built in wardrobe, and began to remove her clothes.

'Oyibo!' Frances shouted, as Nixon ran past.

'Why do you call him Oyibo?' asked Sade.

'That's what his mother calls him. She says he is the reincarnation of a white man. The man used to be a friend of the Eze's, but was killed in a car crash.'

Nixon twisted his face as he stood by the door.

'Carry these things to the girl's room,' Frances ordered him.

'Is Nixon your mother's child?' Sade asked Emeka.

'No! He's Mama Obi's child.'

'I always thought you and Obi were from the same mother.' Sade sat on the bed where she began to feed Saul.

Emeka was determined that she should understand the family structure. 'My mother is the Eze's first wife. I am their first child followed by Chukwuma, Frances, Kennedy, Truman, and Jude. Mama Obi's first child is of course Obi, followed by Roosevelt, Vivian, Bogart, Nixon, Kechi and Ezinma. Baby is the Eze's third wife, but she has failed to produce.'

'But she's still trying.' Frances sniggered.

'Well, she's still very young. She's only twenty.' said Emeka.

'She told someone that they did not circumcise her properly so she became infected. Yet every night, I hear her sneaking into the Eze's room.'

They all laughed.

Frances continued, 'Do you know she does not even know her father? They say her father was a white trader. Her mother must have been one of these street girls.' Frances hissed in disgust.

There was a knock at the door and Baby appeared.

'Mama Emeka asked if you will like rice?' Baby asked Sade.

'She will eat anything,' Emeka responded, determined that Sade should not be given any preferential treatment.

'As long as you don't put too much pepper,' Frances scolded.

Baby approached Sade and Saul.

'Such a beautiful baby!' she cooed touching his soft curly hair. 'Let me carry him,' she offered, reaching out her arms. Sade surrendered Saul to Baby who held him against her cheek. Listening to her singing an Ibo lullaby, Sade felt sure that she was going to like the Eze's junior wife. She appeared to be a caring and gentle person.

'So from now, we have to call Sade "Mama Ironsi".' Francis declared.'

It was an obvious slant at Baby's barrenness.

'Of course!' Baby smiled affectionately. 'But Emeka can still call her Darling.'

'You better hurry up and have your own,' said Frances.

Baby handed Saul back to Sade; her eyes were full of tears.

'Let me go and prepare the food,' Baby told Sade before hurrying out of the room.

'But what's your problem?' Emeka scolded Frances.

Frances hissed. 'Isn't it because she's seen money she carried her fat "nyash" to meet the Eze. As far as I'm concerned she's the equivalent of a prostitute.'

Emeka stared at her in shock.

'It's true!' Frances shrugged, 'Why else will a fine young girl like that enter the bed of an old man?'

'Don't ever let me hear you repeat that again,' Emeka warned.

'You think I go about telling everybody?' smiled Frances. 'I'm only telling you because you are my brother.'

TWENTY-FIVE

THE FOLLOWING MORNING Sade was awakened by the loud ringing of a bell. She shot up in bed, unable to comprehend where she was or what was happening. Saul stirred in the cot besides her bed and Emeka jumped up.

'What the hell is that?' she demanded, looking at her watch. It was five o'clock.

'The prayer bell!' Emeka replied.

'What?'

She had slept little all night. It was hot and uncomfortable sharing a single bed with Emeka.

'Come on, get up!' Emeka insisted, pulling his dressing gown down from the wardrobe door.

A child screamed out in agony and Sade hurried out of bed. Emeka opened the bedroom door, and Jude ran past, his face covered in tears.

'What's the matter with you?' Emeka demanded.

Jude was in too much of a hurry to answer. Within seconds Mama Emeka appeared. In one hand she held the prayer bell and in the other, a long cane.

'Come on! Go prayer room!' she shouted at Jude.

'Good Morning Mama!' Emeka greeted. He recalled the many times he too had felt her cane.

'Doctor! Good morning!'

Mama looked in at Sade who greeted respectfully.

'Carry Ironsi go prayer room!' she ordered.

The large room allocated for family prayers had an altar at one end, adorned with a crucifix, a Bible and white candles. Sade joined the rest of the family, kneeling down on raffia mats. The service conducted by the Eze was exceedingly well attended.

After the service Mama led Sade into her own bedroom.

'Sit down!' Mama ordered Sade.

With Saul in her arms she sat down on Mama's large double bed. The room was quite unlike her mother's room. There was no perfume on the dressing table, no frilly curtains over the window and no sexy negligee lying across the bed. Instead there was one long wardrobe, packed with expensive wrappers and head-ties.

Frances came in carrying a large bucket of water. Sade watched as she lay some utensils out on the floor. One large enamel bowl, a tiny stool, a kettle of boiling water, a towel and a face flannel.

'Bring my pickin!' Mama ordered as she balanced on the tiny stool. Unashamedly she pushed up her wrapper, exposing her obese legs. She stretched her legs over the enamel basin. Reluctantly, Sade handed Saul over before sitting down to watch. She prayed that the tiny stool would not collapse under so great a weight. With Saul on her fat laps and her wrapper rolled between her legs, Mama ordered Frances to pour the hot water into the bucket of cold water at her side. Having tested the temperature with her free hand, Mama reached for the Lux beauty soap.

'Let me collect the baby soap.' Sade protested.

'This one good!' Mama responded, working up a lather in her hand before rubbing it over Saul's skin.

Sade watched helplessly as the dirty water trickled down Mama's legs to the large enamel basin below. Mama then proceeded to exercise the child, bending and stretching his limbs. Saul screamed and trembled in discomfort.

'Cry no go kill am!' Mama tried to reassured Sade.

Resting Saul on his stomach, Mama now parted his buttocks with one hand. Holding a wet flannel high above his anus, she allowed the water to trickle into him.

Sade jumped to her feet, reaching for the towel. She felt herself going dizzy. Mama turned Saul over, pressing his abdomen with the wet flannel. Rapidly, Saul expelled the contents of his bowel in squirts and blurts. Holding Saul upside down by his ankles, Mama now gave him a good shaking. He stiffened, changing colour. Sade held out the towel to take the child. Impressed by her initiative, Mama accepted it. She spread it out over her lap whilst reaching for a bottle of surgical spirits. Sade felt sick with anxiety. She was trembling in shock and rage.

When eventually Mama handed the sobbing child back, Sade hurried out of the room. She found Emeka in the bedroom where she confronted him in whispered hysterics.

'Go and sit down!' he scolded. 'What do you know about bringing up children? And if your mother was so perfect, where are all her children that died?'

'You bastard!' Sade cried, trembling in temper. 'I should have known better than to marry a bush man like you.'

Emeka scoffed.

'Bush man like who? I was educated in Britain! And where have you been?'

He grabbed his towel and escaped to the bathroom.

After breakfast, Sade joined Emeka on the balcony. Surrounded by his brothers and sisters, he was in his element. She looked down on the children as they chased the chickens and goats around the garden.

'And you allowed them to commandeer your Mercedes,' Frances shouted provocatively at Emeka.

'What did you expect me to do?' he snapped.

'D-d-d-don't mind her.' stuttered Roosevelt.

'Isn't that your husband's car?' Vivian, one of Emeka's sisters, asked Frances.

Suddenly Frances dived down behind Sade and Saul. 'I'm dead-oh!' She appeared very agitated.

Sade looked down the driveway to see a white Peugeot approaching the house. It pulled up in the driveway, and three men got out.

'S-s-s-so why are y-y-you hiding?' asked Roosevelt screwing up his eyes in frustration.

'What's your business?' she retorted.

They all laughed.

'Don't tell him I'm here,' Frances begged Emeka.

Emeka, Chukwuma and Vivian made their way downstairs.

'I'm dead-oh!' Frances kept repeating, pranced up and down the balcony.

'T-t-that's very good f-f-for you,' laughed Roosevelt, happy that someone could put her in her place.

'Look at your mouth like f-f-f-f.' Frances hissed. 'Idiot!'

'D-d-d-don't let me beat you-oh!'

'C-c-come and beat me now.' said Frances, imitating his stutter. As Roosevelt got off his seat, Frances placed one hand on her hip. 'Put one finger on me and I show you pepper!' she warned, pushing out her chest.

'Frances!' Emeka shouted from downstairs.

'Eh!' she responded.

'Come downstairs!' he ordered.

'G-g-god saved you t-t-today!' Roosevelt hissed, as Frances hurried off.

'What's going on?' asked Baby, coming to join them on the balcony.

'Her h-h-husband has come to collect her,' Roosevelt laughed.

From downstairs they could hear Frances' occasional outbursts.

'It's a lie! It's a lie!' she protested about something.

'That girl is so bold.' laughed Baby. 'Look how she's even shouting in the presence of the Eze. She's not afraid.'

'D-d-d-d-don't m-m-mind her. N-no wonder h-h-her husband is always b-b-beating h-her. I d-d-don't blame him. If I were him, I w-w-would b-b-beat her too.' Roosevelt blinked in frustration as he struggled to get the words out.

'Why did he beat her?' asked Sade.

Baby shrugged not wishing to involve herself in gossip.

'S-s-she was insulting h-h-his mother. S-s-she's always looking for t-t-trouble. When she s-sees the trouble, she will run a-a-away.'

Baby bent her head down in laughter.

After about an hour, Frances came out of the house, escorted by her husband and his entourage.

'The Eze has sent her back to her husband,' laughed Baby.

'Are y-y-you going?' Roosevelt shouted down at her mischievously.

Frances eyed him contemptuously.

'Leave her alone,' Baby laughed quietly. 'You're looking for her trouble. Let her go in peace.'

Frances ordered Oyibo to collect her clothes, before setting off to her husband's house.

TWENTY-SIX

AFTER A WEEK in Umuahia, Sade felt certain that just one more day would drive her insane. After prayers one morning, she locked the bedroom door to prevent Emeka's escape.

'When are we going back to Lagos?' Her voice was calm and determined.

'You've asked me that question one hundred times, and I've told you. I do not know.'

Emeka slipped on his sandals and attempted to leave.

'I've asked you that question a hundred times and now I want a proper answer.'

'Where's the key?'

'I have it.'

'Then open the door, I'm going somewhere with the Eze.'

'You are just trying to be evasive,' Sade sighed. Obstinately she sat down on the bed.

'Believe me, I am not.' Emeka reached for her hand and sat down beside her. 'I intended to talk to you, but right now I have to go out. The Eze has organised a job for me at the Queen Elizabeth Hospital. I'll be starting work next week.'

'What the hell are you talking about?' she flew off the bed, 'Did you bother to consult me when you were making these arrangements? You think I'm going to live here? And what about my A level? You promised my father that I could continue my education in Lagos.'

'Look!' shouted Emeka, standing up to meet her. 'I don't see why I should have to explain to you. You know the situation we are in. We were forced to flee for our lives. Do you think that I ever want to go through that again?'

'But things have calmed down,' Sade pleaded.

'What has calmed down? What the hell do you know? The bodies of Ibos are still arriving home. In their hundreds! And you tell me things have calmed down. Haven't you heard the people crying out for weapons?'

'But what about our house in Lagos? And the hospital? And what about Mercy?'

'Sade! A friend has informed me that the house and hospital have been completely looted. Even the light bulbs and fixtures have been removed. So don't talk to me as if I am responsible for this whole mess. As for Mercy, I don't know what has happened to her, but she's no longer there.'

'Well, I can't stay here.' Sade leant against the window sill. 'You have to give me some money. I'll go to Benin with Saul.'

'Open the door!' Emeka's voice was full of aggression.

'Not until we've reached an agreement. I want to leave tomorrow morning.'

He began to search for the key.

'Open the door,' he demanded.

'Not until you give me some money.'

Emeka banged his fist against the wooden wardrobe. 'You can leave anytime you like,' he said. 'But there is no way you will take my son out of the East.'

'How dare you!' Sade began to cry. 'You know that I can't leave without my son.'

There was a knock at the door. It was the Eze.

Sade threw the key at him. He stared at her in rage as the key struck his forehead. Slowly he bent down, picked up the key, unlocked the door and left.

After breakfast, Sade prepared six feeding bottles. With Saul in one arm and a large bag in the other, she sneaked out of the house. Walking down the main road she attempted to flag down a taxi. Her mother would pay once she arrived in Benin. A large American car came splashing through the rain puddles and pulled up in front of her. She looked into the back seat expecting to find Emeka and the Eze but a bearded stranger eagerly wound down the window.

'Good morning to you,' he smiled. A deep tremor echoed from his voice like that of a base drum.

'Morning!'

'Can I drop you somewhere?'

Sade realised that he could be the answer to her problem.

'I want to get to Benin.'

'No problem at all. We can drop you at the motor park.' The stranger opened the door and Sade bit her lip apprehensively. The man excitedly clambered to the other side of the seat. She contemplated. She heard a woman shouting. Looking across the road, she spotted Frances trying to cross. Pretending not to have seen her, Sade jumped into the back seat. Before she could shut the door, Frances was banging on the car bonnet.

'Wait!' she shouted at the driver.

Frances grabbed the car door. She curtsied slightly, greeting the man next to Sade.

'Where are you going?' she asked Sade, still studying the strange man's face.

'Nowhere!'

'Nowhere?' Frances now stared into Sade's enraged eyes.

'Please excuse me,' said Sade, trying to shut the door.

'Where's Emeka?' Frances demanded.

'He's gone out.'

'Gone out to where?'

'Go inside and find out,' Sade snapped.

Realising that something was wrong, Frances grabbed Sade's large bag containing the milk bottles.

'You better wait till Emeka comes home.' Frances waddled like a duck back to the Eze's 'palace'.

Without Saul's food it was now impossible for Sade to travel.

She held her head down, sighing in defeat.

'Is there a problem?' the man sounded very worried.

'No!' Sade got out of the car.

'Let me give you my card,' the stranger insisted, opening his briefcase. 'If I can be of any assistance, do not hesitate to call me.'

Sade accepted the small business card, and walked back to the house. Frances, Vivian, Mama Emeka, Mama Obi and Baby were all waiting for her in the driveway, surrounded by the smaller children.

'Sade?' Mama Emeka stared in disbelief. 'For where you dey go?'

Sade was huffing and puffing in rage. Ignoring Mama she walked straight up to Frances who cowered slightly.

'Where's my bag?' she demanded.

Frances knew that Sade would not be stupid enough to hit her, whilst carrying a two week old baby.

'Who do you think you're talking to?' Frances shouted, placing her hand on her hip. 'Do you know who I am? Or do you think I want to eat your bag?'

'No wonder your husband is always beating you. All you can do is go about interfering in other people's affairs. The first day I arrived, I saw the kind of person you were. A useless gossip,' Sade scolded. 'Baby, you said was the daughter of a street woman. You said she did not know her father and went as far as to call Baby a common prostitute.'

'Sha!' shouted Mama Emeka in shock.

'Why?' shouted Baby. 'Let her finish what she wanted to say. You people should come and hear-oh.'

'Ahh!' chorused Mama Emeka and Mama Obi, their mouths remaining open in shock.

'I'm not lying,' Sade continued. 'She said these things in Emeka's presence. She said that Baby carried her fat nyash to the Eze because of money. You can go and ask Emeka.'

'That I carried my fat nyash to Eze because of money?' Baby

repeated. 'Frances! Because I've been keeping quiet with you all these days?'

'Heeeey!' Mama Obi declared, clapping her hands and roaring with laughter. Kechi who was seven and Ezinma who was five years old nervously tried to hold their mother's hand. Nixon her nine-year-old albino son stood defensively in front of her.

'No-oh!' Baby shouted. 'This is no laughing matter.'

She took the head tie off her head, using it to secure her wrapper. Sade moved away, standing by the front door. Baby tried to approach Frances, but Mama Emeka stopped her advance.

'Mama Emeka!' Baby cried trying desperately to get past. 'I just want her to tell me, who is a prostitute. Let her tell me where she saw my mother. She said that I,' shouted Baby thumping at her own chest, 'am a prostitute.'

In a speed that amazed even Sade, Baby ducked under Mama Emeka's arm, grabbing Frances by the collar and twisting the fabric to get a firm grasp. Frances responded by also grabbing Baby's blouse. Mama Emeka re-tied her wrapper.

'Leave my dress!' Frances demanded but Baby intentionally ripped the cotton blouse.

'Ehnn!' screeched Frances, trying to rip open Baby's blouse. 'I will naked you today.'

Baby delivered one sound punch which Frances responded to by scratching three bloody lines down Baby's face. Baby went mad. The blood poured down as both women wrestled, biting, kicking and punching. Trying to separate them, Mama Emeka used her fist, hammering Baby on her head. The rage on Mama Emeka's face made her wide nose snort and flare, like that of a horse. The whites of Mama's normally small beady eyes were on show, as were her beautiful set of pearl white teeth.

'You will kill me today-oh! You will kill me today-oh!' Baby cried and screamed, attracting the attention of passers-by.

Baby tried to punch Frances yet again but Mama Emeka came in the way, receiving the punch straight in her eye. Mama held her face as though she had been blinded.

'Ehnn!' shrieked Mama Obi.

Bogart and Kennedy, the seventeen-year-old boys, came out of the house. Bogart grabbed Baby, pulling her arms behind her back. Truman, who was fifteen, tried to pull Frances off, but ended up with three sound slaps.

'What's happening! Why are you people acting like market women?' Chukwuma yelled on his way out of the house.

Sade picked up her bag which Frances had dumped on the door step. In the bedroom she placed Saul in the cot. She sat down on the bed wondering what to do next. She thought about the stranger. Perhaps he could help. She knew that if Emeka found the card, he would certainly destroy it. Pulling out the bottom drawer of the chest, she placed the card on the floor, before returning it in place.

Suddenly the bedroom door flew open and Emeka stormed in. His eyes were red with anger and for the first time Sade was terrified of him. He slammed shut the door and locked it.

'Have you seen my mother's face?' he demanded slowly moving towards her. He seized her arm but she slipped from his grasp and ran to the other side of the bed. He walked towards the wardrobe and Sade knew he was going to take out his horse whip. She banged at the bedroom door, screaming in vain for help. The whip caught her across the back, hard and stinging. She turned putting her hands up to protect her face. He raised his whip again and brought it down across her shoulder. Sade fell to her knees, crouching to protect herself. He grabbed her hair, pulling it with great brutality as he kicked her in the stomach, in the chest and in the face. He hit her again and again until she lay motionless.

'Let that be a lesson to you!' he warned kicking her for the last time before he opened the door and left.

Sade lay on the floor sobbing desperately. Every part of her body hurt. She hated him intensely and wanted revenge. Slowly she got up but collapsed back on the bed. Did Emeka really believe that he could dominate her through violence? Emeka might have won this battle but he certainly hadn't won the war.

TWENTY-SEVEN

SADE SAT IN the lounge with the rest of the family, listening to the news on the radio. There had been rumours of Biafran Independence and everyone wanted to hear the Declaration for themselves. The heavy rain poured down outside and the dull room fell into a deadly silence as the broadcast began.

'Fellow countrymen and women,' came the voice over the roaring thunderstorm outside. 'You, the people of Eastern Nigeria:

'Conscious of the supreme authority of Almighty God over all mankind, of your duty to yourselves and posterity. Aware that you can no longer be protected in your lives and in your property by any government based outside Eastern Nigeria.'

Sade looked around at the faces of eager anticipation. She did not want Biafran Independence. She wanted to go back to Lagos.

'I, Lieutenant Colonel Chukwuemeka Odumegwu Ojukwu,' the stranger's voice proceeded, 'Military Governor of Eastern Nigeria, by virtue of the authority and pursuant to the principles recited above, do hereby solemnly proclaim that the territory and region known as and called Eastern Nigeria, together with her continental shelf and territorial waters shall henceforth be an Independent Sovereign State of the name and title of "The Republic of Biafra".'

The silence in the room was immediately shattered with laughter and jubilation. A frantic glow of pride and joy lit up

Emeka's face. Mama Emeka began to clap, dancing and singing in Ibo. Sade watched unenthusiastically as the junior wives and children joined in the chorus. She could not share in their pride. Their cause meant nothing to her. Treacherous thoughts rushed through her mind. What right did the Ibos have to isolate themselves from the rest of Nigeria? What right did they have to claim the rich oil fields that belonged to all Nigerians? After all, the oil was not on Ibo land! It belonged to the people of the Delta. In the days that followed, Sade watched in desperation as the expatriates hurriedly left the sinking ship. The white businessmen took flight. The English schoolteachers and headmasters abandoned their schools and the white wives hurriedly abandoned their black husbands. Sade also felt that she had the right to escape the impending doom but before she had the chance the Nigerians attacked and she was trapped. Filled with the frustrations of a caged animal, she watched for the slightest chance of escape. The increasingly long days rolled by and her spirits dropped. All Emeka's attempts to revive them with unwanted gifts and kindness failed.

One afternoon, while Emeka was taking his siesta, she made her way downstairs. Shutting the door, she sat in the lounge next to the telephone. She planned to contact the bearded stranger. Nervously, she took out the card hidden in her bra. Lifting the receiver, she found that the line was dead. Trembling in frustration, she looked at the address on the card. Emeka had forbidden her from leaving the house unescorted. As a jeep pulled up in the driveway, she stuffed the card back down her bra. Looking out, she saw Boniface approach, dressed in the new Biafran uniform. Sade opened the front door and invited him in. She sent Jude upstairs to call Emeka, who appeared within seconds.

'Brigadier!' Emeka shouted in delight.

'Doctor!' Boniface responded, jumping from his seat to shake hands.

'You know he's a Brigadier now!' Emeka told Sade jovially.

'Congratulations!' She sounded genuinely pleased for him.

'This calls for celebration! Please sit down!' Emeka told Boniface.

They were joined by the Eze, Chukwuma, William and Roosevelt, all anxious to catch up on the latest news.

'We must stand our ground and fight!' shouted Boniface. 'Look at how we Ibos were driven from the North. Like dogs! We will now show those bloody Nigerians that we are men.'

'Do you know what we are faced with?' Emeka demanded.

'Of course I know what we're faced with,' Boniface shouted in excitement. 'The federal troops have over 85,000 trained soldiers against our volunteer army. But our men are committed to the cause. And we are fighting on home ground. We have the people behind us.'

'But Nigeria is armed to the teeth,' Emeka stressed, concerned by the speed of events. 'And they have been supplied with the most modern weapons by Britain and Russia. Their supply of arms is unlimited.'

'Are you telling me what they have and don't have?' Boniface demanded aggressively. 'Of course I know all this, but we have to make a stand. Or do you seriously expect any Ibo soldier to return to the Nigerian army? After what we've experienced? Or do you expect the Ibo people to return to the North? Where they will live in fear and wait for the day that the Northerners will again rise up against them?'

'I personally never expected the Nigerians to attack,' said the Eze. He looked old and tired, his face drawn in sadness.

'We must hold out for a few months. The Nigerians will realise our determination to succeed.'

'What areas have they taken?' asked the Eze in a low and sombre tone. He sat forward on his throne resting his elbows on his knees.

'They attacked Ogoja, a town near the border with the northern region, taking Nyonya and Gakem. But this was just a diversionary attack,' said Boniface, filled with excitement. 'The real attack came near Nsukka where they managed to advance inland by about four miles. Then we held them back. They captured Nsukka, raising it to the ground. But we are holding them back.'

'But Radio Nigeria has been broadcasting the fall of numerous towns,' insisted the Eze in disbelief.

'Can you believe the Nigerian broadcasts?' Boniface laughed. 'It's just government propaganda to demoralise our people.'

Boniface realised the power that the Eze had over his own people.

'So you mean they have not reached Enugu?' asked the Eze.

'Certainly not, Eze. I was in a meeting in Enugu just two days ago and I can assure you that life is carrying on as normal. Even the expatriates are still there. So far the only other place they have succeeded in taking is Bonny Island, where the oil loading terminal for Shell petroleum is located. I'm not trying to say that we are having an easy time. The front line is hell and our men are being slaughtered like goats.'

'Where else are we to run to!' interrupted Chukwuma overcome with emotion. 'So they have murdered us in the North, they have murdered us in the West and now they are following us to our own land to murder us.'

'There can be no more running.' Boniface was adamant. 'We must stand and fight.'

'Please help me get into the army,' said Chukwuma. 'I went to enlist, but I was told to wait.'

'Everyone wants to enlist,' Boniface laughed, proud of his new found authority. 'Come to my office tomorrow and I will sought you out.'

'I will c-c-come with him.' insisted Roosevelt.

'No problem!' Boniface turned to the sombre Eze. 'What we need now are funds to purchase arms. The people have been donating the little they can, but it's not sufficient.'

The Eze pondered and shook his head sadly. 'I have a

meeting tonight with some former politicians. You better come with me so that we can discuss the matter further. But we must get recognition from the outside world. If they are sympathetic to our plight, they can supply us with arms, or at least the funds to purchase the arms.'

'That would be wonderful,' Boniface smiled, realising the potential. 'In the meantime, I would suggest that you get labourers to cover the roof of the palace with palm leaves. You must camouflage the building from air raids. I would also recommend that you build a bunker.'

The Eze looked very disturbed. He pondered again. 'Emeka! Tomorrow you arrange for labourers to start work,' the Eze instructed solemnly. 'I have been hearing rumours that the Nigerians are imposing food blockades.'

'Eze! It's true! The Nigerians think they can starve us into submission. They are aware of our dependence on imported salt and protein. The situation is made worse by the influx of millions of refugees and panic buying. And traders are hoarding goods to hike up prices.'

'So what can we do to help the people?' asked the Eze.

'We are setting up intensive chicken and egg-rearing farms. Kwashiorkor is caused by a lack of protein. Working with the relief organisations, we can beat the problem.' Boniface tried to assure the Eze.

The following morning, The Eze sent Mama Emeka to market with the driver and two houseboys. They scoured the markets. In the evening they returned with cartons and crates of foodstuff, stacking them up in the food store. There were cartons of soap, toilet paper, baby food, tinned milk, sugar, Bounvita, margarine, sardines and corned beef. There were boxes of stockfish, yams, bush meat, and alcoholic and soft drinks. There were sacks of salt, onion, gari and rice. She purchased everything she could lay her hands on, even bunches of unripe bananas. The key to the store was kept tied on a rope around Mama's neck.

TWENTY-EIGHT

MAMA RANG THE bell for prayers and Sade joined the rest of the family in the prayer room. The children sat quietly on mats in the centre of the room, whilst the adults occupied the soft chairs surrounding the room.

'What of Eze?' Mama Emeka asked Baby, assuming that she had spent the night in his bed.

Baby shrugged. She did not know where the Eze was. Emeka hurried out of the room, returning moments later with a most peculiar look on his face. He called his mother out of the room and whispered something to her. She began to cry like a child. Mama Obi quickly jumped to her feet.

'Wetin happen?' she demanded. 'What of Eze?'

'Eze is sleeping.' Emeka responded. It was against the custom to announce an Eze dead. An Eze could never die.

Ripping the head-tie off her bald head, Mama Obi began to cry and bang her chest in confusion. The adults knew instantly that the Eze was dead and the house was thrown into a state of turmoil. The family demonstrated their grief, filling the early morning air with endless blood curdling wails. All the family photographs were taken down from the walls and the curtains drawn. Emeka and his brothers tore their clothes, whilst the female members of the household stripped themselves of all jewellery. The smaller children clung to the adults, crying in confusion.

Now head of the household, Emeka sent the houseboy to call the village elders and traditional priests. They arrived within a very short time and began to organise various burial committees. There was a committee for compound cleaning, one for uniforms, another for wake keeping. The list was endless. The lounge was designated as the Eze's final resting place and one committee set to work emptying the room of all furniture to dig a grave.

Frances and Sade were given the responsibility of cleaning out and decorating the Eze's bedroom where he was to be laid in state. It was the largest and most luxurious bedroom in the house. There was one door leading off to a private bathroom and a second door to a balcony. The floor was covered in a red silk Persian carpet and red velvet curtains hung across the windows.

Sade and Frances spent hours winding yards of white ribbon around the posters of the king-sized bed. They covered the mattress in a new white satin sheet before the Eze was brought back into the room. Six men struggled to place the wooden coffin on the bed before Emeka removed the lid. The Eze was adorned in brand new regalia. On his head, he wore a golden crown and in his hand he carried the staff of office. He was dressed in a new white damask cloak.

The family sat around the Eze's corpse, praying and singing hymns. Mama Emeka and the other wives were comforted in their own rooms by relatives and friends.

Three days after the Eze's death, the elders appointed a senior member from the council of chiefs as the new Eze and at last the burial could take place. The preparations where enormous. Women were brought in from the village to do the cooking. Two cows were purchased at exorbitant prices and tied up in the back yard. A large canopy was erected on the front lawn. Musicians were employed and arrangements were made for the Ijele, King of Masquerades to attend the funeral.

Sade saw little of Emeka as the preparations went ahead. He remained guard over his father's corpse every night. When she did see him he was shouting and cursing people in frustration.

Five a.m. on the day of the Eze's burial, Sade was awakened by the sound of women shouting and banging enamel pans in the back yard. Jumping out of bed, she rushed to the bedroom window. About thirty women had arrived from the village. Using three building blocks as a base, they had constructed about twenty wooden fires. The women cut up branches, sticking them into the block surrounds. As it was August there was a lull in the rainy season, but the damp wood was extremely difficult to light. For hours the women blew into the concrete surrounds, occasionally wiping the tears from their smoke filled eyes.

Sade watched as the children helped to catch and tie down three goats and several chickens. Filled with excitement, Jude and Oyibo dragged one obstinate goat to the far side of the compound. There Chukwuma and some men had set up a slaughter ground. Ruthlessly, the men slit the throats of the screeching animals, allowing the blood to trickle into the ground. The children crowded around. The slaughter seemed to act like some sort of magnet.

The dead animals were piled high on banana leaves that had been laid on the ground. Gradually they were collected and taken to the cooking area. The chickens were dunked in boiling water, making it easier for the woman to pull out the feathers. The goats were thrown onto the open fires. The stench of burnt hair was everywhere. It took hours to burn and shave off the hair, before the animals were slit open.

In the night Sade joined the rest of the family in Mama Emeka's bedroom. An elder was describing to them how the grave had been dug. The Eze would have a 'room and parlour'.

'Will anybody follow him?' Frances enquired.

Baby held her breadth. Her wide eyes fixed on the elder. Without replying the man walked out of the room.

'You can be so stupid!' Vivian scolded Frances. 'How can you ask him such a question?'

'Who is stupid?' Frances retorted. 'I will deal with you today.'

199

Mama Obi stared at Frances. 'Your trouble is too much!' she sighed.

Frances hissed and stormed out of the room. With Saul tied securely to her back, Sade followed.

'Don't mind them,' she told Frances.

'If I get that Vivian, I will so pepper her! Or has she forgotten that I senior her?'

Frances pushed open the door to the girls bedroom. Ezinma, Kechi and Frances's three children all slept in one bed. Frances sat down with the children whilst Sade sat on a bed opposite.

'When are they going to bury the Eze?' she asked Frances.

'Tonight!'

'Why in the night?'

Frances looked up at Sade. 'Because that is when the spirits of the dead can be evoked. They will accompany the Eze into the spirit world.'

'Where is the spirit world?'

'They say it is the same as this world in every respect except it is dimmer. Like a shadow land. There people do not have the joy of life but only the shadow of that joy. When the sun sets on this world, it rises on the spirit world.'

'Will we attend the Eze's burial?'

Frances scoffed.

'Women and children don't attend burials. In fact only Emeka will be there.'

'Will they bury anyone with the Eze?'

'Do I know?' snapped Frances as she recalled the incident with Vivian.

'Is it just anybody that they catch and bury with the Eze?' Frances laughed. 'Don't worry! It's only in the olden days that wives and slaves were buried with the Eze.'

'But why?'

'To serve him in the spirit world. It would be like an indication of his greatness on earth.'

'So why did you ask if anyone will follow the Eze if such

200

practices no longer go on?'

Frances was now obviously irritated by Sade's persistent questioning but Sade was determined to get answers.

'Will they kill anyone at the Eze's burial?'

'Sade, stop asking me all these questions! Go and ask your husband!'

A bell rang and an elder ordered the whole family to the prayer room. Frances woke up her three children, whilst Sade pulled Ezinma and Kechi into the crowded room. There she removed Saul from her back and sat down. The smaller children lay down on the floor and fell asleep. It was close to midnight and the Eze's burial was about to take place. The door was locked so nobody could get out of the room. Looking around the room Sade realised that Baby was missing. The adults sat in silence, staring morbidly into space. She could not intrude upon the silence.

At about four a.m. there were terrible screams. They were quickly followed by wailing. Then there was the sound of gunfire. The door was unlocked and the family emerged. Sade tried to find out what had happened to Baby but no one was prepared to talk about it. The celebrations carried on for three days and nights but when the festivities were over, there was a strange new emptiness in the house.

TWENTY-NINE

WITH THE DEATH of the Eze, Emeka inherited his vast fortune, but also the enormous responsibilities that went with it. As a true patriot, he continued to work at the Queen Elizabeth Hospital. The hospital was now desperately short of staff and Emeka decided that Sade should help with the war effort. Returning home one afternoon, he informed Sade of his decision. She had been taking her siesta at the time, but flew off the bed.

'I don't want a bloody job!' she shouted, staring at him in blind rage. 'I want to return to Benin. You have no right to keep me here against my will. I'm not your bloody slave.'

'Just watch how you talk to me,' Emeka warned, moving aggressively towards her. He pointed his finger in her face. 'I am your husband and it is your duty to obey me.'

Sade pouted and twisted her lips, moving away from him. Since their arrival in Umuahia he had beaten her up several times in an attempt to crush her defiant nature.

'You need to do some work,' Emeka insisted, 'The experience will be beneficial to you. Right now the hospital is desperately short of staff. We can hardly manage to keep going.'

'Sure they're bloody short of staff, because anybody with an ounce of intelligence would have packed up and gone.'

'Because they are a bunch of cowards,' shouted Emeka. 'When this war is over, they'll all come flocking back. But it will be those of us that have contributed to the war effort that will be the ones to really enjoy.'

'I'm not working there,' Sade shrugged.

'You are working there.'

Sade was quiet as she realised a possible means of escape. If she could save up her salary, perhaps she could find a way out of Biafra.

'How much will I get paid?' she asked.

'There isn't even enough money to pay the qualified staff. You will work on a voluntary basis.'

Sade began to laugh, she laughed until she collapsed on the bed crying in despair.

'I have no time for such theatrics,' said Emeka on his way out of the room.

The following morning, Emeka drove Sade to the Queen Elizabeth Hospital. He took her to the casualty ward where he introduced her to his friends, Dr William Amadi, and his English wife Becky. The red-haired Mrs Becky Amadi worked as matron incharge of the casualty ward.

'So I'm leaving her in your safe hands,' Emeka told Becky. 'Don't worry, we'll take good care of her.' Dr Amadi responded, his face glowing with a lustful grin. He put his arm around Sade. 'If you need anything, don't be afraid to come to me.' Dr Amadi sounded patronising.

Emeka hurried off to the operating theatre, and Becky led Sade onto the ward. She was pleasant and taught Sade the basic nursing skills. Becky's treatment of the black nurses was however very different. She was quite obnoxious, treating them with contempt. Her office at the entrance to the ward was out of bounds to all the nurses. Sade however was encouraged to keep her company.

'Are your parents still together?' she asked Sade one day. Sitting behind an old desk, she dragged hard at her cigarette while waiting for Sade's answer.

'Yes.'

'I have three children like you. All girls unfortunately. You know what Nigerian men are like! They must have their sons?' Becky blinked, her eyes filling up with tears and her face glowing red.

'Maybe the next one will be a boy,' said Sade trying to console her.

'If there is a next one!' Becky rolled her eyes. She stubbed out her cigarette.

One morning, Becky told Sade to send the other nurses on break. Filled with self importance Sade walked down the ward checking on each nurse before sending them off for a break. Naji, an emaciated little boy, called out for a bed pan and she asked Grace, one of the older nurses to attend to him.

'You can see to him!' Grace responded, obviously resentful of the preferential treatment Sade was receiving.

Naji cried, forming additional wrinkles over his already withered face. The junior nurses giggled as they hurried off the ward.

'You better do as you're told, right now!' Sade scolded. 'Or you're sacked.'

Grace began to shout, bringing Becky storming down the ward.

'Sade! What is going on?' she demanded.

'I asked Grace to take a bed pan to Naji and she told me to do it myself.'

'Who is she to tell me to take a bed pan to a patient?' Grace shouted. 'I am a qualified nurse.'

'Either get on with your job, or get out!' Becky told Grace.

Filling the air with many hisses, Grace collected the bed pan and went to attend to Naji.

'Don't take any notice of her,' said Becky as they walked back to her office. 'It will take some time for them to get used to you. You know you're much younger.' Becky sat down behind her desk. 'How old are you anyway?'

'I'll be eighteen next month,' Sade averted her eyes in temper.

'We'll have to arrange a big party for you,' Becky laughed.

Sade slumped into a seat. She wondered how old Becky was. She had to be in her late twenties. Becky fanned herself with an old newspaper.

'I can't stand this heat. It's just so humid,' Becky panted. After lighting another cigarette Becky spoke again.

'I suppose after the war you'll start training to be a nurse?'

'That's the last thing I want to do.'

'I thought your husband said you wanted to do nursing.'

'Emeka has his own ideas,' Sade replied. 'I wanted to study Law but the war has disrupted everything.'

'It's terrible, isn't it. One of the nurses, Ndali, was in Nsukka University. I understand that when the federal troops took Nsukka they destroyed the University. It's such a shame.' Becky dragged hard at her cigarette once again.

'Well, you'd better call the nurses back or they'll be out there all day,' she ordered.

Sade found the nurses sitting outside on the long veranda.

'Those Nigerian bastards think they can defeat us,' Ndali was shouting out. 'In our own land? Because they saw us running from the North they think we are cowards. Let then come! We will kill them one by one. Look at that stupid Gowon with his mouth like "swift police action". So what happened to his "swift police action"?'

'Till the last man!' shouted another nurse, her arm raised in defiance.

'Excuse me!' Sade interrupted. They all turned and stared at her. 'Matron wants you back on the ward.'

Ndali eyed Sade contemptuously. Sade turned and walked back to the ward. The nurses followed. They made fun and pulled faces behind her. Suddenly there was the screeching sound of a fast, low flying jet engine. The ward was thrown into a state of turmoil as the anti-aircraft guns blasted out at the enemy aircraft. By the time the first bomb had exploded, Becky and the terror stricken nurses were flat on the ward floor. Sade glanced up at Naji, the emaciated little boy. He screamed in terror and tried to pull the drip out of his arm. Instinctively Sade rushed to stop him.

'Get down!' Becky shouted at her.

Sade's thoughts turned to Saul. She couched down at the end of Naji's cot, covering her head with her arms. A second bomb exploded and the building shook. The glass shattered in the windows. The air cleared to a tense silence. The silence was quickly overcome by wailing. The nearby school and market had been hit. There was frantic activity everywhere with people shouting and screaming in panic. Hastily the dead, dying and wounded were rushed in. Sade watched in shock, unable to comprehend the instant chaos. Within minutes the ward had swelled from just one room to encompass the hall, corridor and veranda. There was no way the small, ill equipped medical team could cope.

'Nurse!' a woman shouted at Sade.

She turned to see a market woman struggling to carry a little girl, while a baby screamed out on her back.

'I beg you!' the woman shouted in panic. 'My child!'

The little girl lay still in her mother's arms. Sade looked around for help but all the nurses were busy. She took the child and lay her down on the concrete floor.

'What happened to her?' asked Sade trying to feel for a pulse.

'People were running,' the woman cried. 'They push her and mash her with their leg.'

Sade rushed off to look for Becky. She found her on the veranda attending to a middle aged woman. The woman was awash with blood and screaming in agony.

'There's a little girl in there that's been trampled,' Sade told her, 'She's unconscious and I don't know what to do.'

'Get Grace!' Becky responded impatiently.

Sade rushed back onto the ward looking for Grace. Grace was attending to a woman with a severed leg. Ndali was helping Grace but Sade pulled Ndali away.

'Come over here quickly,' she insisted, her voice almost breaking.

Sade led her to the little girl.

'Do you know what to do? She's been trampled.'

Ndali felt for a pulse. She had no stethoscope to check for a heart beat.

'She's dead!' said Ndali, hurrying back to Grace.

The girl's mother walked to and fro hitting her own head before returning to shake her daughter's body. She refused to accept that her child was dead. Sade was trembling in shock. She felt the woman's pain and loathed the devilish people that created and supplied the weapons. The people that grew fat on blood money. They did not have to see the dying children and wailing mothers. They did not have to look into the faces of the victims and explain why. They remained devoid of all responsibility and accountability, immune from prosecution. Here in Biafra it was the innocent that were the victims, not the men in power.

The woman persisted, shaking the body of her child. Sade felt sick and rushed out of the congested ward. She ran out of the hospital and onto the road outside. The road was littered with discarded shoes from panic stricken victims. Still there were children crying amongst the bodies on the roads, desperately searching for their parents. The bodies had been strafed. Sade flagged down a taxi. They passed a house that had been completely gutted by a bomb. A little girl was being dug out alive from beneath the rubble and in front of the house a car was ablaze. The bloodied body of a man hung out of the front seat. People rushed to and fro, throwing buckets of sand into the flames. Sand made available by a bomb crater at the side of the road. There were severed bodies scattered everywhere with entrails hanging out and limbs blown yards from their owners. A white reverend father walked about in obvious shock. He made the sign of the cross over the dead, stumbling about in confusion.

The taxi pulled up outside the Eze's house and Sade rushed out. Running into the house, she found Saul in the kitchen, wrapped on Mama's back.

'Let me have him,' Sade cried, taking him off her back.

'Where Emeka?' asked Mama, staring at Sade in panic.

'He's at the hospital,' Sade cried as she made her way to the dining room. With Saul in her arms she sat down crying uncontrollably. The taxi driver stood by the front door demanding his money.

'You no pay am?' Mama asked Sade.

'I had no money,' she sighed deeply.

Mama paid the taxi driver and sat with Sade.

'Make you no cry, my pickin!' she repeated, rubbing her back. 'Make you no cry!'

THIRTY

SADE WAS WAKEN by Emeka. Without words he demanded his marital rights, clinging like a leopard, heavy and exhausting. Eventually he got up wrapping a towel around his waist and setting off for the bathroom. Sade lay in bed watching the rising sun. Life for her had lost all meaning and purpose. She thought of all the sacrifices she had made. As the tears rolled down her cheeks, Emeka returned from the bathroom.

'What's the matter with you?' he demanded.

'I can't take any more. Please let me go home.'

Emeka sat down on the bed next to her.

'I know what you're going through. When the war is over, things will be different.'

'This war will never be over,' Sade sobbed.

'What do you mean? Didn't you hear the news? The Biafran troops have occupied the Mid-western State. They will soon be in Lagos. Once we take the capital, we have won the war.'

'If the Biafrans have taken the Mid-west, the roads to Benin will be clear. I beg you. Let me go home.'

Emeka jumped off the bed, his moment of patience gone. 'This is your home!' he scolded. 'The sooner you get that into your fat head the better.'

Slinging off his towel, he got dressed and went to work. Sade tried to console herself with the news that the war would soon be over.

In the afternoon, Emeka returned home with Boniface. The

men appeared very excited about something. Soon after Dr and Mrs Amadi arrived and Sade went to join them on the balcony.

'I heard the Nigerian Head of State attempted to flee the country in his private jet!' Dr Amadi announced. 'The bloody coward! I wonder where he was running to?'

'To the North of course.' laughed Boniface. 'When there is trouble every rat will find its hole. It was only the intervention of the British High Commissioner and American Ambassador that persuaded him to stay.'

'As if they have not created enough chaos in Africa!' declared Emeka.

'It's most unfortunate,' said Boniface sadly. 'For had he fled the war would be over by now.'

'If only these bloody Europeans will stop interfering in our affairs,' said Dr Amadi, averting his eyes from Becky. 'Can the Nigerian High Commissioner in London order the Queen to shoot the Irish for demanding their independence? What God given right do they think they have to control us?'

'Well, all is not lost,' said Boniface. 'We did not want the Mid-western region in the first place. So our withdrawal is of little consequence.'

Sade suddenly realised what all the excitement was about. Emeka's prediction was wrong. The war was not going to be over in a matter of weeks and the capital was not going to fall. Her eyes filled up with tears.

'Are you allright?' asked Becky placing her hand on Sade's knee. Sade nodded and quickly composed herself. 'When can we expect you back at the hospital?' Becky asked.

'I can't go back. All I want is to get away from this place.'

'I don't blame you,' said Becky dragging at her cigarette. 'I'm flying out with the children next month.'

Sade's heart skipped a beat.

'But Emeka said there were no flights.'

'It's a private flight to Dahomey. We'll have to get another flight from Dahomey to London. The important thing is to get out of Biafra. Why don't you come with us? Perhaps you could fly from Dahomey to your parents in Nigeria. I hear Lagos is quite untouched by the war.'

'She's not going anywhere,' Emeka interrupted. 'Her place is with her husband.'

Becky looked embarrassed and the men fell silent. In despair Sade stared down the driveway. A ragged looking woman with three men approached the house.

'Obi!' someone screamed downstairs.

'It's my sister!' cried Emeka jumping off his seat and rushing downstairs.

Sade followed. There was pandemonium as Mama Obi rushed outside with all the children. Obi and the men were led into the dining room. The two week trip through the bush had sent Obi into premature labour but her tears were for Sarah.

'They are killing all Ibos. They will kill her,' Obi cried. 'We have been trying to console her,' said one of the men whom Sade identified as Joseph, Mrs Udochi's houseboy. 'The child's father is Bini so she will be safe with him. And they are not killing small children.'

'We should have brought her,' Obi cried.

'Sarah could not have survived the trek through the bush,' said Joseph. His voice was pleading.

'Clive's mother will take care of her,' said Sade.

'I know,' said Obi. 'But she will miss me. She was crying when we left.'

'Have the Federal troops retaken Benin?' Sade asked Joseph.

'Yes Madam!'

'Were many people killed?' asked Sade staring at Joseph in panic.

'It could have been worse,' Joseph shrugged. 'The Biafran troops had already withdrawn long before their advance. So there was no fighting. But when the Federal troops came into the City, they came in shooting down everything that moved. The main roads were covered with bodies.'

'What of my parents?' Sade cried, looking anxiously at Obi.

'I didn't see them. But if anything had happened to them, we would have heard.'

'But why didn't you stay in Benin until things calmed down?' asked Sade.

'Some of your people were collaborating with the Federal troops, identifying Ibos amongst them,' Obi responded, her voice full of hatred. 'Clive hid me in the roof, with bats and lizards.' Obi began to cry again. 'When they started rounding up all the Ibos in Benin, Clive decided I should flee with Joseph. We heard that one Nigerian commander had given orders for the execution of every Ibo male over the age of ten. We did not know what would happen to the women that were rounded up, but I heard some of them were raped.'

'What of Innocent and Patience?' Sade asked.

'I don't know,' cried Obi doubling up in agony.

'Take her to hospital–now.' Mama Obi pleaded with Emeka.

'There's no point,' he responded. 'There are no drugs and the beds are full.' Emeka turned to Sade. 'Help me get her upstairs,' he ordered.

Obi's condition appeared to be deteriorating fast. They almost had to carry her up to her mother's bedroom where she collapsed onto the bed. Sade watched as Emeka examined his sister. He looked very anxious and concerned. It was going to be a breech birth and most of his surgical equipment was at the hospital. Unable to cope with Obi's screaming, Sade left the room to attend to Saul. She collected him from one of the housegirls and sat alone in the dining room, feeding him. Obi's screams persisted. Suddenly Mama Obi started shouting and there was a rapid shuffling of feet coming down the stairs. With Saul in her arms, Sade got up to see what was going on. Emeka and Mama Obi were struggling to get Obi back downstairs. Obi was haemorrhaging, her clothes saturated

212

with blood. Emeka was in a terrible state.

'Open the door!' he shouted at Sade who instantly obeyed.

They bundled Obi into the back seat of the car and Emeka sped off to the hospital.

Sade went upstairs to her bedroom. The children were all asleep and the house seemed abnormally still. After she had changed Saul, she placed him in his cot. She heard a car pull up in the driveway and was followed by the sound of wailing. Unwilling to accept what she already knew, Sade rushed downstairs. Emeka was leaning against the dining room door.

'What is it?' she demanded. The tears that rolled down his face sent her cold.

'Obi is gone!' he replied turning away hopelessly.

Sade collapsed in tears. She had never really wanted Obi to die. She cried even harder as she pictured Obi's body dumped against some blood soaked wall in the mortuary.

The following morning Obi was laid to rest in the graveyard of the Roman Catholic church.

THIRTY-ONE

FROM THE KITCHEN window, Sade looked out onto the back yard. One of the house girls knelt over a large flat stone grinding pepper. As she moved to and fro, her ebony body glistened under the mid-day sun. Still the children played, the cock crowed, the goats mated and the hens laid their eggs. Life carried on regardless of death.

Mama walked past the kitchen and saw Sade standing there, staring into space. She did not like it.

'Come! Follow me go market,' she ordered.

Bogart announced that there was no petrol in the car because the driver had wasted the little petrol left by driving around looking for petrol. After insulting the driver, Mama gave Sade a large umbrella to shade herself from the sun. With Saul wrapped securely on her back Sade set off with Mama and Bogart.

Half an hour later they arrived at the market and Mama began to bargain with the malnourished women sitting next to virtually empty trays. Luckily she had bought two sacks of salt before the Nigerian blockade because now salt was worth its weight in gold. 'Come buy!' one old man pleaded.

Displayed on his wooden slab were lizards, frogs and a large bush rat.

Sade followed Mama's determined step. Kwashiorkor children gathered around them begging for money. Sade felt sick and thought she was going the pass out in the heat.

'I'm taking Saul home,' she told Mama.

'Wait now!' Mama insisted staring at Sade in confusion.

'I haven't fed him! I'm going home.'

Sade set off on the return journey. Halfway to the house Bogart came running after her.

'Mama said I should tell you to start cooking the soup,' he panted, walking alongside her.

'Go back to help Mama carry the shopping,' Sade insisted.

'She said I should send the driver,' he replied, dropping his head in embarrassment. Sade realised that he had really been sent to guard her.

Emeka returned home to find Sade in the bedroom with Saul. He sat down on the bed.

'I was told that you abandoned Mama in the market!'

'I came home to feed Saul. And apart from that I could see no point in walking around the market when I have no money.'

'If you want money you should be prepared to work for it,' Emeka sighed.

Sade realised his ploy. Obviously Mama was tired of playing the prison warden and wanted her to return to work at the hospital.

'If only my father knew the way I am being treated!' she cried. 'You think because you paid him dowry you can keep me here as your slave. Once I tell him how you've beaten me, he will return your dowry to you.'

'Please shut up! I have headache,' Emeka responded, tossing himself backwards on the bed.

'What married woman do you see going to the market with no money? I'm treated worse than a housegirl!'

'Get me a bucket!' Emeka ordered.

Ignoring his request Sade persisted.

'Never in my life have I been without money.'

Suddenly, Emeka reached over the side of the bed and was sick. Sade stared in rage.

'So why couldn't you go to the bathroom?' she scolded. 'You

know that there's no disinfectant. Supposing Saul catches something.'

Emeka tensed up.

'Now the room bloody stinks!' said Sade grabbing Saul from his cot and storming out of the room. She made her way downstairs. In the back yard she found the housegirl and sent her to clean up the mess.

Darkness fell and Emeka's condition continued to worsen. He was sweating abnormally and sank into delirium. For two days and nights Sade sat at his bedside. She wondered what would happen to her if he died. Emeka was not important enough to expect an escort into the next world. She thought of Baby. Every time she had brought up the subject of her disappearance Emeka had responded sternly. He wondered why she was so concerned about Baby. Mama Emeka had told her that Baby returned to her people. If Emeka died, would Mama allow her to return to her people? At the back of her mind there was always the possibility that Baby might have escorted the Eze to the other world.

On the third night, Emeka tossed and turned violently, his perspiration soaking the bed. Sitting by his bedside Sade watched the shadows caste over his sleeping body, by the flickering candle. Suddenly, Emeka sprang up in bed.

'They are trying to kill me! No! No! No! They are trying to kill me!' he shouted in wild panic.

The bedroom door was flung open and Sade jumped off her seat. Mama stood by the doorway looking like a ghost in the night.

'No! No! No! They are trying to kill me!' Emeka persisted.

'Who want to kill you?' asked Mama staring at Sade accusingly.

'It's the fever!' said Sade reaching for a wet flannel to wipe the sweat off his face.

'Look! Look there!' shouted Emeka as he pointed to the end of his bed. 'He has a dagger! He has stabbed me!' Emeka collapsed back onto his pillow.

Sade recalled her sacrifices to the god of the sea. Could the god have sent this spirit to kill Emeka? But she had not asked the god to kill him. It was Emeka's spirit that said it was not going to stay long in this world. And now she would get the blame and stand accused of witchcraft. She began to cry. If Emeka died she would be killed too!

'No cry,' advised Mama. 'They no fit kill am.'

Sade sat next to Emeka, urging him to sit up and drink some water. She held the glass to his lips and he drank eagerly. When he had finished he suddenly grabbed her arm.

'Darling!' He was sober. 'If I should die…!'

'You are not going to die,' cried Sade trying to pull away from him.

'Listen to me!' he insisted. 'If I should die, I want you to stay here with Mama.'

'No!'

'Yes! You must stay here. I want my son to know he is an Ibo man.'

Was Emeka such a fool? Did he not know how desperately she longed to return to her people? Could he not see that Saul was too fair to be his child? Too fair to be an Ibo man?

'He's not going to die,' cried Sade as she looked up at the old woman's face.

Mama left the room, returning moments later with a bottle of native medicine and her cane. She forced Emeka to drink the bitter concoction before she settled down at his bedside. While Mama whipped the spirits and prayed, Sade attempted to reduce his temperature by persuading him to drink water. By the morning, Emeka was weak but without fever. Sade felt exhausted but relieved that he would survive.

THIRTY-TWO

CHRISTMAS DAY ARRIVED without ceremony. There were no Christmas decorations or presents for the children. Sade felt very sad. In the coolness of the morning she took the children into the garden to pick greens. It was a beautiful day with clear blue skies and the air was heavy with the dust of the harmattan. The children were playing, joking and teasing each another, while Saul toddled about. Kechi and Ezinma ran after him checking on everything he bent down to pick up. The driver helped the children by climbing the trees to pick the fruit.

Suddenly there was the sound of an aircraft and from the top of the mango tree, the driver began to shout.

'Nah bomb-oh! Take cover-oh! Take cover-oh!'

After witnessing several bombing raids the driver was rather paranoid. He had often said that the safest place was up a tree since 'they no dey bomb tree'. He always refused to go into the bunkers because he had seen many people buried alive when the walls collapsed.

As two MiG 17 fighters and one Ilyushin bomber came slicing through the sky, the children screamed in panic, abandoning the leaves and unripe fruit they had collected. Sade snatched Saul off the ground whilst grabbing Ezinma's hand. They all ran to the house for cover, collapsing on the dining room floor. The onslaught appeared to go on for ever. The house shook and the glass in the windows shattered.

'They are targeting the house,' shouted Bogart getting to his feet. His face was full of confusion and panic. 'Let's run to the bunker!'

The younger children screamed in protest. They were too terrified to run back outside. Bogart set off with Kennedy, followed by Sade, Saul and Ezinma. The brothers were halfway through the long garden, when one of the MiGs screeched across the garden strafing them. Sade dived for cover, pulling Ezinma down, while shielding Saul with her own body. When the air cleared the two boys were still lying on the ground. Sade and the children rushed to meet them. There was blood everywhere. She screamed as the sirens went off again. Emeka and the rest of family ran out to meet her. Mama Obi grabbing the blood-covered body of her son Bogart, while Mama Emeka flung herself over the body of Kennedy. The whole family cried. Later on Emeka arranged for the bodies to be wrapped in raffia mats and carried to the churchyard. The church was now in ruins. There the men dug a grave next to Obi and her stillborn child. After a brief prayer the bodies were lowered into the ground. Watching the heavy earth thrown down on the bodies, Sade knew that her escape was now critical.

The following afternoon Boniface arrived in an army Landrover. He was to take Emeka to Uli Airport where they had arranged to collect medical supplies for the hospital. Sade was aware that Uli was the only link left with the outside world, and so insisted on following the men. She knew that it was from Uli that Becky had escaped with her three children.

They eventually set off with Sade sitting between the men in the front seat. The potholed roads stank of death and there were roadblocks every few miles. The abandoned farms were covered in sharp stakes ready to receive any attempted parachute landings by the Nigerian army. Dried out palm leaves camouflaged the existence of every house from the sky.

After about an hour they arrived at the airstrip and a gang of heavily armed soldiers approached them. The loss of Uli Airport would have been a devastating blow to Biafra, so security was extremely tight. Recognising Boniface they were allowed to wait for the arrival of the relief plane. Boniface parked next to the dozens of Red Cross Landrovers, their newness contrasting sharply with the row of old mammy wagons.

Staring ahead she realised that the landing strip had been covered with thick leafy branches.

'These white people are wonderful!' said Boniface, his face glowing in admiration. 'Do you know they even flew in their own fuel.'

'It all boils down to one thing,' Emeka responded sternly. 'The Bible in one hand and the gun in the other. 'They are nothing but a bunch of hypocrites. Do you know how much money Britain is making by supplying Nigeria with the weapons to kill us? If they stopped supplying the weapons we would not need their so called relief supplies.'

'That is true!' said Boniface thinking deeply. 'But still we should be grateful. They do not need to help us.'

Emeka scoffed.

'Help us! Do you really believe they want to help us? They are killing us. Just as they did to the indigenous people in America, Australia and New Zealand. The only difference now is that they are supplying our brothers with the weapons, to do the job for them. This so called relief is no more than a propaganda exercise! Apart from that, it is an excellent opportunity for them to monitor the progress of the war.'

Sade sighed deeply. Surely Emeka was becoming irrational.

'If they genuinely want to stop our suffering,' Emeka persisted, 'these so called relief workers don't need to come here. All they need to do is pressurise their governments to stop shipping arms. People know these weapons are not used for ornamental purposes!'

The mosquitoes buzzed, hovered and landed, attacking their victims with a vengeance, and the three constantly slapped and scratched their legs and arms.

'Colonisation!' hissed Emeka in disgust. 'The Queen of England has made us second class citizens in our own land.'

Sade recalled a placard she had seen in one of the many demonstrations: QUEEN ELIZABETH MOTHER OF GENOCIDE. She read without understanding the relationship between a far away Queen and the woes of Biafra.

'The vast majority of our people are excluded from education and government. Here in Africa! And why? Because they are unable to communicate in the language of their former colonial masters.'

Emeka rambled on and Sade tried to study her surroundings. Apart from the relief personnel and military there were no private operators advertising at the airstrip.

Once darkness fell there was frantic activity everywhere. Soldiers began to clear the landing strip. Surprisingly it was no more that a stretch of road surrounded by bush. There was the sound of an aeroplane engine high in the sky. As the plane approached the noise grew louder and louder. Suddenly the landing lights went on and a Hercules freighter touched down on the runway.

Leaving Sade in the Landrover, the two men jumped out and disappeared into the darkness. Sade felt afraid being on her own in such a sensitive area but glad she had made the trip. She knew that if she remained at home she would never make the necessary contacts. She had to return to work at the hospital. Perhaps Dr Amadi would tell her how he got Becky and the children out.

After a very long wait the men returned accompanied by soldiers carrying boxes of medicine. One of their friends in the Air Force had supplied them with gin, brandy and whisky brought in from Portugal. After loading the provisions in the back, they anxiously set off for the return journey to Umuahia.

THIRTY-THREE

EMEKA RETURNED FROM work to find Sade playing with Saul on Mama's bed. Saul was now a bonny little toddler with soft wavy black hair. On seeing his father, he jigged and reached out his arms. Emeka picked him up and tossed him into the air. In Emeka's dark hands the child appeared almost white. The difference was striking. Luckily no one had questioned the fact, attributing his light complexion to his white grandmother.

Emeka put Saul on the floor and he toddled off. He approached a basin of rain water from the leaking roof and Mama grabbed his arm. He threw himself on the floor, crying and kicking to break free. Mama picked him up and swung him under her arm and onto her back where she tied him securely. The old woman had lost so much weight that the skin on her arms now hung down like empty sacks.

Emeka looked at his watch and reached for the transistor radio. He tuned into the BBC World Service and an English voice filled the air. The music indicated that the news was about to follow. They listened anxiously. There was to be yet another 'final offensive' into the Ibo heartland and Umuahia was to be captured as a wedding present for the Nigerian Head of State.

'Which kind wedding present be dat?' demanded Mama enraged. 'Nah God go punish dem!'

Umuahia was already a scene of devastation and the Nigerian air raids had become a daily occurrence. Many of the

222

inhabitants had already fled their homes to the relative safety of remote villages, but there was no safe haven.

Suddenly there were excited voices coming from downstairs. Chukwuma had returned home from the front line and the family gathered around to welcome him and hear the latest news.

Chukwuma was obviously in a great deal of pain. His feet were in dirty bandages and only the sign of the rising sun remained intact on his dirty and tattered uniform.

'What do your leg?' demanded Mama.

'Nah bottle Mama!'

'Bottle?' Emeka puzzled.

'The enemy knew we were fighting with bare feet so they scattered broken bottles around their positions,' said Chukwuma, falling backwards to lean against the front door. Placing an arm on Jude's shoulder, Chukwuma struggled into the dining room where he sat down. Emeka, Mama Emeka, Sade and Mama Obi sat at the table with him, while the children stood against the walls.

'Didn't they treat your feet properly?' asked Emeka.

'Not really! There's still glass in my soles.'

'So what's our position?' Emeka asked anxiously.

'Brother! The situation is acute,' Chukwuma shook his head. 'It's only the equipment we capture from the enemy that we are able to fight with. Our men are fighting in the boots and clothing taken from the dead. We have no ammunition and for days we have been fighting without food.'

'They no give you chop?' asked Mama Emeka looking shocked.

'Believe me Mama. For seven whole days, I have not eaten.'

Mama immediately set off for the kitchen. She instructed Jude to collect a bowl of hot water so that Chukwuma could soak his feet.

'But what of the Research and Production Board?' Emeka asked as Mama left.

'They have been able to supply locally made foot cutters, ogbunigwes, grenades and various sorts of mines. But the locally produced weapons are not enough. Our situation is desperate.' Chukwuma paused. 'Brother! We have lost Onitsha!'

There was a frantic look on Emeka's face.

'Now the enemy is bringing troops into Biafra across the river Niger,' Chuks continued. 'Believe me Brother! Our men have done their best. Against all odds we fought to hold Onitsha. On several occasions the Nigerians attempted to cross the Niger but we sank their boats. The Nigerians suffered heavy losses. As a result they had to abandon further attempts at crossing the Niger by boat. In the end they marched their soldiers northwards to take Onitsha from a landward approach. Our militia men were alert and warned us well in advance. They reported their war cry, "Anicha sosai!". This means "Destination Onitsha!". To take Onitsha, they had to march 68 miles. We tried everything to hold them back. Our troops laid mines, rockets and ogbunigwes. They felled trees to block the roads and laid traps for the armoured vehicles. Unfortunately we were fighting a losing battle. We did not realise they were advancing with a force stronger than the whole Biafran army put together. They had a convoy of heavy road construction equipment for clearing blockades and rebuilding bridges. The enemy was equipped to fight indefinitely without re-supplies. And us? We could not even last one day without supplies.'

'So the road to Umuahia is wide open!' Emeka was in despair. He placed his elbows on the table, supporting his head in his hand.

'Our men are not making it easy for them,' said Chukwuma adamantly. 'The roads are littered with their bodies as well as our own. And we successfully eliminated the vast majority of Mohammed's Division, of around 20,000 men. They have to fight for every inch of ground.'

Jude returned with a bowl of hot water for Chukwuma's feet and Emeka ordered the child to take off the bandages. Jude knelt down and began to undo the strips of cloth, but Chukwuma tensed up in agony. The dried blood had caused the bandages to stick to the wounds. Chukwuma screwed up his face and Emeka cracked.

'Leave it!' Emeka scolded Jude before ordering all the children out of the room.

'Just soak your feet like that!' Emeka ordered Chukwuma. 'It will make the bandages easier to remove.'

Mama Emeka returned with a sparse meal of boiled stockfish in cassava leaf soup and semolina. She placed a small bowl of water on the table where Chukwuma washed his hands. Eagerly he reached for the glass of water Mama had provided, gulping it down in seconds. Taking a handful of the semolina, he rolled it into a ball before dipping it into the watery soup. The stockfish was tough and occasionally he had to remove the fibres which became stuck in his teeth.

'What of Roosevelt?' Mama Obi enquired.

Chukwuma glanced at her and stopped eating. Chukwuma put his head into his hands.

'Answer now!' Emeka demanded. 'What of Roosevelt?'

'He was killed in shelling.' Chukwuma cried.

'Roosevelt?' cried Mama Obi leaping to her feet. She stared at Chukwuma in disbelief. 'My Roosevelt? Why? I told him not to go!'

Chukwuma struggled to walk to the car and Emeka drove him to the hospital where the glass could be removed from his feet. There was no anaesthetic to numb the pain but at least the rest of the family could be spared his screams.

The worst part about Roosevelt's death was that he had not even received a Christian prayer at his burial. His body was dumped on the mounting pile of Ibo dead. The blood of the Ibos moved down from North to South and from West to Eastern Nigeria.

THIRTY-FOUR

SADE LAY AWAKE in the darkness, unable to sleep owing to Mama Obi's crying. The family was shrinking fast. Sade knew that if they did not find a means of escape, they would all perish. Now that the Nigerians had established a strong foothold in Biafran territory, there was little to stop their ruthless advance.

Emeka returned home late that night, but Sade was waiting up for him.

'You have to get the family out of here,' she told him. 'Can't you see we don't stand a chance? The air raids are getting worse and you heard Chukwuma. The Nigerians are armed to the teeth.'

'Shut up!' Emeka snapped, now tense and exhausted. 'Just leave me alone.'

'Please! I don't want to quarrel with you. Just tell me what your plans are.'

Emeka sat down on the bed looking defeated.

'Boniface will keep me informed.'

Sade knew that putting additional pressure on Emeka would only make him aggressive.

'I've been thinking about returning to my job in the hospital.'

Emeka glanced up at her. 'Grace is now in charge of casualty. You won't be able to work with her.'

'There must be something I can do?'

'If you're serious, you can assist me.'

The following morning, Emeka escorted Sade on to the male

surgical ward. It was heavily overcrowded with wounded army officers and infantry men. The ward possessed a strong sickly stench, which Sade was now able to identify as gangrened flesh. Most of the dirty, verminous men brought in had the most hideous wounds and many suffered from shell shock. As though hypnotised, they stared blankly into space.

Walking down the ward, one soldier continually cried out. He was in agonising pain, from a leg that no longer existed. Emeka tried to convince him that it was not possible to feel pain in a limb that had been amputated, but to him the pain was real and unbearable. The rest of the groaning and delirious men almost all suffered from malaria. Unfortunately the hospital had run out of quinine to treat them. The men continued their battle, against the flies that plagued the wards all day and the mosquitoes that attacked at night.

Emeka and the rest of the medical team worked with a vengeance in the humid, intense heat. Sade grew to respect and admire him for his strength and determination. For days he worked without sleep. On the other hand, the relief workers, who appeared to be using the war zone as a training ground, were replaced on a regular basis.

One morning a soldier was brought in on a makeshift stretcher. He was almost delirious with fever and moaning in agony. Two tree branches had been roughly tied around his leg, and the stench was nauseating.

'Come here!' Emeka ordered Sade, bending over a bed as he examined the patient. The leg was swollen, inflamed and full of pus.

'We have to amputate immediately.'

'But there's no more chloroform,' Sade responded, not wishing to be a party to such cruelty.

'So what's new?' Emeka sighed. 'If we do not operate he will die.'

'If you do operate he will die,' said Sade, recalling the last patient to lose his leg.

'And when did you become a doctor?' Emeka scolded.

She pouted. The illiterate soldier moaned in agony. He did not know the meaning of amputation, and he did not care. All he wanted was for the doctor to stop his pain.

'At least the operation will give him a chance,' Emeka spoke aloud to himself.

Reluctantly, Sade joined the masked medical team in the operating theatre. Emeka ordered her to hold a basin of surgical equipment, while four men held the patient down on his stomach. Emeka wiped the sweat from his forehead on the sleeve of his white cotton coat. Suddenly and rapidly, he sliced into the mortified flesh. The soldier screamed, struggling to break free. Sade watched the stars encircling her, then there was blackness. Time went by without her knowing, until she found herself on the floor. One of the male nurses was trying to revive her. The patient was still howling uncontrollably and Sade hurried out of the theatre.

Sitting on the veranda, a trickle of blood ran down her face from a cut to her forehead. At the far end of the compound, hundreds of women queued, with babies wrapped to their backs. Under the mid-day sun, they waited for the distribution of powdered milk.

Sade stood up, and walked over to casualty. She found Grace sitting in the office.

'Good afternoon!' Sade greeted.

'Good afternoon.' Grace responded, with an air of contempt. 'What happened to your head?'

'I fainted.'

'Maybe you're pregnant?' Grace lent back authoritatively in her seat and folded her arms.

Sade sat down on the opposite side of the desk. She felt sickened by the realisation. 'Please let me have some water.' she gasped.

Reaching for a glass, she poured Sade some water.

'Is Dr Amadi about?' asked Sade.

'He's gone to join his wife in England.'

Sade was close to tears. She was however determined not to break down in front of Grace. She recalled her last escape attempt and the bearded stranger. Perhaps he could help!

'Please lend me some money. I'm not feeling well at all and my husband is in the operating theatre.'

'I have no money!' Grace shrugged.

'Please! I'll give it back to you tomorrow. I just need enough to get a taxi.'

Grace hesitated before reaching for her handbag. She gave Sade enough change for her to get a taxi home.

Sade arrived back to find the house empty. Expecting the routine bombing raids, Mama and the children were taking shelter in the bunker. Sade hurried upstairs. In the bedroom she pulled out the bottom draw of the chest. To her surprise she found a bundle of letters. She took them out before feeling about for the stranger's card. To her relief it was still there. Flicking through the pile of letters, she found two envelopes with the sign of the Red Cross. They were addressed to Mrs Sade Nzeogwu (that was her!) c/o Dr Emeka Nzeogwu, 52 Nzeogwu Road, Umuahia. She was Mrs Sade Nzeogwu so they had to be her letters. But what were they doing on the floor beneath the draws? Emeka must have hidden them there!

She removed her letters from the pile. They had been opened. Her hands were trembling as she removed one letter from the envelope. It was from her mother. Hardly able to concentrate she read the date. The 3rd of October 1967. She must have written immediately after the Biafran withdrawal from Benin. That was six months ago. Quickly she began to read.

Dear Sade,

Your father and I have been worried sick about you. We have written about twenty letters to you, and had no reply. Please reply this letter through the Red Cross. Just let us know you are well. Sister Philomena introduced me to a man working with the Red Cross, called Mr Williams, and after explaining your situation, he agreed to get this letter delivered to you. He said you should contact a Mr David Cole in Umuahia. Mr Cole will help you get out. You are still registered under my British passport which was issued in London, in 1950. The passport number is ZN 415. It was issued under my married name, of Mrs Susan Uwaifo. My maiden name is Smith. My address at the time was 12, Glover Road, Clapham, London. I hope this information will be of use to you. I am enclosing fifty pounds sterling, which your father was able to change on the black market...

Sade returned to the envelope but the money was gone. She emptied out the second envelope to find just another letter. She cried in fury, struggling to read on.

Clive received Emeka's letter which had been posted from Nigeria. He must have given the letter to someone leaving Biafra to post. The news it contained came as a terrible shock. Clive sent Obi back to the East thinking she would be safe there. It is so sad for Sarah who is growing into a beautiful little girl.

I worry about you all the time. The news about Biafra is horrific. You must get out. Life in Benin is far from being peaceful but you will be safe here. We also experienced bombing raids by the Nigerians, while the Biafrans were in occupation, and when the Federal troops re-took Benin, they set up road blocks searching for Ibos. One evening the night watchman told me that the villagers had sent him to meet me. They wanted money or threatened to report me for hiding Ibos. Innocent and Patience had been hiding in the bush for weeks. I had been sending the Cook with food to them. Luckily I told him that they were no longer with me, or I would have been blackmailed forever. Your father decided that they had to leave. I just hope they arrived back in the East.

Food is now very scarce. Luckily when the war began, I went shopping and bought in bulk. I purchased salt, flour, rice, oil, margarine, and sugar. The large farm at the side of the house has proven to be a Godsend. The tomatoes we harvested six months ago I preserved and still use them for stews. We had such a large harvest that I even ended up making tomato jam. I think your father is a bit sick of the tomatoes now. We also live off the fruit trees as they come into season and we are eagerly awaiting the corn harvest.

It is impossible to buy bread now, so I make our own. The kneading is hard work, but with the help of the cook, we have fresh bread twice a week.

The relief food donated by various European organisations is now on sale in the market. A few men who knew the right people were able to obtain large quantities which they are now selling at exorbitant prices. One of the men has even built a mansion with his profits from selling American relief agency rice. I suppose it is better to pay for it than not to have any at all. As your father says, 'monkey dey work, baboon dey chop' [Monkey works for the baboon to eat].

There are now just a handful of Europeans left in Benin, mostly from the Roman Catholic church. Mr and Mrs Udochi left for London with Clive, Sophia, Marilyn and Sarah. Sophia and Marilyn are to continue their education in England whilst Clive and his parents hope to find work.

Please write back immediately and let us know if you need any help.

All our love,
Mum and Dad.

Without hesitation, Sade picked up the second letter which was also from her mother.

231

My Dear Sade,

I can't understand why you have not replied my letters. Don't you realise what you are putting me through? I do not know how to tell you this, but I must. Your father was arrested by the military governor for allegedly attending a meeting with the rebels. The conditions in the jail were terrible but I managed to get food to him every day. We were later informed that he had died of a heart attack. His body was released for burial only after desperate appeals by the family. It looked as though he had been tortured. We laid him to rest in the Roman Catholic churchyard.

Sade collapsed in tears, struggling to comport herself as she continued to read.

Circumstances have changed so drastically within such a short space of time. It all seems like a nightmare. At your father's burial three women came forward, claiming they had children for him. One of the women had three boys, another two boys and the third one a daughter. It would appear that your uncles knew about their existence, but left me in the dark.

Recalling Idowu's utterances Sade was overcome with guilt. She should have been loyal enough to inform her mother. Sobbing desperately, she continued to read.

I know your father wrote a will, because he showed it to me. I have searched everywhere and asked everyone, but no one claims to know anything about it. Before he died, he told me that he had given a copy to your Uncle Samuel, but he knows nothing about it. Your father's so called first son is now twenty-three years old, and has claimed the property under native law and custom. The three boys from his so called first wife arrived to occupy the house. When I protested my clothes were thrown out onto the driveway. The two sons from the second woman occupied your father's bungalow and like hyenas they are all fighting amongst themselves. After nineteen years of sacrifice, I am now destitute. I can't continue. I will be flying back to the UK next week. It might be easier to contact you from there.

All my love,
Mum.

Sade cried without relief. How could Emeka have opened and read such personal letters? How could he have kept such shocking news from her? She searched through every envelope and letter in the vain hope of finding the fifty pounds. The word 'Darling' at the top of one letter captured her attention, and she could hardly prevent herself from reading the letter.

'Since I left the hospital, I've been missing you badly. Frances gave me the money you sent. Thank you so much, I was penny-less at the time. How is Ironsi? I hope he is not giving you too many sleepless nights. You know what they say? The child that says his parents will not sleep, will not sleep either.

'Last weekend was fantastic. I will never know how you and Boniface manage to get so much booze for your parties. The answer to your question is Yes. I will meet you at Boniface's guest house on Saturday night. But make sure you don't stand me up again.'

Sade looked at the name at the end of the letter.

'Love and kisses,
Ndali'.

Ndali? The nurse at the hospital? Her guilt over Saul left her

233

in an instant. She was enraged. What right did Emeka have to possess and control her, when he could not control himself? Desperately, she wanted to confront him. At the same time, she could not understand her jealousy. Why should it suddenly upset her if Emeka took another woman to his bed? Had she really fallen in love with him?

Suddenly, the screeching noise of the Nigerian air force filled the air. Struck with panic and trembling wildly she threw the letters back in place. As fast as her legs could carry her, she ran downstairs. As she ran through the garden, one of the fighter bombers flew overhead. She lay flat on the wet ground, under a tree. The Ilyushin bomber was flying so low that she could clearly see a white man in the pilot's seat. Emeka had often told her about a white south African mercenary that nicknamed himself 'Genocide'. She wondered whether this could be the man. There had to be a place reserved for him in hell. Recalling how Kennedy and Bogart had been strafed on the ground, she again got to her feet, running quickly for the bunker. Urgently she lifted the zinc door. The family stared up at her in petrified silence.

'Ah Ah! I think say you follow Doctor go hospital,' Mama Emeka puzzled.

Panting and trembling, Sade climbed down the wooden ladder into the dullness of the earth. The family sat on concrete blocks. It had rained and the floor had become flooded. A bomb exploded somewhere nearby and the earth trembled. The children cried in contagious fear. Sade prayed that the cement walls would not collapse and bury them alive, but still the grave bunker offered greater protection than the houses.

Sade sat down next to Mama who was carrying Saul. Looking at her son, she saw Clive's face. She hated Clive and never wished to see him again. Yet there could be no escape from the past. She was united with him forever, in the form of Saul. She reached out to take him but he violently rejected her.

'What of Doctor?' Mama asked, looking gravely concerned.

'He's in the hospital. I fainted so he told he to return home.'

'Sorry-oh!' said Mama, looking at the cut on Sade's forehead.

Sade had grown to love and respect Mama for the strength that she found in times of crisis. She pitied her pain and anguish. She did not deserve this kind of life. She was too old to be running in panic down a hole in the ground. Suddenly it occurred to her how similar Emeka was to his mother. He too possessed that discipline and persistent determination to succeed. Now she could understand Emeka's obsession with duty and she knew that the fight was literally 'till the last man!'

Sade began to cry, burying her head on her lap. Mama scolded her for being so weak. Sade was unable to identify the greatest cause of her depression. Was she mourning for her father, or was she crying because of the way her mother had been treated? Was it self pity or rage over the deceit of her husband and father? Or was it just because of the injustice of the world?

'Wetin do you?' Mama demanded, as the smaller children watched her anxiously.

'I have pain,' Sade cried.

'Pain? For where?'

'In my head!'

'Ah Ah! You tell Doctor?'

Sade shook her head still sobbing bitterly.

'Auntie, don't cry!' pleaded Kechi who placed her tiny arm through Sade's.

Between her fits of tears Sade thought of Mr David Cole. Could he have left Umuahia? At least now she had her mother's passport details. She would find a way out of Biafra.

THIRTY-FIVE

SADE EMERGED FROM the darkness of the bunker with Saul sleeping in her tired arms. Mama struggled up behind her, her arthritic joints making her climb very painful. The hurricane lamp that she carried exposed the faces of frustration behind her, the children eager to be released from the family tomb. The bombing raids were over for the day and the warm night air smelt of death and burning. Although the Eze's house still remained standing there were bomb craters all over the garden. The cries in the darkness indicated that other families had not been so lucky.

The hungry children gathered around the candle lit dining table. Jude quarrelled constantly with Oyibo over the ownership of a spent hand grenade and Ezinma and Kechi quarrelled with Frances's three children over anything and everything. The children argued and squealed as the adults prepared their food. Eventually Mama Emeka found her cane, lashing out violently. As the children sobbed Mama sat by the dining room door tapping her cane on the floor.

In the kitchen, Sade put two scoops of powdered milk into each of eight plastic cups. She placed the cups on a tray. Even though she was now recognised as a fully fledged member of the family she yearned for the life that was over.

'Bring the milk now!' Mama Emeka bellowed as the children continued to cry. Mama's voice was near breaking and she sounded defeated.

After topping up the cups with cold water, Sade carried the

tray into the dining room, placing it on the table. Within seconds it was emptied. Naturally the children could not understand the reason behind their suffering but they could sense the fear from the adults. They knew that they were in danger and their faces were full of confusion.

Sade went outside where a makeshift kitchen had been erected. Vivian and Frances sat on cement blocks cooking on a wood fire. They were boiling the stockfish for the family supper.

'Is it ready?' Sade asked.

'It's too tough,' responded Vivian, testing the fish with a fork. 'And I left it to soak since morning.'

Frances threw in one chopped up pepper and some green leaves she had picked in the garden. Apart from a bit of salt the soup was complete.

The sisters began to discuss events at the 'cook house' where they worked. They were very proud of their contribution to the war effort.

'What do you do at the cook house anyway?' asked Sade.

'We purchase food stuffs, cook it, and take it to the soldiers on the front line.'

'We also feed refugees!' added Vivian.

'Have you ever taken food to the front line?' Sade asked Frances.

'Of course! Yesterday we carried food to my husband. He's in the front trenches near Ameke.'

'Where is that?' asked Sade.

'It's around six miles from here. We walked it.'

Sade felt sick with shock. Of course she had heard the shelling as part of the daily background noise, but it never occurred to her that she was now a mere walking distance away from the front line.

'Oh my God! How can you sit there so calmly when the fighting is just six miles away? What are we going to do?' she cried.

'They can never take Umuahia!' Frances responded confidently.

'That is what Emeka said about Onitsha and Enugu.'

'But this is the Capital. With our bolt action rifles and our ogbunigwes we will defeat them!' Frances said adamantly.

'Till the last man!' shouted Vivian throwing her arm up into the air in defiance.

Frances and Vivian began to sing one of the many front line songs.

Take my boots off when I die
Send my clothing to the camp
Give my gun to someone else
To fight for fatherland.

Suddenly Mama Emeka shouted from the house. 'You people should be there singing! The children are hungry, so stay there and be singing!'

Sade knew that Mama was not shouting because the children were hungry but because she was afraid of crumbling. Sade also knew that if Mama crumbled the whole family would collapse behind her.

After the children had eaten Mama sent them all upstairs to bed. In the near darkness the adults ate their meal. No one spoke. Sade picked at her food. She tried to swallow the semolina but it stuck to her throat like glue.

'I think we should take the children into the bush,' said Sade intruding on the silence. 'Maybe we can find a way to cross into the Cameroons.'

'Don't be stupid!' Frances scolded. 'You want us to take the children into the bush? What will they eat in the bush? At least in Umuahia the Red Cross will supply us with food.'

'We have to get out!' shouted Sade in frustration. 'When the Nigerians arrive, we will be raped and the children will be killed like goats.'

'Sha!' Mama scolded. 'No talk bad thing!' Mama's attitude was that if anyone mentioned such a disaster it could cause the disaster to happen.

Sade sighed in frustration.

'We have to watch and pray!' concluded Frances.

Sade could not bear the suspense any longer. She took Saul upstairs and tried to force him to sleep. He kicked and screamed for Mama, arching his back in defiance. Sade slapped him hard and he bawled. Eventually he fell asleep and Sade placed him down in his cot. The shelling had died down but she could not feel safe. She longed for Emeka to return from the hospital. With the fighting so close he was bound to do something.

Hours passed by and the rest of the family fell asleep. Sade paced the bedroom floor determined to remain awake. She was determined to confront Emeka.

Suddenly a car pulled up in the driveway and Sade rushed downstairs. It was Boniface wanting Emeka.

'He's still at the hospital,' Sade informed him. 'Why not wait for him?'

'No! I'll come back later,' replied Boniface walking back to his Landrover. Determined not to lose him, Sade followed. 'Boniface! Have you heard of a Mr David Cole working with the Red Cross?'

'Yes! Of course! He gave me the letters for you.'

Boniface was unsuspecting.

'He gave you the letters?' asked Sade.

'Yes! Didn't Emeka tell you? Mr Cole asked me how he could contact you because he had a letter for you from Nigeria. Naturally I told him I would make sure that you got the letter.'

'How can I contact Mr Cole?'

'Emeka knows him. Ask him to take you to the refugee camp where he works.'

'Please take me there. It's very important.'

'Now?' asked Boniface reluctantly.

'It would mean so much to me. Please!'

Boniface shrugged.

'Okay get in.'

Sade wanted to run upstairs to collect Saul but knew that would arouse too much suspicion. She jumped in to the passenger seat and they set off.

Umuahia looked as though a powerful hurricane had passed through, followed by a mighty earthquake. Obviously Umuahia was going to be the Nigerian Head of State's wedding present after all. Sade was determined that she and Saul would not be part of the gift of death. As they drove past a gutted building, she recalled the face of a child she had seen being dragged out alive from beneath the rubble. Feeling sick with anxiety, she stared ahead down the dark street illuminated only by the headlights of the Landrover. An unearthly calm hung over the town. Sade knew that it was the calm before the storm.

After about half an hour, Boniface turned off the road into the grounds of an old school. The headlights illuminated the Red Cross flag on the roof, demarcating it as a refugee camp. He stopped and they got out. They walked through the long rooms which were now free of desks and chairs, but overly burdened with desperately malnourished women and children. The helpless victims lay down on raffia mats with their few possessions on the floor beside them.

'Mr Cole!' Boniface suddenly shouted.

A European man looked up from the end of the room. In white shorts and long white socks he looked quite comical. On his shirt sleeve was the sign of the Red Cross and his head was covered by a beret. He could have passed for a boy scout master.

'Ah! Brigadier! I'm so glad to see you!' shouted Mr Cole. 'I'm in the process of organising volunteers to evacuate these people. I desperately need your help.'

Sade was determined to get attention.

'Good evening!' she said to Mr Cole who responded.

'This is Dr Nzeogwu's wife,' Boniface told him. 'You must remember him from the Queen Elizabeth Hospital.'

'Of course! And a very good doctor he is!' said Mr Cole sounding a bit patronising.

'You remember some time ago, you gave me a letter to deliver to Mrs Nzeogwu from Nigeria?'

'Yes! Of course!'

Sade knew this was her last chance to escape.

'I wonder if I may speak to you in private?' she asked.

Boniface appeared rather astounded.

'Well it's a bit difficult!' replied Mr Cole who appeared sensitive to Boniface's reaction.

'It's okay, I'll wait for you outside,' said Boniface heading back to the Landrover.

'What can I do for you?' Mr Cole asked Sade.

'I need your help,' she pleaded. 'My mother wrote to me asking me to contact you. I thought you would be aware of my situation?'

'I'm sorry! The letter came to me and I passed it on. That's all. What exactly do you want?'

'I need to get out of Biafra. My mother is now in London and I want to join her there.'

'Do you have a passport?'

'I was registered on my mother's British passport. I have the details.'

'So you are British?'

Sade hesitated. She did have English blood and she was registered on a British passport but she did not feel British. Neither did she feel Biafran or Nigerian.

Mr Cole continued.

'We might be able to help you but time is running out. Can you make your way to Uli Airport tonight?'

Sade's heart skipped a beat.

'I have no transport.'

'What of the Brigadier?'

She realised that there was no alternative but to confide in Mr Cole.

'I don't want Boniface or my husband to be told anything or I will be prevented from leaving. My husband has kept me in Biafra against my will. Please help me.' Sade began to cry.

'I'll see what I can do!' said Mr Cole. 'As you can see I'm very busy. We have to evacuate this camp tonight and we don't even have a place to go. You have caught me at a very bad time.'

Sade collapsed on her knees crying and pleading not to be dismissed. Mr Cole was obviously very embarrassed and irritated by her display.

'Can you leave immediately?' he demanded.

'Yes!' she cried, rising to her feet.

'Okay! Write down your address and I will send one of our drivers to pick you up.' He handed her a notebook and pen.

Thanking him, she quickly wrote down the address and drew a small map.

'You must be ready by midnight,' Mr Cole warned.

'I will be ready! Please tell the driver not to approach the house. I'll meet him outside on the road.'

Sade handed him back the notebook and he slipped it into his shirt pocket.

'Please don't forget.'

'I won't! Don't worry!' he said, patting her on the shoulder.

Impatiently, Boniface came to meet them.

'Mr Cole, I have to go,' he insisted, jumping into the Landrover.

Sade shook hands with Mr Cole, before hurrying into the Landrover.

'So what did you have to discuss that was so confidential?' asked Boniface, as he drove off.

'It was about my mother. I don't know if Emeka told you, my father died.'

'He didn't tell me! I'm so sorry,' said Boniface.

'I wanted to know if I could send a letter home, through the Red Cross.'

Boniface pulled up in the Eze's drive way. To Sade's relief, Emeka's car was not there.

'I hope Emeka has petrol to get home,' Sade feigned concern.

'I better drive to the hospital. I need to see him urgently,' Boniface responded.

Sade jumped out of the Landrover, wondering why Boniface needed to see Emeka. Perhaps he was going to report her? Or did he have a rescue plan for the family?

'Thank you for taking me,' said Sade, shutting the Landrover door.

Trying hard to control her excitement she hurried into the house. To her relief Saul was still asleep on the bed. Picking up a torch she looked at her wrist watch. It was already eleven o'clock. Tilting up the edge of the mattress she collected the letters that her mother had written and placed them in her handbag. With no money, she was completely at the mercy of the Red Cross. Opening the wardrobe she wondered what clothes to take. Taiwo had told her that in winter, England was like a freeze box. She had no suitable clothes.

At the slightest sound Sade rushed to the window in panic. If Boniface informed Emeka about her visit to the Red Cross, he would certainly be on his way back home. In fear of her life, she stood on a chair reaching on top of the wardrobe for Emeka's pistol. He had taught her how to use it, but the thought of killing another human being petrified her. She loaded it and placed it in her handbag. A car pulled up outside the house and she felt sick with anxiety. Gently she reached for Saul, praying that he would not wake up. With his head resting on her shoulder, she picked up her handbag. After peeping down the dark corridor, she made her way out of the room. Holding onto the banister rail, she sneaked downstairs. Slowly she opened the front door and set off down the dark gravel driveway. The crunching sound of the stones grated through her body, forcing her to walk on the grass verge. By the gate she spotted a Red Cross Landrover and hurried across the deserted road. She ran around to the passenger side and climbed in banging the door.

'Good evening!' Sade panted. 'You were sent by Mr Cole?'

'Yes Madam! Good evening!'

'Please let's go!' said Sade placing Saul spread eagle over her torso.

Lackadaisically the man started the engine and they set off. A car approached and Sade ducked her head down. When it had passed, she turned to see Emeka pulling up in the driveway.

'Go faster! Go faster!' Sade ordered.

Sensing trouble the driver put his foot down on the accelerator. Emeka continued down the driveway.

Sade could picture what the uproar would be when he discovered she had escaped with Saul. Only when they arrived at the outskirts of Umuahia was she able to relax. She had not slept properly for nights and unwittingly drifted off to sleep. She was awakened by the overpowering stench of death. By now she could identify the stench of rotting flesh without having to see it. The Red Cross driver had pulled up at one of the numerous checkpoints approaching Uli Airport and a soldier carrying a sub machine gun shone a torch into her face. The driver knew the necessary codes and signals to get them through and they were allowed to proceed at walking pace, and without the headlights. High in the sky above droned the fearful engines of the Nigerian Air-Force. A bomb landed somewhere in the distance and all Sade's tension and anxiety returned. She thought of the Red Cross relief plane that had been blasted out of the sky by the Nigerians. She had come too far to turn back now.

Eventually the driver pulled up at the heavily guarded airport and jumped out of the Landrover. Sade remained in her seat with Saul as he set off to talk to someone.

'We have to wait,' he informed her on his return.

After what appeared like a lifetime of waiting, a soldier approached the Landrover opening Sade's door.

'Follow me!' he ordered her.

Sade stared at the driver in panic. Had Boniface radioed the Airport to have her arrested?

'Have a safe journey Madam!' the driver told her.

Sade thanked him and apologised for not being in a position to give him a tip. She struggled out of her seat, Saul feeling unusually heavy in her arms. Perhaps it was because she had become so weak. The soldier led her past a group of white men, whom Sade guessed were relief workers or mercenaries. Before she knew it she was standing before the gangway leading into the aircraft.

'Safe journey!' said the soldier in the darkness.

'Where is the aeroplane going?' she asked him.

'Cotonou!'

'In Dahomey?'

'Yes! From there you can make further arrangements.'

Sade climbed up the gangway with the soldier watching from the ground. She looked into the dimly lit interior of the aircraft then out into the darkness. The soldier waved goodbye and slowly walked away. She knew exactly how he felt. He too probably wished that he could climb aboard the aircraft and escape into the unknown. Feeling absolutely exhausted, she went to look for a seat. The aircraft was full of families all sitting in that too familiar deadly silence.

By the front of the aircraft she got a seat. Looking out into the African darkness she recalled the many climbs down the bunker. She thought of the Eze, now resting in his room and parlour. Obi and child in the church yard cemetery along with Bogart and Kennedy; Roosevelt in some unmarked mass grave and Baby disappearing in the night. She thought of Oyibo, Kechi and Ezinma and began to cry. She was overcome with guilt. She had abandoned them to die. Holding tightly onto

Saul, she told herself over and over again, that there was nothing she could do to save them. Looking down at her sleeping child she gently kissed his head.

Suddenly the aircraft doors banged shut and the pilot eased the aircraft to the point of no return. The screams of the engine intensified as they sped down the runway, hurriedly leaving the hostile earth. Sade shut her eyes and surrendered herself to destiny.

THIRTY-SIX

EPILOGUE

IT WAS A week to Christmas when Sade and Saul eventually arrived at Gatwick Airport in London. After months in a wretched refugee camp, Sade managed to contact her mother who sent her the necessary documentation for her to obtain a passport. Although it had been a night flight, Sade had been unable to sleep. In the dull light she read her mother's letter for the tenth time.

...Thank God you were able to escape before the fall of Umuahia. I feel sure that with Emeka's army contacts he would have been able to get the family to safety. There is no point worrying about them now because there is nothing that you can do to help them.

Kehinde is now back in London. Understandably he was unable to return to Ibadan University after Taiwo's death. He informed me that Idowu got married to one Johnny Brown. I hope they will be very happy together. Clive, Sophia and Marilyn called to see me last week. I felt very ashamed that they found me living in a run down council flat. Once you arrive we can apply to be rehoused, especially with the new baby on the way.

Anxiously Sade felt her bulging belly. The last thing she wanted was to bring another child into the world to suffer. The DC 10 aircraft taxied to a halt and Sade looked out of the small porthole. The wet black runway glistened and sparkled from the lighting and the white substance that covered the ground she guessed was snow. A Nigerian sitting next to her stood up and pulled his hand baggage out of the luggage rack. Sade felt glued to her seat. She dreaded the thought of leaving the security of the aircraft.

'Is this yours?' asked the man pulling down a large shoulder bag. It was all she possessed, containing a few clothes donated to her by the Red Cross.

'Yes! Thank you!' she responded reaching for the bag. With Saul still sleeping in her arms she struggled out of her seat. Slowly they disembarked.

'You didn't bring a coat?' asked the man, turning back to look at her.

She did not respond. She was embarrassed at the second hand clothing they wore and conscious of the fact that the jumper had lost its shape. Her shoes were far too tight, affecting the way she walked.

'You are really going to suffer!' said the man as they walked down the stairs to a waiting bus. After a short trip, they arrived at the huge plush terminal building. She wondered how she would ever find her mother. Shivering from the cold, she followed the man to the section dealing with foreign nationals. Although she held a British passport, she did not feel British. They queued for almost an hour before it came to their turn. The Nigerian man handed his passport to the immigration officer who checked and stamped it before letting him through.

Sade handed the officer her passport.

'You should be at the other section,' said the officer as he examined her passport. 'Where were you born?' he asked.

'London!'

'What of the child.'

'Nigeria!'

'May I have his passport?'

'He hasn't got one.'

248

The officer stared in disbelief.

'You better come this way!' said the officer leading the way into a side cubicle. There were blue upholstered chairs on either side of the desk.

'Sit down!' he ordered.

With Saul still asleep in her arms she obeyed.

'Now then!' said the Officer. 'We seem to have a bit of a problem. Your passport was issued in?'

'Cotonou! Dahomey. We were flown out of Biafra by the Red Cross and I was able to contact my mother in London. She sent our tickets and the documents I needed to get a passport. I tried to contact my husband in Biafra to get my son's birth certificate, but the Red Cross were unable to locate him.'

Saul woke up and sat staring at the strange looking man on the opposite side of the table.

'My mother arranged to meet us here,' Sade persisted. 'Please let me go out to look for her. She might think that we have not arrived.'

'What's her name?' asked the officer, his blue eyes showing no sympathy.

'Mrs Susan Uwaifo.'

'I'll make an announcement to let her know you're here.' He stood up, abruptly leaving the cubicle.

Saul was now wide awake, and struggled to get off Sade's lap. She put him to stand by her chair, but he ran off. Grabbing a pen from the holder he began to scribble all over the wooden desk. Sade stood up and snatched the pen out of his hand. She placed it back in the folder. Defiantly, he returned to the folder.

'Come here!' she whispered grabbing his arm. Throwing himself on the floor, he accidentally banged his head on the metal table leg.

'I'll beat you!' she warned forcing him to his feet.

'I beat you.' he cried smacking her leg. 'Naughty!' he scolded.

The door opened and the officer entered with Mrs Uwaifo. Sade rushed into her mother's arms and they both cried in relief.

'I'm sure this can be sorted out in no time.' said the officer, 'I'll just collect the necessary documentation.' He left them alone in the cubicle. Saul ran into one of the corners in confused defiance.

'Come and say hello to your grandmother,' Sade told him.

Saul refused. Occasionally he peeped up at the strange woman that was his grandmother.

The immigration officer returned and after the necessary forms had been completed they set off by train for Mrs Uwaifo's one bedroom flat in Brixton, South London.

Books by post

Ace Books are available through mail order or from your local bookshop.

Further copies can be ordered direct from the publisher by filling in the form below.

Please enclose a cheque or postal order made payable to Ace Books to the value of the cover price and allow the following for postage and packing:

UK: £1.00 for the first book, 50p for the second book and 30p for each additional book ordered.

OVERSEAS & EIRE: £2.00 for the first book, £1.00 for the second book and 50p for each additional book.

Ace Books, 133 Condell Road, Carey Gardens, London SW8 4HS.

Name_____

Company _____

Address for delivery_____

_____

_____

_____

Country _____ Post Code_____

Tel_____

Prices and availability subject to change without notice.
Allow 20 days for delivery.

Books by post

Ace Books are available through mail order or from your local bookshop.

Further copies can be ordered direct from the publisher by filling in the form below.

Please enclose a cheque or postal order made payable to Ace Books to the value of the cover price and allow the following for postage and packing:

UK: £1.00 for the first book, 50p for the second book and 30p for each additional book ordered.

OVERSEAS & EIRE: £2.00 for the first book, £1.00 for the second book and 50p for each additional book.

Ace Books, 133 Condell Road, Carey Gardens, London SW8 4HS.

Name_____

Company _____

Address for delivery_____

_____

_____

_____

Country _____ Post Code_____

Tel_____

Prices and availability subject to change without notice.
Allow 20 days for delivery.